"Not so fast Flo-Jo. We have some things to discuss," the man growled.

Jai tried to shake loose from his grip, which turned out to be a fruitless effort. The heat from his hand snaked through her in a lazy path, which riveted her to the ground. "I won't run," she said, and he quirked an eyebrow in disbelief. "I won't," she repeated, her body in flames beneath his stimulating touch.

He let her go and took a step closer to her.

"I'm Jailyn Wyatt of the Creative Forces advertising firm. I'm here at the inn on business. You scared me, and I ran for the same reason."

"I should've expected as much," he said, his gaze lingering on every curve of the feisty, five-foot-six-inch, cinnamon-colored woman with huge jet-black eyes, impossibly long lashes, and glossy, kissable lips. She was a lissome beauty without a speck of make-up and was decimating his senses.

"And you, sir, are?" she asked, rubbing her arm. It didn't hurt, but she could still feel his touch trying to tattoo itself on her skin.

"Caleb Hamilton Vincent, owner of the inn and your client."

"Oh crap!" she said in Spanish.

"Oh crap is right," he agreed in English. "That one I understood."

If You Were Mine

J. S. Hawley

Kensington Publishing Corp.
http://www.kensingtonbooks.com

DAFINA BOOKS are published by

Kensington Publishing Corp.
850 Third Avenue
New York, NY 10022

All Kensington Titles, Imprints, and Distributed Lines are available at special quantity discounts for bulk purchases for sales promotions, premiums, fund-raising, and educational or institutional use. Special book excerpts or customized printings can also be created to fit specific needs. For details, write or phone the office of the Kensington special sales manager: Kensington Publishing Corp., 850 Third Avenue, New York, NY 10022, attn: Special Sales Department, Phone: 1-800-221-2647.

ISBN-13: 978-0-7582-1936-7
ISBN-10: 0-7582-1936-9

First mass market printing: February 2008

10 9 8 7 6 5 4 3 2 1

Printed in the United States of America

Dedicated to
my mother, Doretha "Rita" Hawley,
and my daughters, Ajah Sahara and Chantel Jacklyn.

And to my daddy, Edward "Buddy" Winston Hawley.

Though you walk with God,
I've seen your footprints in the sand,
dancing with mine.

J. S. Hawley

Acknowledgments

I'll just say one huge THANK YOU to everyone I work with now and have worked with in the past and to those who are no longer with us.

I'd like to thank my "street team"—Henri, Carolyn, Michelle, Simpson, Yvonne, Rachel, and Qumyka. My thanks go to my nephews, Daniel, Cameron, and Justin (my personal bodyguards) for holdin' it down. To Berto; Jaiana; Jus; Jarick; and JHS 231 (class 821), Thalisia, Jocelyn (Myra), Shanice, Nikkia (Glad you're back, baby girl), and Anthon. My gratitude goes to Ms. Bell, Ms. Fuentes, Ms. Pickney, Ms. Perry, Ms. Sookram, and Ms. Nixon. All girls need women to look up to and to look after them. You've helped to raise some fine young women. And I wish to thank P.S. 147, Ms. Cohen, Ms. Emmanuel, and Mrs. Gerst. (My baby is in caring hands.)

To my dad's fam, The Hawleys and the Marshalls. Y'all know who you are. (There's a lot o'ya'll.) To the matriarchs Aunt Lolly and Aunt Helen, I give my praises. To the rest, thank you for supporting this endeavor in all ways. To Jer, Ro, Nik, and the girls. To my big bros Edward and Lawrence. (My friends think u 2 r characters in my book or a lifelong figment of my imagination.)

A special thanks to Savy's Café (Devon and Artis, the Chef), Skylark Lounge (Yvonne), and Vicky and Melissa (hairdressers) for lending your venues and style to my success.

To the reviewers, readers, e-mailers, buyers, my editor, and everyone, T H A N K Y O U !

(& 2 think this is what I call short ☺)

(& I love Puddin'.)

Prologue

The sun was making a slow ascent into the sky, the night still dominating the land. She walked fearlessly by her father's side. Age, time, and words were irrelevant as they enjoyed the brisk wind pulling at their clothes. Raindrops fell silently through the trees, creating a distinct harmony with the melodic sounds of nature, adding to their high spirits as they pranced to music only they could hear.

The sun's rays began beating down on the land, decimating the rain, scorching the earth, causing a desolate wasteland to stretch before them. In the brightness of day, screeching wheels were heard. Horses on a death ride shook the ground that they walked on. She grabbed for her father's hand as gunshots rent the air, but he was too far away. She screamed for him without sound and tried to go after him, but he moved swiftly.

She turned away from him as the men caught up to him. She was helpless to stop the massacre, but she refused to watch the men attack her father with sticks, or lasso him and drag his inanimate form from the back of a truck, or beat him with their fists and kick him with dirty, heavy boots. They would lynch him and set his body on fire. She had seen this merciless dawn in her mind too many times not to know how it ended . . . .

But none of that happened.

She looked back to see her father take flight, merging with the darkness, which always protected them, a smile on his face. The darkness stole over the other men, and she could hear their horrific cries grow faint. She had no fear of the dark. Her father was coal black and her savior, the night their refuge. But now he was gone, and night and day vied for the sky over her.

Her loneliness was but a flicker in time as she stood in a wheat field rippling with beautiful brown whispers in the wind. A man of monumental proportions stood before her, completely nude. He faced away from her. His hair, a wild lion's mane, brushed his wide shoulders and stopped midway down his powerful back in a sleek mass. His narrow hips jutted forward, and his buttocks were tight and round as he stood on proud legs. He was the color of sepia: the sun lit him from behind, but the darkness defined him. The lines of his physique created caverns of shadows on the hard planes of his face. He had the profile of a king, the body of the gods, the strength of a man. . . .

Her weariness taking hold, she lay down in the cool shelter of darkness that the tall, majestic stalks offered. Moving stealthily, he came to her, gathering the light within him and presenting it to her. He lowered his imposing form with grace. She was transfixed by the ebony darkness that this honey-colored man exuded, but she was not afraid. A defined arm snaked across her stomach, deft fingers sprinkling her with a myriad of sensations. The long fingers of his other hand reached up to bury themselves in the thickness of her ink black tresses. With feline movements, he tantalized her body, his muscled limbs exploring each unfamiliar area, making it indelibly his. He gathered her into a soul-sealing embrace and held her until he owned her mind.

He moved over her as if the elements existed within him. He brushed his lips over her throat like a soft breeze while direct-

ing the wheat to sing a heavenly song above them. With his fingers, he traced the path from the curve of her breasts down the length of her womanly form. With powerful legs, he nudged apart her supple thighs and moved over her like the clouds moving over the earth. He worshipped her toffee-enhanced skin like the rain revitalizes the ground. The hard mahogany buds of her bared breasts arched up to the torrent of tender kisses he showered upon her. She opened to him the way nature flourishes in the sun and accepted him like the night enveloping the world in its grasp. He burrowed so deep within her delicate paradise that he couldn't think without her hearing it. With each stroke into her receptive femininity, another prayer was enticed from his lips. Through her physical body, he tried to touch her heart.

She responded to him without reservation. She gave what he had spent time nurturing with his own gifts, and he watched her surrender herself to him. Her earth-toned hues glowed like the sunset. Her arms encircled his neck, and he lifted her from the ground. She greeted him in ecstasy, her legs wrapping around him, drawing him deeper with each glorious thrust, their joining divine.

Her body had been erected for him; this she knew without doubt. When his hardness pressed insistently against her tight sheath, her slippery softness molded to him, to fit around him like no other. When his firm erection blazed a fiery path into her petal softness, her dark haven greedily met each swift stroke of his growing fullness. With each encouraging moan from her lips, he pressed deeper into her slick, wet heat until the walls of her body stretched to fulfillment. The stirring pulses of his manhood touched the passion-soaked center of her womanhood, pushing her higher and higher until she soared outside of herself when she felt him spilling white, hot fire into her and setting her core ablaze with his pleasure. His mind fractured when a wave of savage pleasure carried him above and beyond himself, his life force flooding her. First, he was taken up into the bright heights of heaven and then released into the cool, welcoming womb of the obsidian dark. He let himself fall to a place he seldom visited, but with her, he had no fear, no shame, no loneliness. The coal blackness became a refuge, and she his savior.

He shifted his weight, but she was gone, and it was darker than he remembered. He saw her then, plunged in shadow, half nude, her legs crossed at an odd angle to act as a desk. He glimpsed paper, which was luminescent against her cinnamon skin. Her pencil was moving with swift, long strokes that reminded him of their lovemaking, and he ached for her. Her head was bent, her hair partially covering her pixie-like features, her raven eyes visible through her even darker curls. His own skin called out to him. The faster she worked, the more he felt the caress of soft lips on his shoulder, the feel of her hands down his spine and over his buttocks, until he could sense her everywhere.

She sat in the darkness of her room, sketching without the aid of light. She had a clear picture of him in her mind, as if he stood in the room with her. With each stroke of the pencil, she grew more confident. When it was done, her ache well sated, she lay down to rest. The mysterious man was forgotten as light began its duel with night.

He bolted upright, his skin hot, his clothes soaked with perspiration, his heartbeat erratic. A stewardess was talking rapidly about isolation, an itinerary, a virus. Dumbly he nodded, wondering if hallucinations of beautiful women were a sign of a deadly virus, because if so, he would be one of the happiest dead men walking. Soon his dream was forgotten, buried in the darkest recesses of his mind.

Chapter 1

"Good morning. Creative Forces—Media Blitz. We take care of all your advertising concerns in a pinch. We're a one-stop public relations shop; we'll make you hot, and we make you rich. This is Jai speaking. How may I direct your call?" She laughed inwardly at the corny line, and although the challenge was to rhyme taglines, not make up corny ones, she still gave herself an air tally. Good thing there were so few early morning calls.

"Hello, Jai," a male voice purred. She quickly swung her feet off the desk, as if the caller could see her lounging with her feet up. During the scramble, things flew in all directions, and she knocked her blue soda all over the reception desk.

"Mon Dieu!" she hissed softly so the caller couldn't hear her. "Mais c'est impossible."

"Is everything all right, Jai?" She froze at the deep baritone, which sent tremors down her spine. The way his voice played over her name . . . "Jai? Are you still there? Can you hear me now?"

"That's an old joke," she answered, with a giggle.

Wait. Giggle? Jailyn Wyatt did not giggle like some debutante on the red carpet, responding to a reporter. No, Jailyn Wyatt laughed raucously. Hers was loud, gut-wrenching laughter, usually punctuated with snorts and eyes tearing up.

"It is old, but it is as memorable for Verizon as "Where's the beef?" is for Wendy's. Can you do something like that for me, Jai? Make me go down in history?"

Jai wanted him to go down all right, but history had nothing to do with it, and if he kept saying her name like that, she'd do just about anything. "Jai?" the voice asked abruptly.

"Do I know you?" she asked, still dazed.

"Not yet, but if all goes well, I should be making your acquaintance soon."

Jai wasn't sure if he was the man of her dreams or a stalker. Her big-city suspicions were kicking in late, as usual. "How do you know my name?"

"You gave your name when you answered the phone," he stated, with a perturbed edge.

"Oh right, right," she said, waving a hand as if that would clear her mind, but his milky voice was drowning her in delicious vibrations. She could practically see him: a tall, muscular, sexy African-American male with soft, sensitive eyes that would melt a woman like butter on a George Foreman grill. She gave an inward sigh. At this hour she expected a potential client, a client inquiry, an ex-client, or an employee calling out for the day, not a voice that could talk her out of her panties. Ice-cold soda dripped into her shoes, which she had kicked under the desk, and onto her naked toes.

"Ça va," she mumbled, searching the immaculate desk for napkins or tissues. *Mickey has to keep some around. Everyone has a fast-food drawer.* Jai had three filled with every condiment known to man, plus napkins, but of course, that was all the way down the hall. Each of Mickey's drawers turned out to be impossibly neater than the last. At a glance, she could see the unending office staples, pens in every color, sharpened No. 2 pencils, file folders, computer supplies, and the like. Not a catsup pack to be found or a napkin with a big ol' *M* printed on it. "Ohhh, maybe on the coffee . . ."

"Excuse me?" the voice asked in unexpectedly clipped tones. If Jai hadn't been on a salvage mission, she might have hesitated for longer than a second.

"Oh no, excuse me. . . ." Jai's eyes frantically scanned the counter where the clean coffeepot stood alone. She was starting toward the cabinets when the phone clattered to the floor. "Hello? Are you still there?"

"Yes," he said, drawing out his reply, making her breath escape her in unsteady little spurts.

"I'm so sorry. It's that . . . no, no, no!" she shouted as the Windex-looking liquid made a beeline for the computer. "Merde! Ce foutu damnation éternelle!" she blurted in French as she looked at the date book she had absentmindedly used to stop the flow of fluid.

"Maybe I should call back at a better time?" the voice inquired in formal tones.

"No, um, now's okay. Who do you want to talk to?" Jai asked, helplessly watching the blue runoff drip to the carpet. She hoped the expensive stain-retardant carpet performed as advertised, since there were quite a few dark puddles growing on the plush burgundy sea. "I'm sorry. Whadja say?" Jai murmured, only half listening, hypnotized by the blue invasion.

"I didn't *say* anything," replied the smug voice, mocking her.

"Well, I can't read minds," Jai answered, getting annoyed at the anonymous caller. She needed him to state his business so she could deal with her more immediate problems. She strained to hear his barely audible breathing sounds and began to wonder if he was an obscene caller. "My apologies for the distractions. How may I direct your call?" she inquired professionally, while distractedly wiping her hand on her jeans. The voice came back at her modulated, causing a cascade of tingles at the nape of her neck.

"I'm not sure with whom I should speak."

"Then let's begin with the reason for your call," she said, concentrating on the subject and not the sound of his voice.

"I run a well-established construction firm, and I've decided to branch out in a different direction. Your company came highly recommended. I . . . ahem . . . I want to work with a firm that will allow me to have a say through the entire process, real intense one-on-one interaction. My prior ad firm . . ."

"If you don't mind me asking, who would that be?"

"Fine Gold Artistic Visions."

Finney Whiney, as the firm was called throughout the industry, spent more time whining about clients than properly representing them. "Fine Gold is known for promoting expansion businesses because of the public relations department . . ."

"I'm not expanding. I am revamping the entire corporate structure. They are trying to convince me that my reputation will cause clients to continue to utilize my services and will draw in new ones, but what they are failing to consider is that I am discontinuing certain services completely. I was told your company could accommodate all my needs. I've heard good things about you . . . Jai. Your company, that is."

He spoke as if the words were an incantation and could make all of his wishes come true if he put his soul into each syllable. Jai felt his voice through the phone line as it spread fairy dust around her. At the sound of her name, she practically swooned, and she put a hand on the desk to keep from falling. The cold liquid on her fingertips brought her back to reality. She wiped her hand on her shirt as he continued to talk, as if brokering a deal in an opium-induced haze. The language he was using kept her senses reeling. Words like *intimate*, *intense*, and *hard* blazed a trail of double entendres across her brain. His voice was taking on a more arid quality, and Jai transformed it into a broad-shouldered, thirty-something, virile man with piercing eyes. She imagined a proud black man dressed in fashions out of *GQ*. . . .

The phone went silent in her hand, and she wasn't sure what he had said or if they were the company to service him. . . . "Me refiero a ellos," she said out loud in perfect Castilian, her voice a rough whisper. ". . . I mean your company."

"Excuse me?" he responded, his voice capturing her anew in a web of sensuality.

"Nothing. Sorry. Please . . . continue."

"As I was explaining, I desire the right connection with the right people or person to handle my business. My employees say I'm a taskmaster of sorts." His voice sent a fresh wave of desire through her. He continued speaking in the same slow cadence. "But I believe when paying for services . . . they should be fulfilled no matter the hour. I rise early and work late. I do not ask anything of my employees that I am not willing to do myself. I am involved in every aspect of my business intimately. . . ." *There's that word again,* Jai thought as she was transported to a close encounter of the sensual kind. And for the first time in weeks she felt guilty that she hadn't bothered to dress better.

"Miss, Miss?" said the caller. The two words ran together and sounded like "psst, psst." And then the "psst, psst" rose in volume and became an incessant noise trying to drown out his soothing voice. "Jai? Are you with me?"

Her eyes opened, the "psst, psst" pulling her back from the comfort of the cocoon she had been ensconced in. The "psst, psst" became the harsh "drip, drip" of soda flowing off the desk and into the metal art deco wastepaper basket. "Jai? I've spent the last ten minutes talking, and I don't think you've heard a word I've said. This has been a total waste of my time," the voice complained in plaintive tones, as if nothing disrupted his calm demeanor.

"Qu'est-ce que ça peut bien faire?" she huffed in French patois, looking at the mess and finding herself angry with the caller for being the initial cause of the chaos, for making her want to change her dress, and for now telling her off in the sexiest voice she'd ever heard. "Tu tienes que aprender ha oir . . ." She threw herself across the desk to try and save the one picture that was there of Mickey's wedding day. But there, at the bottom, Jai saw the little ocean of soda seeping into the frame. "Fuckin' shit."

"That one I understood. You have the foulest language I have ever heard at this hour of the morning," the voice reprimanded.

"Then you need to get on a subway at seven a.m. in Manhattan," she countered, finding her backbone.

"No, I don't. Your language is inappropriate and unnecessary."

"How do you know? Are you here with me? I could be on fire, for all you know. . . ."

"Are you?"

"What?" Jai asked, her tirade interrupted.

"I asked, are you on fire?" The voice was quiet and subdued.

"No," she answered, now feeling his exasperation. "I'm trying to point out—"

"Well, then, your language is unnecessary. Your behavior, your tone—"

"You need to ease up. I'm having a thing here. Maybe if you—"

"I don't care." The voice had a no-nonsense, don't-you-dare-utter-a-sound tone. "This is a business call. You do realize that, don't you, young woman? Do you know what that means? It means, I call you up to retain your services, and someone knowledgeable and pleasant tries to impress me." His voice had gone up in volume, and Jai could feel his contempt through the phone the same way she had felt the imagined seduction. "And if that's the most creative language you've got, then maybe I've called the wrong place."

Panic flew through Jailyn. She couldn't lose another client. "No, wait. Honestly, I am sorry. . . ."

"Sorry is a state of worthlessness and inferiority," he stated, goading her.

"I apologize," she ground out.

"For what? Being rude, ill-mannered, and downright nasty, or for lacking the common sense to have apologized before pissing off the client?" the voice asked sarcastically, still sounding pleasantly composed.

"What've you got stuck up your butt, dang?" Jai took

a deep breath and tried to explain. "Again, I apologize for having taken up so much of your time, but I spilled some—"

"I'm not getting paid to listen to you."

"Could you please give me a chance to explain, and could you reconsider?"

"No," the voice said flatly. "I'm tired. I lost out on my bid for a very large, multimillion-dollar resort deal in Hawaii to my ex-partner. I had a crappy flight. I haven't had a decent meal in days, my luggage didn't make it back, and I need a shower and my bed. But first I wanted to stop in the office, make this one call, and conclude this last piece of business as a favor to a friend, but obviously, you have no clue as to how I do business. I like order and organization." His voice barely changed an octave as he continued reminding her of her faux pas. "In fact, I'm sure few of your clients would have accepted your halfhearted apologies. Some might even say this type of treatment is abhorrent. And look at that. I've managed to say all of that without one single, solitary profanity."

"But you see how nicely I listened to you, and not a single dollar has changed hands," she goaded, throwing his words back at him.

"You're supposed to. I'm the potential client, and you're supposed to be trying to impress me!" His voice was sexy even when he was yelling at the top of his lungs.

Jai couldn't help but smile. She had made him lose his composure, and she was ready to turn the tables. In a calm and collected manner, she said, "Creative Forces doesn't need favors, nor do we have to impress anyone. Our work speaks for itself. We are a creative force to be reckoned with. We have designed some of the biggest campaigns in New York. We have successfully worked in the most challenging areas of advertising. It will be your loss if you don't come in and speak with us."

Jai had wasted enough of his time and her own. His voice might be gorgeous, but he could be ugly as a rock. It was time to put up or shut up. She continued. "It would be a shame not to schedule an appointment and see our portfolio. We've been known to put out some impressive work and fulfill client needs and wishes."

"Is this how you impress new clients, shouting and cursing before you get to the sales pitch? You seem ineffectual as a secretary, and that isn't a good first impression, nor does it leave me secure in the knowledge that your company is very capable. I plan to check into more established firms."

"We've been open for eight years and have captured some of the largest accounts in the city. I look at my company as original, progressive, and unique in its approach and outlook. You won't get that from older firms. We have steadily been gaining respect in our field and have established ourselves as a viable competitor. Perhaps when you cease being so rigid and uptight, you'll be more in a position to appreciate the types of new directions we can take your company in."

"With you answering the phones—"

"God dang . . . ," she uttered, along with two other oaths, which caught in her throat. A slew of foreign phrases flew out of her mouth as she tried desperately to sop up some of the spill with the bottom of her shirt. Jai was pissed at the devastation she had caused in Mickey's neat little world. The calculator floated by, the glass blotter was making rainbows, and the phone lay face down on the floor. Everything had been touched by the far-reaching tentacles of the maniacal blue soda. "Dégueulasse . . ."

Jai leapt at the computer keyboard, and the phone swung into a puddle with an awful squish, splashing her shoes and feet for good measure. The reception desk officially resembled a big, blue, sticky Jolly Rancher that had melted in the sun. She made one last-ditch effort to shift things out of the way of the expanding mess, and then she finally righted the culprit. Belatedly, she remembered the phone. "Hello? Hello? Ah, motherfucking merde," she said to no one and then began laughing hysterically. *Only in my world*, she thought. *Only in my world.*

Chapter 2

"So word around the office is our shining star went nova this morning." Paul Reynolds lounged against the door frame, much as he had three years ago, when he first began working at Creative Forces. And just like three years ago, he was justifiably conceited, with the smell of good breeding coming through his pores. The only thing different now was she was wiser.

"Mon Dieu, get out of my office, Reynolds," replied Jai. "When we broke up, you gave up your drop in unannounced privileges. Schedule something with my secretary." Jai continued working, barely giving him a glance. She was finishing the panels for a storyboard based on the blue fiasco, her mind's eye picking up the tiniest details and transmitting them to her pencil. "I'm not in the habit of repeating myself, Reynolds," she said after a minute.

"First, stop speaking in tongues, you witch. Second, we didn't *break* up. I dumped you," he said casually. Jai ignored the correction, not wanting to give him the time of day. "Third, your secretary never seems to be where you left her, and lastly, I'm not in your office."

"That nose of yours is at least a foot over the threshold." Paul flinched, and Jai took some pleasure in irking him. She leaned over and tapped her secretary's extension.

Rosalind Clark's perky, Caribbean-accented voice sang over the speaker. "Yes."

Jai didn't bother to look at Paul as she proved her point. "Ros, would you please be so kind as to get someone to take care of cleaning Mickey's desk for me?" Jai knew she wasn't focused enough to handle the task. "Tell Christian to replace all of Mickey's office hardware. I've already compiled a list of styles and serial numbers. Anything we don't have, replace with the newest model."

"Anything else? Do you need some trash removed from your office?" Rosalind remarked, always aware of Jai's comings and goings.

"Yes. I have rewritten Mickey's date book, so you can get that when the cleaning people are done. And please, get me Jude on the phone."

"Why? Are you going to recommend she fire Reynolds?" Rosalind asked, and Jai was certain the girl knew he was standing in her office. "He insisted I hurry and make copies for him, and suddenly, he's nowhere to be found. That's a waste of resources, which you should report to the board."

Paul winced imperceptibly but quickly found his voice. "You taking orders from your secretary?"

"Ros, please get Judith on the phone for me," Jai said, then clicked off the speaker. "And you get out."

"I hear you lost another account. A big account, lots of money," said Paul.

"*We* didn't *have* anything, but I *had* a phone call."

"And to think you even blew that. At this rate, I'll have this office sooner than expected."

"Dave wouldn't be happy to find out that you've usurped him in the hierarchy of importance around here."

Paul stepped into the sparsely decorated space. "Dave would be happy with that cushy spot upstairs, next to Judith. This, however, would be perfect for my account team. As soon as you and those street thugs you call student trainees get the boot, I'm having the carpet ripped up, the walls painted, the furniture burned. . . ."

"Be happy you still have a job and that Dave is too busy actually doing his job to notice you trying to bump him out."

"Dave deserves a promotion. The man can soothe all you artistic types and trim a budget all in three hours." This was a truth Jai and Judith discussed frequently. Dave DeAngelo was the most qualified traffic manager they had ever had, but he could never take over the coveted "fifth seat" on the board of directors. "And he was smart enough to hire me and help me get promoted. With him on the board, I'll probably end up with a seat right next to him." Paul walked closer to Jai to deliver his kill shot. "It's a shame you don't run the joint. If you did, maybe I'd still be warming your bed, keeping you from being grizzly so early in the day."

Jai swiveled in her chair to face him squarely. *How dare he gloat, to her of all people, about his ability to use people!* She folded her arms across her chest, and Paul dropped his superior stance. "You still mad that your pretty little wife left you?" she shot at him, with precision calm.

Paul's face reddened. His lovely, precious, little Erika had turned into a vicious nighttime soap opera character, and their divorce was being played out in the society pages every week. It was tabloid fodder that Erika

Winston-Reynolds, of the Boston Winstons, was now dating her attorney, who was ripping into every asset, liquid or otherwise, with a hint of Paul's smell.

"You're crazy, and you don't even bother to hide it. First, you seduce me. Then you try to smear my name, get me fired, and ruin my marriage. And today you throw a public tantrum at our newest, potentially most lucrative client, and your work isn't as refreshing as it once was."

"Strange how only one of my character flaws has nothing to do with you."

"Maybe you need another vacation. I mean, aren't you due for another change of scenery, or is your father—"

"If you finish that sentence, I will make sure you have nothing left to live for." Jailyn walked over to where he stood, stopping an inch from him. "You may have dated me to get that promotion, but we both know if I invited you into my bed again, you'd be there with bells on." Jai could feel his body tense as he took a tentative step back. She knew her work wasn't nearly on par with what she had done in the past, but she was working her tail off to compensate.

She continued. "On my worst day, my numbers surpass yours. And it's only gonna get worse for you once Erika officially takes all of her friends and connections back. You may be charismatic, but that alone won't be enough to sway the country-club set. You asked me once, 'What is Mayflower to Middle Passage?' Well, sweetheart, how does it feel to be the Titanic?"

Paul clenched and unclenched his fists. "Don't pretend the Reynolds name doesn't carry its own prestige."

"The Reynolds legacy will fade, but Winston diamonds are forever."

"How dare you! You really do believe you belong on that imaginary pedestal you made for yourself. Trying to compare my pedigree with your upwardly mobile black behind."

This time Jai was ready. Paul Reynolds no longer had the power to hurt her. "As usual, you're way off base when it comes to me. You thought dumping me and marrying Erika was going to do me in. You had us both thinking that she won the pot at the end of the rainbow. But now I know there isn't enough gold in all of Ireland to pay for a lifetime of marriage to you. You're fool's gold, shiny and pretty on the outside and nothing of worth on the inside. And people are starting to see the façade, like when you were trying to steal my clients. It didn't work. They left rather than deal with you. Guess my upwardly mobile black behind trumps your recently dumped white behind." Jai took a steadying breath and backed him into a mental corner. "And for the last time, Reynolds, get out."

Chapter 3

Quinn's Pub was a small, out-of-the-way place on the edge of the city. It was all wood and alcohol. No chi chi, frou frou trappings like at the trendy Midtown and uptown bistros and cafés. You didn't get a menu at Quinn's. You got a burger and fries, Buffalo wings and fries, or pastrami on rye with fries. Quinn did not cook, so if his cook showed up, you ate. If not, then you drank.

Quinn was a nice-looking, burly guy, with slick gray hair and a ruddy complexion. His eyes were an intense aqua blue and held fathoms of wisdom. Quinn had a friendly, fatherly face. He always had a sympathetic ear and an understanding smile. It's what made him a stereotypical bartender and a great friend.

"You don't look so good, li'l girl. What happened?" Quinn asked. He pulled out a special bottle he kept just for her in the "strictly for show case," as he called it.

"Bad day is all," Jailyn said, moping at the bar.

"Goat dung! Now if'n you need me to call some of me friends wit bats, we'll handle the bastard right nicely. I'll get you some fries while you describe 'im so I don't hurt the wrong lad."

Jailyn laughed without censure. It warmed Quinn's heart to know he could still bring a smile to her face. It had been hard on Quinn, losing his best friend, but it was even harder watching his best friend's daughter deal with it. Quinn and Ed had forged a fast and easy bond. It was just as easy for Quinn and his wife, Gwen, to befriend the whole Wyatt family. When his Gwen died, the Wyatts had been there, alongside his sisters, doing everything to keep him and the bar going. When Ed died, Quinn was there for Doretha and Jailyn Wyatt. He felt privileged that the women came to him in times of crisis. As a result, he was developing real feelings for Doe, as he called Doretha, and planned one day soon to ask her out on a real date.

Quinn came out of the kitchen and scooped Jai beneath one meaty arm. "John, I'm takin' lunch," he yelled over his shoulder.

"Bring me back something," said a voice from the kitchen.

"Whaddaya want?" yelled Quinn.

"Anything I didn't cook!" Everyone in the place yelled. It was an old joke at Quinn's Pub, but something about screaming like that released a lot of pent-up frustration. They slipped into a clean booth, and Quinn slid a half order of fries in front of Jai. She covered her fries in a layer of salt and shoved one in her mouth, scalding herself with hot oil.

"Nothing much different there. You act like you don't see the steam," said Quinn.

"I'm hungry," she said in her defense, waving five fries in the air to cool them and then ramming them into her mouth.

"So whatever is botherin' you ain't affected your appetite. And you say it ain't a man, so no one needs a talkin' to, and I spoke to yur ma jes the other day, so it ain't family." He ran a weathered hand through his soft silver hair. "Must be money." He pulled out a twenty, which made her choke up a fry. When she was a kid he would give her Kennedy half dollars when he couldn't get her to talk.

Even though she didn't need the money, she snatched it from his light grip, drew some odd little picture on it, and stuck it in her pocket. *Nothing much different there,* he thought. He was used to her drawing on anything she could find.

She took a sip of the sparkling raspberry drink to clear her throat. "I think my lunar cycles are clashing with the rising tides, causing a temporal shift in my personal equilibrium. But not due to outside influences, like you would suspect, but to some sort of internal disruption of my Zen alignment. It's like my karmic circle has a hairline fracture that's making my skin not fit."

"Uh-huh." Quinn nodded, his brows knitted in concentration.

"Too existential for you?"

"Just a wee bit, me love. Try again." Quinn wiped salt off a fry and popped it into his mouth, giving her time to get to the crux of the matter.

"I blew another account today."

"Uh-huh. Which one?"

"I don't know."

"You don't know? So how do you know you blew it?" he asked, blowing a ton of salt off of a fry and wincing at how much was still left.

"Because when the guy called, he had this "Do Me, Baby" vibe with this "Forever My Lady" melody, and I was all ready to let him have my children. I didn't hear business. I heard headboards thumping. And then he hung up."

Quinn smiled at her description. Her powers of description were what put her at the top of the advertising game and were one of her most outstanding characteristics. The fact that they seemed to be back in full force was a positive sign that she was finally bouncing back from the loss of her father. He raised a brow at Jai showing interest in a guy. Other than that slickster, Paul, Jailyn hadn't shown any interest in men in quite some time. She had dedicated herself to her small company, right out of college, and had managed to put it at the forefront of the multimedia promotions industry—without becoming jaded by money and by being a face in the media. That is, until the death of her father. Her father was a wonderful but unassuming man, and Jailyn had followed right in his footsteps. Ed had never given himself credit for being an exceptional human being. His daughter was the same way. So as he would with Ed, Quinn offered the best advice he could. "Call his office and apologize."

"I can't. I didn't get a name, a phone number, or anything. My hormones mutinied, and my brain went kablowie. My common sense was taken over in a coup. That doesn't happen to me, Quinn."

Quinn stretched an arm across the back of the seat, studying the young woman and smiling. "Yea, it does, lass. It's been happenin' ever since ye were a wee one."

"Not over a guy. Especially one I haven't seen. And never at work. I mean, yeah, I can get distracted. . . ."

"By bright lights and shiny objects."

"Quiiiiiinnnnn . . ." She dropped her head into her

arms. Her voice started out a whine of desperation and then mellowed, until she kablowied him.

"The lines in the middle of the road still fascinate you at night."

"It looks like plain old paint during the day, and then you see the little shimmery specs. And it not only reflects the light, but it sort of refracts . . ." She looked in his indulgent face before giving up the ghost. "Okay. I get it. I have the attention span of a flea."

"And I wouldn't want ye any other way. But you're right. You've never kablowied over a lad. Now, lass, what are you *planning* to do?" he asked as she added more salt to the crunchy remnants at the bottom of the basket.

"I need to get my head straight."

"Sounds like you're already there." Now it was her turn to give him an indulgent look. It was his love for her that caused him to speak the words. "Stop chasing rainbows, gal. You have all you want and need." She looked up, startled. "Yup, I know all about rainbow chasin'. We Irish have a love for things unseen. Fairies, leprechauns, and rainbows."

"I guess I'm part Irish then. I love rainbows."

"Your daddy comes in here one night, drinkin' himself three sheets to the wind. We get to talkin', and he tells me in great detail about the things in his head. The pictures are so grotesque, I was quaking. I mean, I had a few drinks meself that night, and I barely touch the stuff. Then he tells me about this wonderful wife of his and the babe she is carryin' for him. He makes her sound like this angelic creature, all light and spectral, and I say, 'Like a rainbow.' He didn't get it right off, but I tell him when you spend all your life runnin' from the rain, you'll most definitely miss the joy of seeing the rainbows.

"I remind him how lucky he is to know how special his wife is. She's his rainbow after a life of running away from a nasty storm. I tell him rainbows are so fleeting that most people miss them. Just pass on by without notice. But they're still there, waiting for the perfect conditions. Seemed like your daddy caught that ever-elusive rainbow when he met your ma and when you came along."

Jai had been influenced by her father's perceptions of her mother, and she had been convinced her mother was a timeless being, with the beauty of the ages in her eyes, the wisdom of the ancients on her side, and the grace of queens in her stride. It was part of the reason Jai missed her father so much. She'd never cultivated a realistic relationship with her mother, and without her father's rose-colored vision, she saw her mother as a mortal being whose heart was devastated. They weren't much help to each other at the time of her father's death, and Jai was learning how much her father meant to her mother.

"Too bad it didn't stop him from drinking," she said.

"Wasn't nearly as bad, though," Quinn said.

"Still killed him."

"He still had those demons messing around in his head. It's hard being a man, 'specially when you're told over and over you're less than a man because of the color of your skin. A thing you can't control or change. But your father was one of the most decent men I have ever had the honor of calling me friend. He was funny, kind, and generous to a fault. Just like you." He plucked the end of her nose.

"I feel ashamed. My father's photographic memory plagued him his whole life, while I make money off of mine."

"Don't you dare! Your father never wanted you to see a bad thing. I swore he was gonna blindfold you every time you left the house. He was proud of what you did with it. You can ask anyone he ever talked to."

"I miss having someone who understands what I'm going through, what goes on in my head, who sees the way I see." She let out a deep, anguished sigh. "I miss him. I go to work, close my door, struggle to get the work out, and run out of the office when I'm done, like the place smells like urine."

"And your team, your co-workers, and student trainees? Don't they make it worthwhile?"

"They barely see me. I'm too busy trying to catch up with myself." Jai pushed the salt around with a fry.

"You expect too much too soon."

"I expect to be as productive as I once was," she reasoned in a small voice.

"I don't imagine them nightmares help much."

"They aren't as bad," she said, smiling sheepishly. Quinn and her mother had taken turns sitting up with her through those first days. And only three people could explain what she was seeing, but the one who knew firsthand was no longer of this earth.

"Maybe you need a change of scenery, a fresh perspective. Why not go with your ma to France? It's about time for her to place orders and see her family."

"I'd rather put mustard on my fries. 'Sides, I'm swamped at work."

"Uh-huh . . . ," Quinn said suspiciously.

"So, I'm afraid to fly."

He let out a guffaw, and she kicked him lightly under the table. "You started on the CK thing?" he said, avoiding an impossible argument and a screaming match.

Her smile returned full force, and she sat up in her

seat, her enthusiasm transforming her into one big nervous tick. Her hands flying about, her black eyes flashing, she painted the most hysterical picture of a secretary spilling coffee all over her desk because she could smell the fabulous cologne of the man on the phone, through the phone. Quinn laughed himself all the way back to the bar after seeing her out the door. He'd call Doe tonight and let her know Jailyn had paid him a visit, but he had another important call to place right now.

Chapter 4

Caleb Vincent groaned as he was pulled out of his sleep. The darkness parted for a woman on stage, in a long, pink-colored gown that sparkled with every twist of her curvaceous body. She was in the spotlight, clutching the microphone like she was clutching a man. Her low-pitched voice produced smoky jazz chords with no effort and tons of emotion. Her eyes closed against the bright lights, and her glossy lips moved over the words of the song like a caress, her delicate fingers curled around the mic the way he wanted them to hold him. She started to fade as the phone continued to ring.

"Hello," Caleb answered, his voice scratchy.

"Why do you sound like that at this hour? It's after one in the afternoon. Don't you have work? Are you there with a lady?"

"No, Pops. There's no girl here. I'm jet-lagged." Quinn's assumption and his directness made Caleb smile. It sort of reminded him of his early morning call with Jai, the receptionist. Since drifting off to sleep, all he could think of was the sound of her voice and the hard-on it had given him. Their fight had ignited a brush fire in his veins to the point where he couldn't distinguish between his anger and his libido. The dichotomy had been disconcerting, so he had hung up abruptly and had finished the little office work he had. But that hadn't stopped her from prancing into the twilight of his dreams. "I just got back from Hawaii."

"Did you sound sexy like this when you called Creative Forces this morning?"

Understanding dawned on both Quinn and Caleb at the same time. Word had already gotten out.

"I sounded sleepy."

"That's me friend, and I'll not have you making me look bad," Quinn said, his Irish brogue coming out.

"Comparatively, you have nothing to worry about," Caleb said dryly. "Their receptionist was obstinate and crude. My patience was shot. I'd been dealing with attitudes for days, negotiations were little more than fighting in suits, and there were complications with my flight back. I have a full day tomorrow, so I need my rest. I'll call you later, when I get up." With another hour of sleep, he'd deal with Quinn, but right now his dream girl was waiting.

"So if'n you were so tired, why didn't you just wait to call my friend?" Quinn asked. Quinn never pressed him about business decisions. In fact, Quinn didn't usually get testy with him at all, so Caleb wasn't prepared for his father's backlash, and he wasn't sure how to proceed without getting chewed out.

"I had to rearrange my schedule at the last minute, and I was doing everything in transit or from Hawaii in the middle of major negotiations."

"Uh-huh," Quinn said.

"My secretary inadvertently cancelled the original appointment with Creative Forces without rescheduling."

"So you call back and hang up?" Quinn asked.

If he confessed to his father that he had hung up because the receptionist's voice had given him a hard-on, Quinn would probably laugh his head off and tell all of the patrons in the bar. Caleb was not about to become the punch line in one of his father's great little anecdotes.

"Lad, I asked you a question. Now answer me," Quinn said.

Caleb knew he should acquiesce now if he wanted to get back to bed anytime soon. "Pop, I appreciate your advice, but—"

"You act like this is gonna take all day. What's thirty minutes of your time?"

"About seven hundred fifty dollars," Caleb answered bluntly. It didn't have the effect he hoped for.

His father replied in a deadpan voice, "Just make sure you do it sooner rather than later."

"I don't procrastinate, Quinn. It'll go on my agenda as soon as I go to work, which will be as soon as I get some rest, which will be as soon as I get off the phone."

"Don't you go getting smart with me. I've never asked nothing of you."

"Because you never did nothing for me!" Caleb shouted. The hostile negotiations, the sleep deprivation, and the lack of a decent meal were really getting to him.

"Oh, laddie, don't you have a wee memory."

"Brad left me the company, and his father left it to him, but it was in piss-poor shape when I got it. It's a corporation now, not some local family business. And I'm the one who put it back on the map."

"I'm not the one telling ye that your accomplishment is small. So don't try belittling me pub, because it sure did help when you needed it most, didn't it, lad? When you found out that good-for-nothing stepfather of yours had stolen your mother's money, that the company was worthless, and that he had left her with nothing to raise you."

"I was out of college by then, so don't act like you helped put food on the table and a roof over my head. You gave me one loan a dinosaur's age ago."

"And Tobin?"

"I've tried to pay you back, but I think you like having me owe you."

"You're my son, come hell or high water, lad. I'll always do what I can when you need, whether you ask or not," Quinn said.

"That's right, and that loan is a tangible reminder looming over me. When you call, when you give me advice, when you want me to come down to the bar, I do it because I *owe* you."

Quinn was so quiet, Caleb thought the line had gone dead. Quinn's voice was distant when he spoke. "I can see you woke up today and lost your damn fool mind, so let me remind you of some stuff. First of all, I'm your father. Even after I'm dead, you best not ever get it in your head to speak of me that way, because if you do, it'll take God and the Devil to keep me from throwing a lightning bolt up your behind and cracking you in two. Second, don't you ever speak *of* me in the same breath with that racist Bradley Vincent. God forgive me for speaking ill of the dead, especially the man who raised ya, but, Caleb, I swear if you keep up with your mouth, you gonna find yourself a lonely, bitter man in an early grave. And lest ye forget, ye best not ever speak *to me* in that voice, or I'll make ye eat your words with me bare hands."

"I don't need this right now."

"Like hell you don't! You need to stop thinking of jess yurself. One day you may need another favor, and won't nobody be there for you, just like no one was there for him. Mark my words, Caleb. You ain't far from it. You need people. You need friends, your family, and most of all, love. Sometimes I think your mother and Brad stole that from you, and me alone couldn't give ye enough, but you're old enough to know you need to stop pushing people away and start letting them in."

Quinn was known for bullying people into seeing things his way with just a good old Irish stare. It would be similar to a Vulcan mind trick were it not for the fact that Quinn was a huge man with plenty of bulk to scare most men into seeing reason. Caleb had inherited that trait. With just the right look and emphasis on the right words, most men tended to agree with him. It didn't hurt that he was a big man as well, with that fiery Irish blood pumping through his veins. Caleb and his father could carry on a silent stalemate for weeks, months if need be. Caleb thought about protesting further, but he knew his father would ultimately win. Then Caleb thought about the voice attached to the words that had slayed him that morning. He wished he could wake up to that kind of passion every morning.

"The receptionist cursed at me in three languages, then insulted me. Bad first impression," Caleb told his father, with bitterness in his voice. Yet, he couldn't help but envision a leggy, cat-eyed, blond Brazilian bombshell with full, pink, juicy lips and perky C-cup breasts with ripe wine–colored nipples on honey colored skin. Her scent would evoke images of the beach at sunset, Caleb thought as he shifted. Caleb didn't take unsolicited recommendations, but he was learning to trust his father's instincts. "I apologize for my behavior. Maybe the hostile receptionist rubbed off on me."

"I figured you was ready to move away from artsy fartsy."

"Fine Gold Artistic Visions, Pop. I have a history with them."

"I've always thought their work was stale. Now these people are all about making things fly atcha. Kablowie."

"Kablowie, Pop?" Caleb asked, with a smirk, relieved he and his father were back on an even keel.

"Face it, lad. Even that one phone call was more exciting that any meeting you've had at Finney Whiney."

"Quinn, these guys are way off the beaten path."

"They are a New York company with an impressive roster of clients. They couldn't do that without some business acumen."

Caleb listened to his father spout more facts and statistics, but all he was hearing was the sensual voice of the receptionist in his head. She'd said just as much. He had thought he'd relegated thoughts of her to the dark part of his brain, which he kept under lock and key, but somehow she'd managed to leave the door ajar, and she slipped in and out at will. Now he really wanted to meet the woman that caused a tightening of his groin just at the thought of her. He dated cardboard women who just wanted to be seen on his arm. All of them were beautiful and smart, but they lacked any originality. They were all carbon copies of what society was spitting out at factory assembly-line rates. Meeting someone who thumbed her nose at convention might be interesting. Besides, he could set the meeting, meet the voice, and keep his father satisfied all in thirty minutes.

"I'll fire my secretary, dock my own pay, and call your

friend as soon as I get up. Okay, Pop? But I'm not promising anything."

"Good. Because I don't do bullshit."

"Me neither."

For Quinn and Caleb, that was as good as a promise.

"And I don't think your cousin will appreciate you saying you'll fire her."

"Like she'd ever leave. She's stubborn, just like a true Quinlan."

"Aye to that, son. Aye to that."

Chapter 5

Jai started her morning with her usual hour-long slamming of the snooze button, followed by a forty-five-minute exercise debate, which made it too late to do anything but grab a shower, throw on something, and catch a cab to work.

Jai got out of the cab three blocks from her job and grabbed a chocolate-strawberry-banana smoothie and three donuts, convincing herself the walk would burn up the calories and count as exercise.

The morning was fast paced. Phones rang, and Jai ordered one secretary or another to tackle the calls, because anyone with an iota of authority was out of the office, and she didn't trust herself if Mr. Sexy Voice called. She ran meetings and tackled scheduling with her manic energy. She left no one waiting and wasted no one's time, escorting each client out the door, with laughter on their lips and a sense of accomplishment in the air. When the lunch hour came, Jai felt as though she had waited a lifetime for a moment of solitude. Her first order of business was to close the office for an hour and head to the bathroom. She worked at her tight curls until they were neatly brushed out, gelled to her scalp in front, and tickling the back of her neck, separated by a black headband with silver kitties on it. She applied Mango Tango lotion to her hands and found herself high stepping down the hall, grateful to finally have time to dedicate to her staff and their needs.

The kids were blaring music and dancing around the office, eating pizza, and guzzling red Kool-Aid slushies. Jailyn was in the middle of a rowdy debate about Russell Simmons and P. Diddy having more influence over current trends than Bill Gates and U2's Bono when her intercom blared over all the noise. "There's a suit coming in with Paul. ETA seven. Oh, and woo, woo, hottie alert for all you afternoon listeners."

"Thanks, Mickey," Jai said.

"And could you send someone down to cover for me?" asked Mickey. Her voice dropped to an urgent whisper. "I gotta go again."

"I thought that stopped after the first trimester," said Jai.

"Someone lied to you. Probably some fool man who has never been pregnant," Mickey said.

"I'll send some pizza down for you, too," replied Jai.

"Thanks, Jai," Mickey said.

Jailyn flicked off the stereo, to mock boos and a couple shouts of "shoot the DJ" from her crew. "Attention. Reynolds is back in the building with company. Ros—"

"Yeah, yeah, I'm going," Ros said, without malice. No one took issue with minding the office with Jai. She was known to close the office, order lunch in, blast music, and use the security camera to play receptionist. But lately she and her team were under constant surveillance, so they were all ready to behave themselves and do as she instructed.

"Someone who's dressed nice, relieve Mickey and bring her some pizza," said Jai. Two young women, college sophomores, took up their sketch pads, volunteering happily. They quickly went out the door, hoping to get the first look at the hottie.

Tyrell, a high school sophomore, grabbed a file, slammed a slice of pepperoni pizza on a plate, and shouted around a piece of anchovy pizza jammed in his mouth. "Wait up! You forgot Mickey's pizza."

"Tyrell, stay awhile. Let Mickey have a real break," Jai ordered, helping the other students with the hasty cleanup. Tyrell was her up-and-coming star. Having lived in the worst New York neighborhoods, he lost his father to street violence when he was a young kid, but never once did he allow it to interfere with his responsibilities as an older brother or as a student. Jai tried to make his path easier, and it was paying off.

Jai continued to bark orders. "Someone tell Ros to run interference with whoever is with Reynolds. I don't want to see the guy, but I want deep intel. The rest of you go take up positions at vacant desks. Make sure you work on something relevant please. And don't tie up the phone lines calling each other, and remember I check IMs and cookies."

Jailyn left specific notes for each of the kids, pertaining to their workload for the remainder of the day. She used the last three minutes to gather her campaign for CK hand soap and to escape to the sanctity of the office upstairs. She would devote this time to reviewing the ideas of the students, grading work, and incorporating as much as she could into the campaign.

She went to the end of the hall and took the stairs up one flight. She walked to the office, which most people assumed was vacant. Before she opened the door, she heard the deep voices of men on the other side. She planned to lay a slew of curses at the feet of one Paul Reynolds after she met his client and stole him away. She pasted a business veneer on her face, but then she remembered her clothes. She was wearing her standard uniform of Levi's jeans and a black Betty Boop T-shirt and had bare feet. *Oh well. There goes that,* she thought as she walked in.

Three men were sipping water while conversing. They stopped to watch her enter, as if she were an intruder. Nothing appeared to have been disturbed; even the air barely moved. It was like a scene from *The Godfather.*

"What's up?" Jai asked, walking across the room and sliding her work on the empty desk. Her voice was falsely upbeat. "Where you been hiding all morning?"

"Damage control," the man on the couch answered.

"Meetings," the man behind her desk replied, a mystical vibe floating across the room to greet her.

"Breakfast with the Interplanetary Alliance of the Galaxy," said the third man, from the arm of a chair.

All three had answered in unison, and she didn't know whom to address first, but she had to laugh at the third response. But the man behind her desk helped solve that dilemma. Toiji was a beautiful Filipino man who just turned thirty-seven. He had a head full of jet-black hair styled only by the best. He always dressed in a mix of eclectic styles from throughout Asia, including from his own country, and of course, from America. Today he wore cream-colored, leather slip-on driving shoes, which he removed from her desk without a sound, and a matching three-quarter tunic and harem pants. His fingers were woven together around the bottle he held. He was very stuck on his outward appearance and extremely egocentric. "Judith said we would find you here, but I had my doubts. From the look of this office, I would deduce you never come here."

"There's not enough space for my drafting table and portfolio, let alone a full-sized storyboard," Jai said.

"Why not?" said Christian, from the far corner of the couch. At forty, he and Judith were considered the elders in their partnership. Like Toiji, Christian had an inflated sense of self. He was a single, distinguished-looking, and smartly dressed Caucasian man. Tall, big-breasted women of varying ages and beauty were always competing for his company. "The four of us are in here, and we're not even breathing the same air," he added.

"I've seen her office downstairs, and believe me, she'd work on the ceiling if she could," said Kevin, the third man. "There're sketches, prepped canvases propped against the walls, charcoals, drafting tables, stools, and kids everywhere. I can't make heads or tails of it." Kevin spoke in a rational tone, but he made her laugh, anyway. He was always on her side. Kevin was a type, just not her type. He was a tall, dark, and handsome African American male, was born and raised in Brooklyn, New York, and was thirty-six and single. He fell into the unnoticed group of nice, straight, educated, working black men. A rarity. He winked at her, and their pretend love affair was on again. However, she couldn't take the concentrated looks being thrown her way from the other two.

"What? Get off my back. I know where everything is," she said in her defense.

"Because it's all sitting in a pile on the floor," Kevin said in his lighthearted way.

"What is this? A cleaning intervention?" she asked. Her special gift allowed her to find most anything.

"What's the big deal? It's my office." She was about to sit on the corner of her desk when she stopped and glared at the closest offender. "Toiji, get out of my seat. Please," she said in her feigned indignation. "I don't know how you got in here. . . ."

"You don't lock the door," Christian said.

"I don't know why ya'll are here . . . ," she replied.

"Judith called us," Toiji answered.

Oh, so I've been ratted out, she thought to herself.

"She's working, and she can't cut it short just because you need her," Christian said, his voice turning cold.

She stole a quick peek his way. Lately, she'd noticed little changes with Christian that bothered her. The creases in his pants were not as sharp; he no longer struck a pose when talking to people, but crossed his arms over his chest; he hunched his back when he walked; and he didn't speak to people as much as at them. Though none of those things were conclusive evidence that Christian wasn't himself, the fact that they weren't getting along was proof enough.

"Jai, are you listening to me?" said Christian. This time she looked directly at him. Even in the shadows she saw that his blond hair was thinning and that he was putting on weight. His hazel eyes seemed to have become dimmer. "The world can't stop every time you're in a crisis."

"But you've got us. We'll help in any way possible. What do you need us to do?" Kevin said, sliding into the chair and offering a comforting smile. Toiji, who was now sitting on the opposite end of the couch from Christian, gave a nod of reassurance. She looked at their concerned expressions.

The roles they each had were much the same as they were the day they met. Toiji was the social son, Kevin the obedient child, and Jai the misunderstood daughter. She was the youngest, the most avant-garde, the one most likely to pull a bizarre idea out of thin air and make it work. Consequently, failures were hers alone, but her successes belonged to them all. She didn't go to them with her problems. She shared those with her father. His death had left her with nowhere to turn. It had left her quiet, withdrawn, and introverted.

That seemed to be the cause of the friction between Christian and her. Although the quarterly figures had risen consistently in the past, they had recently taken a serious dive, because she was mentally on hiatus. Jailyn assumed Christian was waiting for her to come out of her funk, and now it seemed like his patience was wearing thin.

"Can't we turn a light on? This can't be good, sitting in the dark all the time," Christian said. "You draw in the dark, too? No wonder you're depressed. This alone is depressing."

"I happen to prefer the dark. It keeps me settled," said Jai.

"You don't seem settled," Toiji remarked.

"I'm fine," she whispered. "I need to keep working. Stay busy. I thought some time off might help. . . ."

"How in the world would that help? You've got clients, students, projects, and coworkers depending on you. Where would that leave us?" Christian ground out, getting to his feet. "All you've been doing lately is thinking of yourself, as if you're the only one with problems."

"Chill, Christian," Kevin said, stepping in front of him. Christian gave him a hard look, but Kevin didn't back down. "Give the girl a break."

"A break? A break! What are you talking about?" replied Christian. "She comes and goes as she pleases, she doesn't meet with anyone if she doesn't want to, she turns down clients without consulting us, and her work is shit right now. In the real world, she'd have been fired."

"This isn't the real world?" Kevin sneered. "That Rolls Royce you have looks awful real, and the house in the Poconos, where you take your women, seems real enough, and, damn, even the tits on those chicks you pay for look real to me. Oh, and let's not forget the hundred-dollar bottles of scotch you buy, and the courtside season tickets you have to the Knicks games, which you give away to your friends because you hate basketball, and your generous entertainment budget. All of that seems damned real."

Jai watched Christian back down, like a wounded animal. A look of quiet disgust was evident on Christian's face. Kevin's was openly hostile.

"I propose a compromise," Toiji said. "How about a working vacation? That should satisfy all concerned. You stay busy, you get to leave and get a new perspective, and you get your numbers back up. And you and Christian get a respite."

"What Ju Ju Bee won't come home, so send the mountain to Mohammed?" Jai asked.

"Nah, we wouldn't do that to Jude," Keivn said, moving away from Christian. "This is a new account. An old construction firm originally from New England, now operating out of New York. When the guy inherited it, it was losing money. He turned it around, made it lucrative. They want a facelift, starting with a property in Connecticut. It's in the file in your drawer."

She reached in and took out five files and held them up.

"What? You said you wanted to keep busy," said Kevin.

He took two files, and Toiji took one. They headed out the door. Christian hung back.

"I told them you'd have some ideas drafted by the end of the week," Christian said, flicking the open file she was holding. "I want them begging us to take them on. Understood?"

"You shouldn't have told them that," Jai said, closing the file and folding her arms across her chest. He might be older, but her father was dead and buried, and even in the best light, Christian wasn't ready to take her on. "I have to meet them first. This is just a file."

"The company is older than both of us combined. Draw a big yellow happy face on it, and make it work. That's why you have this office. You're the mastermind behind all of this. And, quite frankly, the year we all suffered with you is enough to make us walk, unless you make this right."

"No one but you is complaining," she said, leveling her gaze on him.

"How would you know? You've hardly been here. You've been wallowing in your grief for months. We're tired of being depressed for your sake, and we're tired of tiptoeing around your sensitive behind."

"Just because you don't understand what I'm going through doesn't mean it isn't valid."

"I understand he's dead and you're not." Christian's voice was caring, but the words hurt her, anyway.

"Don't overstep your bounds," Jai said.

"Maybe it's time someone did," Christian challenged. "Money is tight, business is slow, and you've been off your game."

She couldn't explain to Christian or anyone what she had been seeing that was hampering her creative flow.

She couldn't explain the vivid nightmares of men chasing her and her father, of the sun burning the earth and making it a barren wasteland, of the men lynching her father so many times, she could no longer count, and of their faces turning to those of strangers before her eyes. The smells of decaying bodies stuck in her nostrils, and the feel of blood and broken bones was familiar to her hands. Lately, the nightmares had all but gone, but she had never told them, and never could, because they already thought she was bizarre. This would definitely get her sent away. She was definitely better. The problem was she had no idea if she would ever be the same.

"When Judith gets back, we'll hire an outside firm to run an audit to see where we stand, do some major marketing of our own, or consider breaking camp," said Jai.

"You don't need to run numbers to see we've had a bad year. And if we decide to close, we need to be in a better position financially," Christian said, talking fast. "You buy low, sell high. And in the future, talk to me before you go running to Judith Gannon," he added in a snide voice as he walked out the door, leaving Jai with a sense that all was not right in Christian's world.

Jailyn took out her cell phone and began dialing the long series of numbers.

"Hello," a happy voice said in her ear.

"Hey, Jude. How's your trip going?"

"What? You didn't read the three-page e-mails I sent you out today, yesterday, and the day before?"

"For real? You know that goat wouldn't make it a block in downtown Brooklyn without someone trying to put him in a pot and sprinkling some curry on his butt."

"Okay, so you got my e-mails."

"And you guys rode all the way up the mountain, but I can't get you to walk a city block?" Jai asked.

"You wrote me that joke last week, so you must really be trying to sell this to the crowd," Judith said as Jai laughed uncontrollably. "Okay, you laugh and keep making up shit, and I'll talk."

"That's why you got caught in the rain. You must have smelled like mildew all night."

"I went over the faxes you sent, and I can't see any pattern. In fact, the only thing I noticed is someone has gone through a lot of trouble to make innocent mistakes look innocent."

"Jude, I was thinking the same thing! Don't they overcharge for American stuff?"

"I saw that. It looks like we charged Spike energy drinks for fifty-two kiosks, but there were only six trade shows and three displays at each. I saw the difference was deducted out, but no checks were cut to the client."

"Or reallocation . . . ," Jai added in a whisper.

"I saw that in the Fanta account, we billed for the posters but only received half the number. The refund came to us, but again, we never cut a check or reallocated."

"Money in a woman's hand will just disappear at an outdoor flea market," Jai said. "So what else can a husband do? Follow his wife? Go shopping with her? Ask for receipts?"

"Yes. I need you to pull invoices from all the departments, from one account for each team. But first pull the time cards. See who's working overtime. I think we'll find discrepancies there, which will tell you which accounts to pull. I also want files on new hires and where they've been assigned. Get me the bank deposits from Christian and Dave. . . ."

"Slow down, misame. That's what I called about. I probably will never date again, let alone that man. Apparently, my contemplative attitude is not well received by all."

"So, Christian is on the warpath again? All right. Use it to your advantage. Use it to tick him off, and get into that office. And get Ros to get you a list of our contractors, with up-to-date contacts. And I want to see a standard contract and what's been going out recently."

"Sounds like a real adventure. Wish I could be there."

"And don't forget to highlight discrepancies."

"I know one clean copy and one with my old voodoo magic. I don't see what this is gonna prove."

"It's going to prove that someone there has scammed a tidy pocket full of change from us, and I can guarantee that whoever it is has a second set of books as evidence."

"I never understood why a criminal keeps the incriminating evidence. I mean, you stole it. Do you really need to account for it, let alone twice?"

"You can't possibly be that stupid. You're not even blond."

Chapter 6

Caleb walked into his office, with a lethal calm. His cousin and personal assistant spun in her chair to gauge his mood. She got up from her desk and followed him in the wake of steam coming from under his collar, trying not to get burned. But, as usual, he glided around the office with his signature aristocratic stealth, which could annihilate a woman's sensibilities and scare a man witless. It was only because she was his cousin that she recognized the telltale signs of suppressed rage: his head sort of cocked to one side, his hand jammed into his pocket, in a fist, and the ruthless glint in his eye.

Saoirse Graham dispensed with the morning pleasantries and went about fixing cups of coffee, while Caleb logged on to his computer and checked his messages. As soon as he pulled out his PDA, she snatched it up and began reviewing his itinerary, downloading anything new to her computer while uploading anything she scheduled in. "Your father called here yesterday," she said. "Couldn't have been more than a few hours after you landed. What does he have? A tracking device on your behind? If so, tell him I need one, too."

"I'm sure he's got someone in the police department tracking me by GPS. He caught me at home. The man woke me from a dead sleep. Ruined a damned good dream, too, and for what? A meeting this morning with his oddball friends?" Caleb complained, taking off his jacket and lounging back in his chair.

He didn't say it aloud, but he enjoyed those mornings when he got to sit and have coffee with his cousin. Saoirse was his aunt Ann's daughter, and she and Caleb were the oldest of the next generation of Quinlans. Although he was older than her by five years or so, they had always been close. He liked her husband, Wallace Graham, a professor of earth science at CUNY, and was more than fond of her twin boys, Ryan the Ruffian and Bryan the Bully. The boys were school age now, and Saoirse, with her traditional Irish name and none of the ways, was as thrilled to be out of the house as he was to have her around. She was an indispensable asset.

"Uh-huh. So at least I know who's in charge," she said, sitting across from him, blowing on her brew. He threw a pencil at her, and she chuckled, glad that she was one of the few people capable of lightening his mood. "So what did dear old dad get you into?"

"I can't figure out which weirdo your uncle is friends with, so I tried not to insult anyone."

"Must have been a real test for you." She ducked another pencil, and he took another sip of the thick black Bustelo coffee.

"That guy Paul Reynolds is using me to get into the inner circle. He's like an upscale car salesman trying to impress the hell out of everyone. I doubt he's Quinn's connect. Christian Meyer is closer to my age, with a gut that makes him look about three months pregnant. He's got a comb-over and plugs. . . ." Saoirse laughed while he went on with his comical description. "He has watery eyes, crow's-feet, and bags under his eyes, like he hasn't ever experienced a decent night's sleep, and yet women are constantly flirting with him."

"Suit?"

"Armani."

"Watch?"

"Movado."

"Rolex is the number one answer," she said like the announcer on *Family Feud*. "Shoes?"

"Alligator. Italian. Dyed."

"Wallet, card, keys, change?"

"Nothing disturbing the lines of his pants and not a jingle to be heard. Business cards are linen stock, embossed, elegant. In a silver engraved case, inner jacket pocket." He contemplated the obvious, knowing his own answers would be similar. He dined at restaurants where he kept an account, had the company car drive him around, and never carried change. "Anyone can pull off being rich these days," he said, disgusted by the knowledge.

"Just long enough to convince the weak of mind," Saoirse added. "Next."

"The Asian dude, Toiji. No last name. Quiet. Spooky quiet, like trying to read me and solve the riddles that will take him one step closer to reaching the answer to carry to Delphi."

"Aren't we all, dungeon master?" she asked, topping off his cup and putting his PDA on his desk. "One name. Very chic. Cher, Madonna, Ciara . . ."

"Ciara?"

"The boys love her, not to mention Graham. Next."

"Kevin Rhodes."

"That sounds familiar and normal."

"Kevin was cool. Tall, well-dressed black guy. Articulate and to the point, he was there to wow the client, secure the deal, and get to work. He's young, but he could be Pop's friend, since everyone is Pop's friend."

"Sounds promising. So are you going to use them?"

"I have no intentions of letting my father's favors put me in a bad situation," he said, his voice curt.

Saoirse knew when the fuzzy morning meetings were drawing to a close, so she got up, taking some of the papers from his desk. "Uncle Quinn is not like your stepfather. He'd sacrifice his own life before letting anything bad happen to you. Just remember that. He may not have been there every day of your life, but he's always been a part of it. When your mother came to him because Brad had used all her money, including your college fund, he had no qualms asking the family to help him out. And don't look at me like that. I've known for a long time, and, no, I wasn't supposed to tell you. No one was ever gonna tell you, because you didn't need to know, and those were his words. He said he didn't want you to feel obligated to act like his son. He wanted you to chose to be his son. I guess he knows you as well as anyone, and he's never steered you wrong."

"They asked about Tobin," Caleb said, speaking into the steeple of his fingers, his eyes shifting to her and then back.

"Yeah, what about him?"

"Wanted to know if we parted amicably."

"Maybe they've heard some rumors that he isn't a particularly nice enemy to have."

"I don't know, but I don't like it. Pop mentioned

him, too, and I'm thinking it's a bad omen. But you've spoken to Quinn about this, and that's their file, so tell me what you think."

"Run the gamut?"

"Yes, and answer any questions you have until you're satisfied," he said in business mode, sitting with his head bent, reviewing some notes she'd left. "I want your opinion."

"Then don't worry about your father. He knows you research everybody and make informed decisions. No bias," she said, giving him a wink and drifting to the door.

"The secretary cursed me out. In three languages."

"Impressive. I've only told you to kiss my behind in English. I'll have to ask her for some lessons in case you get it in your head to fire me," she said, pulling the door behind her as his cup of pencils went flying through the air.

At the end of his day, Caleb dialed the number from his personal digital assistant, reposed in his chair, legs outstretched and crossed at the ankles. He had called Christian after leaving the meeting to find out who he should direct his questions to and to put in a decent word for the receptionist. After seeing her, he wished he had more of his father's patience. He'd also spent an inordinate amount of time thinking about what his cousin told him, and now he wanted to finish his day and go home to bed.

"Jai here. State your business." Her voice held an easy smile. It was a balm for his hectic day, which he didn't know he needed.

"Is that the way you answer a phone? You must not have learned anything the other day, huh?" Jai could hear the joking manner in the unmistakable voice. She didn't know why he was being pleasant, but she liked it.

"This is my private cell phone. I can answer any way I like to, thank you very much," she said, stretching her legs and leaning back in her chair.

"Oh," he said, looking at his PDA like it had done something offensive. "I hadn't realized."

"How'd you get this number?" she asked, hearing the tension in his voice.

"Reynolds. Sorry to have disturbed you at home." His voice was exceedingly polite.

"You didn't. I'm still in the office."

"Oh," he responded, not sounding any better. Jai suspected Paul Reynolds wanted to make her look bad by giving out her private number so the guy would catch her off guard yet again.

"So what's up?" she asked, trying to keep the mood light.

The sensual coolness of her voice made his blood pump faster. "I met with your people. I wanted to apologize for my shortness with you the other day, and I assured your bosses that the phone call was a misunderstanding."

"And what did my bosses have to say about that?" she asked in a snotty tone.

"Don't like them much, huh? I wouldn't, either, if I were you, considering they offered you up like a sacrificial lamb at the altar of me."

Jai's breath caught, and her heart flew up into her throat. She saw her body, seminude in a torn and smudged gossamer gown, splayed before him on a stone altar, with heavy shackles and chains holding her spread eagle. He wore a crown, precariously perched on his head, and some sort of long leather sarong, his bulging pectorals bared to her. The picture shot through her mind in Technicolor 3-D.

She tried to come up with a witty reply, but her tongue lay heavy in her mouth. So the voice continued in her ear. "It's a good thing I'm not into sacrificing pregnant women. Now maybe if you were a virgin, I might consider opening up shop."

Jai jumped up and nearly shook her teeth out of her head. "I'm sorry. Did you say pregnant?"

"Yeah. I saw you when I came by your offices today. You were waddling awful slow, and that would explain your mood swings the other day on the phone."

She stretched her shirt flat and leaned back to make sure she could see her naked toes past her stomach. She found her breasts were in the way. But she was pretty sure she didn't look . . . "Oh my goodness, you think I'm Mickey. She was covering the reception desk at lunch. Michaela Ruiz. Short, fair-skinned Hispanic girl with long, straight dark hair?"

"You forgot pregnant."

"Yeah . . . not me," Jai said, relieved.

"Not you?" he repeated, with heat in his voice, which made the phone in her hand sizzle.

"No. I was hiding in back." Jai's adrenaline kicked into high. "Not hiding from you. I mean, I was in back, but you couldn't know that, and I'm not prone to mood swings . . ." she babbled.

Caleb barely heard a word as he sat back, listening to his fantasy woman rebuild herself in his mind. His hand unconsciously went to his stiffening groin as he imagined her sauntering into his office in a tight suit that emphasized the delicious swell of her backside, and slowly shutting the door. Occasionally, a Spanish phrase or French term or some sort of accent would pop out of her mouth, and he fantasized about making love to her while she spoke intimate words to him in a foreign tongue.

"I apologize for going on like this, but I'm nervous," added Jai. Her hand flew to cover her mouth, and she plopped into her chair, missing it by inches and hitting the floor with a soft thud. She scrambled up, thinking, *What the hell made me admit that?*

"You have a similar effect on me." He paused to let the words and their not so subtle meaning brush over her. "It's refreshing, the way you speak your mind. My dad's like that, so maybe that's why I like you." *Whoa, what am I saying? I should not be flirting with her. She could be as ugly as a troll, and I'd have to see her,* Caleb thought to himself.

"I'm going to thank you for the compliment, although I don't know if being compared to someone's father is a compliment for a young, vibrant woman like myself."

"If you knew my pop, you'd be flattered. Everyone loves him. He's this incredible guy who knows a little about everything and makes it sound like he's Buddha. He's also got the ability to insult someone and make it seem like a compliment. I think he's got a piece of the Blarney stone under his pillow."

"Blarney stone?"

"Irish legend. It's believed that if you kiss this stone, you get the eternal gift of eloquence and bullshit."

"With all your quasi flattery, I guess you inherited the gift, too," Jai said, with her requisite attitude thrown in for good measure.

Caleb was getting accustomed to the don't-mess-with-me edge in her voice. In bed, he figured she was a dominant type of woman, commanding him, "*Harder. That's it. Right there,*" in that voice while he moved in and out of her. He would have her talk dirty to him in the heat of the moment and then would give her all that she asked for until she gave an uninhibited cry of satisfaction. But he'd also heard that women who were dominant in the real world became extremely submissive in bed. He could imagine her eyes partially closed, her body being coaxed open by his touch, her begging for him in a near whimper. *Please. I need to feel you right now.*

Instead, she said, "I have to get back to work." She hastily added, "But feel free to call me . . . at this number . . . if you have any questions about anything. Anytime."

"I don't want to take advantage. Especially if you're busy."

"I'm always available to you. I mean, at this number. You can reach me. Even if I'm busy, I'll make time. That is to say, I make time for all clients. I can even deal with taskmasters. They're my specialty."

Jai dropped her forehead into the palm of her hand. She couldn't believe she was flirting. How was the poor man expected to read deeper into a vaguely opaque, passing hint of a notion of an offer? If she was going to do this, it was time to do it right. She took a deep breath and plunged ahead. "Next time you're around, stop by and say hello. We can get a coffee or something." She knew she'd have to hang up soon or she'd start laughing at her ridiculous attempt at being a sex kitten.

There was no mistaking the change of mood or the loaded meaning behind her words. "Sounds like a plan. You can curse at me live and in person."

"I think we can find something much more productive to do. Go over to Starbucks, have a grande vanilla bean cappuccino with lots of whipped cream and milk." She giggled into her hand at all her kitten references.

"Then I'll have to schedule in some time, but I'm definitely more of an espresso straight kind of guy. No milk and no cream. The blacker and stronger, the better," Caleb volleyed as his manhood responded with rock hard enthusiasm. He imagined his Brazilian bombshell walking toward him, each step slightly worrying the small, tasteful split of her skirt as it crept up her shapely left thigh, her jacket molding her sumptuous breasts and providing peeks of a lace camisole that barely concealed the swell of cleavage. She was deliberately peeling off layers of clothing as she crossed the room, revealing her gorgeous golden curves, her private parts strategically hidden by scraps of pale lingerie.

They must have said their good-byes a while ago, because the monotone male voice told him, "There appears to be a receiver off the hook."

"Ah, motherfucker," he muttered.

Chapter 7

The following day Jai exhausted herself by finishing the campaigns she had in front of her. Three out of the seven went to Toiji in photography, two went to Kevin in copy, and the remaining two stayed with her interns so they could put together the client presentations. Eva had left her a file, which she quickly reviewed, committed to memory, and faxed to Judith in Rome. Ros had set up meetings for her new accounts. However, the construction firm seemed to be eluding her.

"Jailyn," Christian said, calling her from across the lobby before she could reach the door. He caught up to her, breathing deeply from his little ten-foot jog. "Did you speak with Eva?"

"No."

"Oh. Well, you'll have time before your flight to come by here and pick up your tickets, traveler's checks, and hotel reservations. I'm not sure if Eva reserved a car, but that's minor. She can handle that when the two of you land. I hope you don't object to her being your account rep."

"Never." Jai's voice was light and happy.

"Good."

"What's this all about?"

"The working vacation we discussed," Christian said, still breathing deeply, as if he had run miles instead of feet.

"We discussed it, but nothing was decided. I handle my own accounts."

"Everything's been arranged. You've been temperamental, and this is too important to brush aside."

"Yeah, but I'm not going anywhere. Night, Christian."

"Eva will be disappointed."

"Since when do ARs go on location?" she said, as if asking, "Why doesn't Santa deliver mail?"

"Well, I thought you might like the company." His voice annoyed her. It was as if he were doing her a favor, and she was being an ungrateful brat.

"I don't need company. I need a photographer. So as soon as I hire one, I'll make plans to go."

"You're an accomplished photographer. You can take your own photos. This meeting is important," Christian asserted.

"I have meetings scheduled for this week and next right here in New York."

"We'll have Ros reschedule tomorrow when she gets in."

"No can do, boss man. I have four presentations to make, and I'll be meeting with the new accounts. First impressions and all that yazz. Muy importante. So I'll see you tomorrow, and don't work too late." It was odd to see Christian in the office after four, just as it was weird that she was leaving while the sun was still out.

"They'll be expecting you in Connecticut tomorrow, and you will be there," he said firmly.

"Fuck you, Christian," Jai said to his retreating back, her voice still sunny.

"Fuck me? Fuck me!" The hostility rolled off of Christian like heat waves on New York asphalt.

"Sí, no lo puedo creer," she mumbled, shaking her head. "Yo estoy harta y muy cansada. Do you understand, Christian? Leave me the fuck alone."

He advanced on Jai with a treacherous leer. "Who do you think you are?"

"I'm the one who created this," she whispered, waving a wistful hand and taunting him.

"You're also the one who damn near destroyed it," he said, invading her personal space. Kevin appeared in the corner of her eye to intercept Christian. Kevin had come down the hall and had burst through the small crowd of loitering spectators. Paul Reynolds was front and center, anticipating her downfall. Toiji came gliding out of his office on the opposite side of the lobby.

"Christian, let's take this in the office," Kevin said while Toiji sent everyone back to work.

Christian turned and walked into his office. As soon as the door to his luxurious office, with all of its costly amenities, was closed, Christian faced the three of them. "I can't baby-sit one emotionally decrepit individual when I have a corporation to look out for. A corporation that provides for the livelihood of all those faces out there, as well as you, Mr. Rhodes. If she wants to fuck up her own life, fine. That's on her. But you'll not be pointing fingers at me when the money dries up and we're all looking for new jobs."

"Don't you think you're exaggerating?" Kevin said.

"We're talented professionals in a competitive and lucrative field. We'll be fine," Toiji seconded.

"He doesn't care about those things. He cares about

the money," Jai added in a whisper. "Kevin, Toiji, would you mind if Christian and I had a moment alone?"

Kevin and Toiji looked from Christian to Jai and felt as though it was high noon at the O.K. Corral. It was best to scatter, but they had no place to go where they wouldn't get hit with debris, even if they left the room. If shares could be counted as bullets, they would be unarmed men within minutes. No matter what happened, they would be caught in the crosshairs of two formidable opponents.

Jai opened the door, and an eerie feeling swept into the room. Kevin looked into Jai's eyes as he was leaving, and there was no mistaking her strength. The playing field was now level. From the time papers were signed, they had all been considered equal partners and had been treated as such, but it was impossible not to feel the tables of power turning at a dizzying rate. Christian appeared to be the one falling the fastest and holding on the tightest. The door seemed to swing shut by a force of will, the lock clicking loudly into place.

"So, Christian, what is this all about? The company is not in jeopardy of folding, and we're no worse for wear. But this is about money," she said, her eyes narrowing. "Your money."

"So what if it is? I like having money, and lots of it. Who doesn't? It's the American Dream. And you don't have the right to destroy that for me and everyone else."

"Why not? I made it happen. He who giveth can taketh away," she said flippantly.

"You are not God!" Christian yelled, slamming his hands on his desk, making the expensive art on his walls rattle. "You can't deny me shit, and you can't take anything away from me!"

"Then stop blaming me," she said quietly, moving

farther into the room, out of the shadow of the door. "If I'm not God, then I don't have the ability to make or break anything. This company, our partners, our employees, or you, Christian Meyer. So stop acting like your problems are my fault."

"You seem to forget, I invested the biggest chunk, so I stand to lose the most—"

"You've made your money back at least five times over."

"And you've lost us ten times that!" Christian opened his jacket and sat down behind his desk, his normally calm demeanor slipping into place, as if his last statement was irrefutable. "When we opened this place, we agreed on specific positions, titles, and duties. I don't go into anyone's office and tell them how to run their division or do their job, now do I? But I was charged with bookkeeping for the entire business. I account for every penny in or out of this place for everyone, and in the last year the numbers have become dismal. I refuse to stand around and let this continue. If you want me to do my job successfully, then you'll be on that fucking plane, or you'll be running this place alone."

Silence covered the room like a nighttime snowstorm. Quiet, cold, and oddly soothing in its desolation, with an eeriness that made the hairs on your arm stand up. Jai stepped forward and leaned over the desk, looking into Christian's haggard face. Worry lines creased his brow, his skin was rough, and his eyes were murky. He wasn't Christian anymore. He was some desperate, money-hungry piranha who had managed to slither his way into their midst. Jailyn didn't care if he left. He no longer belonged.

"The next time you feel the need to throw a public tantrum, check yourself on the lobby videotape so you can see how stupid you look. . . ."

"You bitch," he said, standing so violently, his chair toppled with a loud bang.

"Shut up. I'm not finished," she said. "I told you yesterday that you can hold your breath until you're blue, kick and scream, whatever makes your world go 'round, but you'll never get me on a plane in this lifetime."

"Then walk," Christian said, with dead calm.

"Don't tempt me. It could be another year before I get back." Jai headed for the door. "And, Christian, you forget? I don't work for you."

"No, but if you want to have a place *to work*, you might want to start paying closer attention to *where you work*, because one day soon it may all just disappear."

"I'm not worried, Christian. I'll always have talent. What about you? If you're worried about money now, imagine if this place closes." Her eyes twinkled when she realized this last shot fired had hit home. "Good night and don't work too late."

Chapter 8

Jailyn Wyatt opened the doors of Creative Forces. She was dressed in a suit of mulberry stretch silk that was feminine, comfortable, and elegant. Her mother had found the perfect shoes: a velveteen pair of three-inch, peep-toe navy blue sling-backs. The final touch—a dark blue, double-breasted, military-style trench coat, complete with epaulettes—was slung over her arm.

She stood her scarred leather portfolio case up against the side of the desk while she flung all nonessential clothing onto the nearby couch. The mostly empty Vivienne Tam pocketbook went zinging over the couch and into the wall when she tossed it like a Frisbee, and the trench coat barely hit its mark, resembling a cape as it hung half on and half off of the couch. She kept on the Ponte knit dark blue blazer, which was supposed to slim her waist and hips, but her reflection in every shining surface in Lower Manhattan, and there were a lot of them, proved she was the victim of false advertising. In fact, the damned outfit seemed to be designed to draw the attention of men, instead of allowing her to blend in with them.

Jai jabbed at the buttons on the console, listening to messages and forwarding them to the appropriate departments. She jotted down each call, noting the time and date and adding her own shorthand notes. She could commit anything she saw to memory, but hearing wasn't her forte. She let out a yelp when she stood up and Toiji was a hair's breadth away.

"Don't do that. You know I hate that," she cried.

"You need to hear as well as you see."

"Fat chance of that grasshopper, so stop with all the Shaolin stuff. And what are you doing here so early?"

"Waiting for you. Word in the bamboo forest is that you defied the almighty."

"Whatever." She shrugged, taking a seat behind the desk.

Toiji tapped in a familiar extension. "Hey, Jesus. She's here."

"Now why did you have to go and do that, tattletale?" she asked.

"I'll get Kev," said Christian. He almost sounded like his old self.

"Kev's here, too?" she asked, sucking her teeth.

"Gang's all here," Toiji said.

"Ya'll really don't trust a sista?" she asked.

"No," said all three men in unison.

"Stand up. Let's see," Kevin instructed while pulling her to her feet.

"This isn't Fashion Week," she said, tugging her hands away from him. He pushed her to the middle of the floor.

"She cleans up nice . . . ," Toiji said. "I like the way the fabric moves. Very different from your usual style. That's something I'd pick out. It's extremely flattering to your shape."

"I like the way it clings. Very nice," Kevin added.

"I like the manicure and pedicure," Toiji remarked. "Shows she pays attention to details."

"Haircut's hot, too," Kevin said. "It shows off her face, with a touch of sophistication."

"Sort of dykish. I am woman, hear me roar, and all that," Christian said, finally joining in.

"It looks good," Toiji said.

"I didn't contradict that. But I think she's still too testosterone driven. Too eager to best a man . . . ," Christian said. "But that might be a good thing in this case."

"How so?" Jai asked, folding her arms across her chest to stop herself from punching him in the mouth. Christian might be feeling all friendly, but she still didn't like his new slithering ways.

"Well, the freelance photographer we send with you may be adverse to hooking up with a masculine female. I want to save you the embarrassment of being dumped by another coworker and having to run away to lick your wounds," said Christian. He seemed to relish his own words, while Toiji and Kevin tried to blend into their surroundings like chameleons. "Oh, and the meeting with one of your clients had to be rescheduled. He has some sort of emergency and has to leave town."

"I still have the presentation this morning," said Jai.

"Ohhh. Didn't Ros reach you at home? Drat," said Christian. "I called them myself and personally apologized on your behalf for canceling. In fact, I cleared your schedule for the next two weeks. Personally. No one seemed to be surprised by that." Christian continued, holding out a thick envelope. "Your flight isn't until eleven. That gives you plenty of time to go home, pack, and get to the airport."

Jai unbuttoned her jacket and flung it haphazardly in the direction of Toijii, who stepped to one side, caught it, folded it, and placed it on the couch. She leaned over, the wrap tank blouse concealing little, and took off one shoe.

"It's only a forty-minute flight, and there's plenty of time in the schedule for sightseeing and pleasure," said Christian. "You and Eva should really have fun. The hotel is excellent for gambling. There's also a state-of-the-art gym you might want to take advantage of. Blue soda does have a lot of calories."

"The place also has a spa, a disco, a salon, and plenty of shows," Kevin added, sounding like a commercial. Jai flung the shoe blindly at Kevin, who deflected it at the last minute. "Hey, we're just the messengers," Kevin protested.

"You take way too much joy in ruining my day," replied Jai.

"Stop being such a spoilsport," Kevin said.

"Yes, this does work out for everyone," Christian said.

"I didn't spend good money on new suits, fight with crowds, and endure coercion from dim-witted salesgirls who don't know the difference between mulberry and plum just so I can get crammed into a tiny, germ-infested tube with a bunch of strangers for forty-five minutes," said Jai. "But you're right, this does work out for everyone, so I guess I will be boarding that plane."

"That money was not wasted," Kevin asserted, eyeing the cut of her blouse with admiration.

"I hate people who don't appreciate their jobs and then have the gall to perform them poorly," replied Jai. "I tried to explain the difference in hues to the salesgirl, but no. The tag says plum, so the color is plum. And I'm so frazzled that I take the proffered 'matching blouse,' which turns out to be the worst combination for a 'healthy' frame."

"The top does the body good," Kevin said, raising his eyebrows.

Jai leaned over and gave him more than an eyeful as she removed the other shoe. "When Ros gets in, tell her to find me a pair of size sixteen, black, stonewashed, flare-leg, button-fly Levi's." She flung the second shoe with such force, you could hear it hum through the air. It made contact with Christian's shoulder, causing sparks of pain, which were evident on his face. Tears sprung in his eyes; a violent curse was on his lips. Kevin and Toiji both winced.

"Duck," Kevin whispered. Toiji laughed and shook his head.

"I will get you two, and soon. Don't turn your back on me," said Jai. With steel in her voice, she added, "One of you can man the desk until Mickey gets in." With icy eyes trained on Christian, she said, "I'll be in my office, working."

Jai pulled out her portfolio case and began working on her sketch, her feet up on the drafting table. Her cell phone rang, and she grabbed it out of her pants pocket. "Talk fast. I got no clothes on."

"And good morning to you, too, sunshine."

Jai couldn't help but smile. Nothing she said seemed to rattle this particular caller. His voice was as smooth as Chablis. "Morning. How are you today?" she replied, suddenly feeling perky.

"Not so good. I'm in the meeting from hell. All-you-can-eat waffle and pancake bar, but wickedly poor company. Then I'll probably have to gas up the Lear and meet Bobby Deniro for lunch."

"Better than three guys harassing you all morning."

"Should I get you a lawyer? First, you're naked, and now three guys are harassing you. I'm not sure if I should be jealous or not."

"Don't be. Christian, Toiji, and Kevin are harmless."

Caleb was glad it was her bosses, and not Reynolds, on her case. At least he knew she was still gainfully employed. "So why is it you have no clothes on?"

"It's a story."

"I've got about ten minutes. Thirteen if I keep moving. Two if I hit a dead spot," he said playfully.

"It's really not that serious. 'Sides, I am dressed. So how about you tell me why you're calling, and please don't tell me it's to gas up the Lear for you." She secretly loved that he called at all. A tingle had started in her chest and was making its way down into her stomach.

"I'd like to invite you to an early lunch if possible, and the Lear is in the shop."

Her hand stopped sketching, her heart ceased beating, and the air refused to enter her lungs. The tingle tiptoed over her skin, leaving a trail of goose bumps on her arms, and she was sure she could hear birds singing.

"Hey, if the Lear is that important, let me see what I can rent on short notice," he added. "I'm sure your boss will give you time off for good behavior."

Reality encroached on her fantasy. Though the urge to blow off work in order to meet the voice was strong, it would make her look more irresponsible than Christian already thought she was. "Sorry. No can do. Busy, busy, busy," she said while shading in areas on her sketch, trying to maintain a semblance of normalcy.

She was about to go to war, and her day was going to be brutal, but she had every intention of making Christian look like the fool, by speaking to and meeting with as many of her clients as she could. It was easy to forget

Christian while listening to the rough voice cascading over her and soothing her hackles. The tingling in her stomach made its way down to her thighs, and his deep, even breaths made it hard to concentrate on his words.

"You gotta eat sometime," he said.

"I'll probably have a sandwich at my desk." She tried to sound nonchalant but thought she sounded more like she was constipated. "Yup. Might even skip lunch."

This wasn't the response he had expected. He was used to women asking him out. And he had expected Jai to sound hyper, jubilant, even angry, but he was insulted that she sounded bothered and put out. "Sorry to have disturbed you. I'll let you go then," he said tersely, not wishing to examine his response, because if he did, he might have to acknowledge just how much he was looking forward to meeting her and that she had gotten to him with her crass language and the sultry way she spoke. He would also have to admit that Creative Forces had made more of an impression on him in two days than Fine Gold Artistic Visions ever did. "Again, please accept my apologies."

"No need. I told you it's no bother. I'm always a phone call away. Maybe we can meet up late next week," she suggested.

"I'll be out of town." His tone was very matter-of-fact. But he didn't want to come off as dry, so he added, "The Lear should be back by then."

"Well, if the three sisters of fate so will it, then kismet will find his way."

Caleb wasn't sure what to make of that cross-spirituality mumbo, but at least it wasn't a "No way, buster. I'd rather burn at the stake like Joan of Arc than have lunch with you." Nor did he imagine she was playing hard to get. Caleb didn't bother with hard-to-get women, because they were often more interested in what could be done for them than what they could do for themselves. But Jai, with her attitude and sharp tongue, was a force to be reckoned with, and the reckoning was coming soon.

"I've got to go. My ten minutes are up, but hopefully, our paths will meet somewhere down the line," said Caleb. It was as close to kismet and fate as he could come.

The door to Jai's office filled with 240 pounds of sand-colored man. He was well-defined muscle from head to toe and was encased in tasteful clothing, which covered his six-foot-four-inch frame. His amber-colored eyes met hers, and an enigmatic smile bloomed on his devastatingly handsome face. She swung her feet to the floor and moved him with the swiftness of her stride. Christian, Toiji, and Kevin presented a united front. Over the phone, Caleb could hear French grumblings, which slid over him like a summer rain. And then he heard her ask in a harsh whisper, "Who the fuck is he?" before the line went dead.

"Meet James Ross, the freelance photographer you requested," Christian answered.

"I interview and select my own freelancers," Jai said, advancing. "How dare you assume control of my work schedule. First, the working vacation, then canceling my meetings, and now hiring my staff. Christian, you've lost your fucking mind."

Kevin put an arm around her waist to restrain her, but the momentum of her words propelled her forward. Christian held up his hands in mock surrender, but his smile was irritating the hell out of her. Toiji tried to block, but she kept closing the space, dragging Kevin with her for the ride.

"And you've got the nerve to walk into my office

without so much as a 'How do you do?' and to bring him with you," she said, jerking a thumb toward her office. "I have no shoes on and am wearing this flimsy shirt." She shook loose from Kevin's grasp and pushed Toiji as she walked back into her office, rapidly speaking French and gesturing wildly. She stopped in the middle of her office.

"Mr. Ross, please forgive my outburst, but it was inevitable," she said in a pleasant voice. "This isn't standard procedure, but then again, we aren't really sticklers for procedure around here."

"Not a problem," said James. His voice was higher than she had expected and lacked the sophistication of her phone friend. At that moment she realized something very crucial. She looked down at the blank LCD screen on her cell phone.

"Houston, we have a problem!" she shouted. She tossed the phone onto her desk and took off running. Kevin and Toiji dodged office furniture as they ran.

Christian, not daring to attempt to outrun her, locked himself in the first available office. "James, if you want the job, call the cops," Christian said in a muffled voice from behind the door.

James thought the playful dynamic in the office would make workdays go by faster, but more than that, he was impressed by the tenacity of the woman in plum. She vaulted a desk in order to pounce on her prey. She didn't let the three guys bully her or get to her. She stood her ground and fought back. Now they ran around the office like it was a playground.

James picked up the larger-than-life sketch she had been working on. Four soft vignettes, the lines so faint, they were like passing thoughts in a dream and yet unmistakably vivid, surrounded a charcoal figure in the center. A man lounged in one pose, his knees bent. He looked to be sitting on a throne. In the other, his repose was more relaxed, and he held a phone to his face, legs outstretched and crossed at the ankles. In the third, he was au natural, perched on the edge of a cliff. Although you couldn't see anything more than his head and shoulders, it was obvious that he was king of all he surveyed. In the fourth, the man was shadowed by the night, which hung low. He was working at a desk, a phone headset at his ear, his shirt somewhat wrinkled. The center picture was the same man. His hands were buried in his pockets, and his face was filled with laughter without laughing at all. His clothes were suitable for a casual day at work or a day at home. Again, he wore the phone headset. But from every angle in every picture, the face James recognized was his own.

Jai came through the doorway, taking gulps of air and dramatically staggering across the room. "If . . . I can . . . survive the next . . . five . . . minutes . . . how about . . . you and I . . . take a road trip?"

Chapter 9

After James agreed to the road trip, Jai cancelled her flight to Connecticut, and invited James to her house to have dinner with her mother and Quinn so she could conduct a casual interview. Although the sketches she had drawn bore an uncanny resemblance to James, there was something that made the face familiar but the man wholly separate and apart, something that during their early Friday morning drive she was unable to flesh out.

He was good-looking, personable, and for all intents and purposes, he was the man in her dreams. They conversed easily on many topics, joked around, and shared the same passion for visual arts. They had so much in common, they quickly established a camaraderie, which would allow them to work well together. And perhaps more. There was no doubt that he was a very attractive man. And his sexy lips were quite a pleasant, unexpected distraction. Sometimes she didn't hear a word he said but sat there, reading his lips.

James felt similarly drawn to Jai. She was a fascinating and unpredictable woman. He liked the organized mayhem of her office, which obviously framed her entire existence. She had introduced him to her staff of excitable teens, who were hopped up on cappuccino, before inviting him to dinner. Her mother had been a gracious hostess, while Mr. Quinn had put him through the Spanish Inquisition. Luckily, Jai and her mom had been great buffers. She and her mother were almost identical in disposition and looks, except that Jai was darker in color. Her mother was more like coffee with heavy cream.

"If you keep staring at me, you'll miss the next turn, like you did six miles back," she said, breaking into his reverie.

James noticed that like most of his male friends, Jai was not in favor of asking directions. But lucky for them, she seemed to have a built-in GPS. Voyager could have used her. James would watch her close her eyes and channel some force that inevitably got them back on track. In reality, Jai was channeling the Internet deity, the patron saint of MapQuest screens. And with James driving like they were in the Indy 500, they made record time.

Jailyn stepped barefoot out of James's Miata and onto a gravel drive, her feet immune to the sharp little rocks. She stood back and watched his massive frame unfold from the tiny car. He was, she had to admit, a divine piece of God's handiwork.

"Catch," he called over the car, tossing one shoe and then the other.

She snatched her knapsack off the backseat and waited for him to round the car.

"Doesn't look like much, does it?" James said close to her ear, his lips inviting her to turn around and be kissed, but the house, with its large, faded pale blue clapboard, was louder. It had a porch and cedar shingles, plenty of level land, flower beds, and an outcropping of trees.

"For a photographer, you have limited vision," Jai replied.

"My vision is twenty-ten. The place is small and run-down."

"It's a quaint country farmhouse that blends with the natural beauty of the historical New England landscape."

"It's a million miles from anywhere," he added, following her as she walked toward the house.

"It's tucked peacefully beyond the woods," she responded. "The gardens beckon visitors and encourage silent reflection." She looked up into his face.

"The wood looks warped, and the windows look drafty."

"The inn boasts original woodwork on the large windows, which offer breathtaking views of the scenery, including the meadow and forest."

"The porch sags, and the steps look as if termites were having Thanksgiving supper. Market that," he challenged, with a bark of laughter.

Bounding up the steps and onto the porch, she swung around on one of the posts and leaned forward, putting her face inches from his. "Your first view of the house is the lovely wraparound porch, which invites you to spend fall evenings watching the sunset create a dazzling light show in the turning leaves or to while away lazy summer afternoons in the hammock, sipping iced tea while enjoying a good book." She finished triumphantly, taking a bow. His laughter rang through the trees.

James worked by specifics: subject, lighting, angles, shadows, colors, and distance. But Jai seemed to redefine conventional methodology and see what needed to be seen. "You don't consider it false advertising?" he asked.

"It's an authentic farmhouse."

"You think it's nice inside?"

"I think it will be a quaint, traditional, and authentic farmhouse. Shall we?" she said, pulling the creaky door open with a flourish.

Ann Mallory had been watching the couple from the time they pulled into the yard. She rushed from the second-floor landing to greet them, mentally agreeing with her brother the entire time. Visually, they made quite a handsome picture, but they had no substantial chemistry. The gentleman was heavy on the looks but light on the intuition, and the young woman was a firestorm of eager energy and life. She watched them enter the foyer and saw the young woman's eyes glitter knowingly. The house had already captured her heart. She heard the young man talking about old men, and Ann thought that would make the already old house look like a retirement home.

"I agree," said an understanding voice.

"Come again?" Ann asked the young woman.

"I said, I agree with you. Old men sitting around, drinking hot chocolate, looking at the fire aren't all that appealing to a younger crowd."

"Oh," Ann said, startled. "I hadn't realized I spoke aloud. I didn't mean to get in the middle."

"No. That's precisely where you should be. I recommend clients have an active role in creating the marketing plans," Jai explained.

"That makes sense. I can see why you've been hired," said Ann. "But I'm not the one you want. I'm more like the proprietress. No, that's not quite right." She squinted, as if expecting James to supply an answer. "I'm more like a housekeeper, I suppose, exceptin' that my friend Dolly Itkins does the cooking, and I do meet guests. But my sister Fidelma is the administrator. My, oh my, young man, you are quite the hunk. Strong and silent. I like that." Ann shot James a wink.

Jai could see that Ann would go right on if allowed. "Well, Ms. Jane-of-all-trades, I'm Jailyn Wyatt. This is my photographer, James Ross."

"Pleasure to meet you both," Ann said, not releasing James's hand. "Especially him."

"And you are?" James asked, with a pleasant smile.

"Oh, how silly of me. I'm Ann. Ann Mallory. And you've got me pegged. I do, do a bit of everything." Ann looked at her watch. "I have enough time to give you the ten-cent tour, and then we're out of here." Ann turned around in a circle, pointing out the living room, the full dining room, the galley kitchen—which, she told them in no uncertain terms, was too small and outdated—and the sitting room, which doubled as a reception area. "All right. Let's lock 'er up and hit the road."

"Where are we going?" Jai asked.

"Oh, that's right. You'd already left when I called," said Ann. "Our toilets are out. Whole basement flooded with human sludge. Luckily, the weather's not hot, or else it'd be like standing in a sewer. I called Krebs to take a look, but he says he wants weekend rates. I say let the new guy deal with it."

"When will the owner be arriving?" Jai asked.

"The man works too hard to actually make a live appearance, but he's just up Hartford way," replied Ann. "He'll probably send someone by Monday. It'll keep till then."

"Are all the toilets out?" Jai asked.

"All but one. The one off the mudroom," said Ann. "Parents had it installed between baby number five and six. It's got its own drainage."

"Then if you don't mind, I'd like to stay," Jai said, her smile brighter.

"Honey, you can do what you want," Ann said, walking toward the door. "Ain't nothin' worth over ten dollars in the place unless you can move the furniture. Now old as that stuff is, I hear it's worth its weight."

James and Jai looked into the living area to take in the Shaker black cherry corner cupboard, the tiger maple coffee table, and the Litchfield sewing desk.

"Okay, kids. Have fun," said Ann. "Me and Dolly are getting a seaweed wrap before we hit the slots. My sister and her husband went out Colorado way to visit his family since we got no guests. There's a kitchen full of food. Dolly cooked for the weekend before the johns went out. So you can stuff yourselves and lay around like stuck pigs. Place is yours."

James looked at Ann, who was hightailing it out the door. "Christian said we'd be at one of the resorts," he said, worried about the lack of brochure amenities.

"We can get a lot of work done with no one to bug us," Jai said. She was so distracted by her attraction to the house, she missed the lecherous smile on James's face. But Ann didn't.

"Let me have him for the weekend. I promise to give him back," Ann said through the screen. "I have a bunch of bingo sluts who'll lust over you while you call out numbers. You're prime rib in these here parts. In fact, I might have to keep you for myself."

She didn't know how well they knew each other, but she was sure the young woman wasn't thinking straight.

A man and a woman alone in the remote little inn was gonna lead to old-fashioned baby making. And just from the sparkle in Jai's eye, Ann knew that the young woman was too in love with the house to notice that young man fawning all over her. "Listen, ain't no public transport this far out, and you could wait on cab service until the cows come home, and they'll still not find you. So leave her your keys. You'll ride with me," Ann said, with a wink to Jai. "Now let's get a move on."

"It might be easier to load your stuff into my car," James said, looking at the light blue Dodge truck.

"Yeah, but then how we gonna get me out? My body don't fold into fourths. So chop-chop."

Chapter 10

Jai took a closer look at the main floor before abandoning it for the next. Walking along the landing, she touched the heavy wood, measured distances by foot, and furiously sketched the four rooms and bath. The attic suite was up a narrow flight of stairs and along a short hall. A king-sized, maple four-poster bed with a blanket rail dominated the room. The cover was white, with tiny, faded lilac flowers all over it. There was a small stool off to one side, as the bed rose up high off the floor. Jailyn kicked off her shoes and dove headfirst into the dozens of down and decorative pillows. She flipped over and allowed herself to sink into the luxurious mattress, enjoying its layers of softness.

She drew the small sitting area under the window, spending a minute trying to make the fussy, spindly-legged chairs look more formidable. She was adding in the matching nightstands, upon which stood identical brass lamps, a cedar chest, and a wardrobe when her eyes lit on the old-fashioned radio perched on the corner of the dresser.

Jai switched on the radio, expecting to hear scratchy

big band music. Instead, the mellow beat of Bob Marley filled the room. She jumped up and leapt around in Marley fashion, clutching an imaginary microphone and belting out "Buffalo Soldier." That bit of exercise and release did her inner child some good. She went into the pristine country bathroom, which had an old-fashioned tub big enough to fit two, and turned the tap, forgetting the water was off. She hadn't asked if there was a working shower. She opened the other door in the attic suite just to be nosey. The small sitting room held a medium-sized bookcase, two comfortable high-backed chairs, a cushy daybed, three brass floor lamps, two scarred coffee tables, and two throw rugs, but in her mind, she saw a dark, heavy bed and a matching bureau, with a mismatched nightstand. Utilitarian blankets and no curtains. All frilly accents had been left behind in the first room, which was awash with light. This room ate sunshine and yet still remained cheery. It came to her that the husband had slept here during childbirth and through nursing so his sleep wasn't disturbed, and when he rose for work before the sun, he'd kiss his wife and new babe and leave them peacefully in slumber.

She could also see the man behind voice here, sitting with his legs stretched out, papers on his lap, hands folded over his stomach, dozing after a long day. An idea began to take shape in her head.

She was retrieving her pad when she heard the creaky hinges of the front door on the fringe of her psyche. She strained to listen, and finally light footfalls drifted up to her. She ran and looked out the window, hoping she had missed the growl of Ann's truck pulling up, but all she saw was bright green leaves waving happily at her.

"James? Ann?" she asked, creeping down the hall and to the stairs. The sounds of the house settling echoed through her head as she cautiously descended the stairs. "Dolly? Ann's sister? Mr. Krebs? Anyone?" She saw a flash of dark blue pants going through the kitchen door. She flattened herself against the wall and pretended she was a ninja, slowing her heartbeat, silencing her breath, and becoming invisible. She chewed her lower lip as she went through the kitchen door. *This is Connecticut, not New York. Not everyone is a serial killer,* she told herself, yet she still felt relief when she spied the Miata safely parked outside.

In one swift motion, she pivoted, planted herself, and punched out. *Tae Bo to the rescue,* she thought. He saw the fist coming and flung open the fridge door, then let it go so she wouldn't harm herself too badly. He heard the power of the punch when her fist made contact. She shook it off, hopping in circles, muttering words he didn't understand. He was starting toward her, an apology on his lips, when her left came out of nowhere, forcing him to eat his unspoken sentiment. His head snapped back, and he howled in pain. She caught him with an uppercut to end his life.

He eyed the petite youngster as she put the table between them, as if he was the one who had attacked her, and sprinted out the door. The tears welled in his eyes from the aftermath of the blow. He heard the door slam and went after her while wiping at his eyes. She was across the gravel drive, running like a true athlete. Her form was near perfection. He'd never catch up to the lithe figure moving toward the road. He was in great shape for his age, but his Italian loafers and dress slacks would hinder his progress, not to mention she had had an incredible head start.

He stepped onto the rickety porch to admire her grace. She nimbly raced over green grass, her slim feet barely touching the ground as she flew. The muscles of her legs flexed of their own volition, and her arms pumped efficiently, expending little, if any, excess energy. When she turned parallel to the road, he saw she wasn't a small stick figure of a girl, but a buxom beauty. Her breasts moved in tandem with her body under a loose shirt; her behind jiggled in the baggy cutoff denim shorts. Dark curls pushed back off her fresh face made her look youthful. But the word that came to mind was stunning.

She was the mesmerizing color of caramel, her carriage resplendent in the noonday sun. When she disappeared from sight, he exhaled a long, unsteady breath, which he didn't know he was holding. He touched his nose, wincing at the pain, but even more disconcerting was the fact that he was sporting a very urgent hard-on.

Jai lay beneath a copse of trees, watching the sunlight dance between the leaves. She'd spent a good fifteen minutes catching her breath and berating herself for leaving the burglar *in* the house. Her insanity extended to forgetting the keys to the Miata, her money, her cell phone, and her shoes. Even though she had managed to stay on the grass, her legs ached from the merciless run. She had stayed close to the road, but not one car had passed, and she hadn't seen a village, town, or house in the distance. The sun was not her friend, and she had been feeling dehydrated, so she'd decided to lie still for a minute and give her body a rest before walking the unending trail.

A sound shattered the peaceful quiet. She sat up and

saw the sun glinting off of the shiny grill before she could make out the form of a car. She took her time standing, figuring she had a bit of a wait since the vehicle had barely come into view, but in minutes the sleek dark blue Jaguar swerved off the road, spewing up dust and dirt.

She swore in patois and jumped out of the way as the figure exited the car and barreled down on her like a hungry bear. She'd barely had time to admire the luxury vehicle when she put her hands up like a boxer, ready to face the glaring man.

"If you hit me again, I promise I will hit you back," he said. His voice made the air around them vibrate.

She squinted up at him, against the sun, and saw the discoloration blooming around his nose. She made a face while lowering her hands. She decided flight was the better option, but then a band of unforgiving iron gripped her arm.

"Not so fast Flo-Jo. We have some things to discuss," the man growled. "Who are you? And what were you doing at the inn? Why did you feel the need to hit me and run off?"

Jai tried to shake loose from his grip, which turned out to be a fruitless effort that burned precious energy. The heat from his hand snaked through her in a lazy path, which riveted her to the ground. "I won't run," she said, and he quirked an eyebrow in disbelief. "I won't," she repeated, her body in flames beneath his stimulating touch.

He let her go and took a step closer to her. She noticed he had changed into a pair of chinos, a white polo-style shirt, and boat shoes to complete the preppie image.

"I'm Jailyn Wyatt of the Creative Forces advertising firm. I'm here at the inn on business. I hit you because you scared me, and I ran for the same reason."

"I should've expected as much," he mumbled, his dreamy Brazilian bombshell going up in smoke as he faced down the feisty, five-foot-six-inch cinnamon-colored woman, with huge jet-black eyes, impossibly long lashes, and glossy, kissable lips. She was a lissome beauty without a speck of make-up and was currently decimating his senses with her self-possessed and sonorous ego trip.

"And you, sir, are?" she asked, rubbing her arm. It didn't hurt, but she could still feel his touch trying to tattoo itself on her skin.

"Caleb Hamilton Vincent, owner of the inn and your current client."

"Oh crap!" she said in Spanish.

"Oh crap is right," he agreed in English. "That one I understood."

Chapter 11

Jai stared up into the swarthy face of her temporary boss. She was staggered by his profoundly good looks. His face was lean and angular, giving it the hard look of granite, but the soft fall of his too-long dark blond locks gave his profile gentle relief. But it was the devastating turquoise eyes that made the fluttering butterflies in her stomach stand stock-still and take notice. His indiscernible eyes bore into hers, and his lush mouth currently formed a grim line.

While looking at him, she realized she was aware of him as a man. For once, she wasn't compelled to capture a subject on paper or canvas. He *was* a brilliant piece of sculpted art, but more than that, he was one sexy motherfucker, and she didn't think she could portray that accurately. He was a living, breathing, flesh and blood, honest-to-goodness sex god. He sang out to her, and she fed on every lilting note. Her fingers weren't itching to draw the fierceness of all six feet three inches of him, the strength of his neck, the hard lines of his mouth, the beginning laugh lines around his eyes, the rich beige of his skin, or the color of his hair. No, her fingers wanted to feel the thick, sinewy muscles of his chest, to draw long, lazy lines across broad shoulders. She wanted to kiss the curve of his masculine jaw and take in a sip of air bursting with the taste of him.

"Sorry. What did you say?" she asked when she heard his rich voice reach her ears.

"Sorry is a state, such as the way one is dressed," he said, scanning her from head to toe, with a frown of disgust coating his fine features. His eyes had become shuttered, and yet she stared at him, fascinated, only giving her appearance brief consideration through his eyes. Caleb was so taken with her that when her tongue darted out and licked her lips, his phallus betrayed the stern message he was trying to communicate nonverbally, and he was forced to say something.

"Well, either way, I apologize for reacting so haphazardly. I'm a little high-strung at times," said Jai.

"Reactionary."

"I didn't say that," she said in her defense.

"I didn't reinterpret *what* you said. I merely added my opinion."

"Opinions are like assholes. Everyone has one or at least knows one," she said defensively, with a neck roll added for emphasis.

"You're reinforcing my assessment," he said, his arrogant posturing already getting on her nerves.

"If you want me to keep walking, you don't have to insult me. I'll gladly keep it moving," she said, folding her arms stubbornly across her chest.

"Another off-the-cuff remark." He held a palm up to stave her off, but he couldn't keep his eyes from dropping to admire the full swell of her chest. Letting her leave might end his problems, but it wasn't an option.

Caleb was already finding himself addicted to her. "There's no traffic on this road to speak of, and it'll be another three and a half miles before you clear my property. It'll be another three miles before you come to the next house. And though it's less than a twenty-minute drive, it's a good two-hour walk to town."

Jailyn walked past him, toward the driver's side of the car, hoping to gain some control over the situation. "You took a nasty blow to the nose. Maybe I should drive, in case you get light-headed or something." The beep-beep of the car alarm made her pull her hand back as if she'd been slapped.

"I drove here. I can drive back," he said, taking a neatly folded dark blue towel from the trunk. The towel matched the car's gleaming paint. "If you're saying you'll take the ride, then here. Sit on this." She gave him a withering look as he laid the beach towel over the white leather seat and unspoiled floor mat. Suddenly, she felt what he felt and was hesitant to get in. The car's interior was showroom immaculate.

"Maybe I should walk back."

"Get in, and keep your dirt to yourself. You've already wasted the better part of the morning with your hour-and-a-half jog, and with no working toilets, it's only a matter of time before *that* becomes an issue." He gave her a shove and was on the road in a flash. The Jaguar XJS sports convertible didn't make a sound as the beautiful flora and fauna became a blur of green and the speedometer hit seventy.

"It would seem we're stuck with each other until they can send your replacement," Caleb said. "I'd like to get started as soon as we get back."

"They aren't going to give you a replacement."

"And why is that? Ideally, it is in their best interest to

appease me," he said smugly as the car hugged the winding road as if it were a straightaway.

"For one, we're a small agency with a heavy workload. As it is, my schedule was inconvenienced to make this trip."

"My apologies for the inconvenience . . ."

"Apology accepted, but had you made the other meetings, this could have been hashed out prior to this unfortunate situation," Jai added.

"Very well. Point proven. There's no need to go on."

"And, finally, I'm the best in my field. Being here and meeting the client are pivotal to my job. Perhaps another company would have settled for pictures and produced lesser work, but I'm more hands-on, and therefore I provide superior-quality services."

"It's all well and good to speak so confidently, but I'll wait until you've actually produced something before I pass judgment."

"I've already done some preliminary schematics and sketched out a couple of ideas."

Caleb didn't know if he'd like her ideas, but he liked the fact that she'd wasted no time in getting to work. "How long have you been here?"

"What time is it now?"

"One fifteen."

"About an hour. I think we got here at ten. Minus the hour-and-a-half jog, plus unloading the bags and a break. Yeah, 'bout an hour of work."

Caleb was impressed that she was conscious of her time as well. He decided that her work ethic suited him, and he might be able to tolerate working with her. "All right, then I'd like to make a few things clear. I'm not thrilled with your attire."

"No compromise there, buddy. I use pencils and charcoals to sketch, and we're on a farm. Next."

"I'm the boss."

"Understood. Next."

"I will not tolerate drinking on the job."

A heavy quiet filled the tiny interior, shrinking it two sizes. He knew he had just crossed some imaginary line in the sand. Her voice was barely audible when she spoke. "I don't drink. Next."

"I won't stand for lying."

"Yet you're willing to take what they print in the papers as gospel?" she asked to his profile since his eyes were now glued to the road.

"No, except that the pictures were very explicit."

"It was two freakin' days."

"Three days of drunken debauchery of legendary proportions that were caught on film and reproduced in every newspaper, including the *Times*."

She sat quietly, more quietly than he thought possible, and for the first time since meeting him, she was physically still. She turned to him as if her neck was stiff.

"I don't like to relive it or talk about it. I can't explain it or excuse it. I accept what I've done and listen to the rumors and speculation without anger. I see distrust on my clients' faces and work hard to erase it. But other than that, I try to put it behind me."

"I need more reassurance than that," he said, waiting two full minutes for her to answer.

"It was the day I buried my father. I only had one father, and it's unlikely he'll die again. I hope that is reassurance enough."

Chapter 12

Jailyn felt the change of energy in the small space. He hadn't given her the look of pity she'd expected or those weak, meaningless words of condolence, and she was grateful for it. People thought her father was a plain old, run-of-the-mill drunk. They didn't understand that he had tried to distance himself from his slave roots and working-class background, only to end up, in his own eyes, mediocre. "My father—"

"I don't need further explanation." His tone was dismissive. Caleb saw her shrink away. "I didn't mean to open old wounds. You seem to have found a better way to handle it. Let's leave it at that."

The Jaguar slid onto the gravel drive in front of the farmhouse. Caleb was out and at her door in seconds. She remained unmoving. "Come on," he said. "Why don't you get cleaned up? I got the water back on, and I'll scrounge around for some eats. We can start work in the morning."

Caleb helped her out of the car, and he noticed how small she was. He felt like a lummox and a giant who had frightened a child, because he saw the lost look in her eye. A strong urge to take her in his arms swept through him, wiping away all of his defenses. Instead, he removed the towel from the seat and briskly walked into the inn. Jailyn stood there, staring at the inn.

He called out to her. "I'm going to ice my nose if you need me." It took a few minutes for his words to sink in.

"Oh gosh, let me help you with that," she cried as she ran over and jumped the handful of stairs. In the kitchen she searched the cabinets and found a Ziploc plastic bag, which she loaded with ice, then wrapped in a threadbare towel. "Sit," she said, maneuvering him into a chair.

She felt dainty standing there in front of him, because when he sat, they were almost eye to eye. Her hand touched the toned muscle of his chest, sending a small tremor down her arm. But it was his languid ocean blue green eyes that caused an earthquake in her psyche.

Caleb's blood was moving at a frenzied pace through his veins as Jai doctored him. After her strenuous run, she exuded scents he had enjoyed as a kid. She smelled like dirt and grass and fresh air. He also smelled her potent femininity, which overrode it all. He squirmed beneath her touch, because he felt like a lion being tempted by a gazelle.

"Keep your head back," she directed.

"I'll do it," he said, snatching the ice pack and rolling his eyes at her.

"Testy, are we?" she said, taking bowls from the fridge and setting them on the table.

"How quickly *we* forget that some stranger decked *us* not too long ago."

"I'm sor . . . I apologize. I hadn't been expecting anyone. Ann said you were in Hartford on business."

"I contacted your office and let them know when I'd be arriving."

"I wonder why they didn't call me?" she said, for the first time aware that she had no idea where her bag was, let alone her cell phone.

"Apparently, you forward your calls to the office when you're traveling," he said. His icy gaze met her embarrassed one.

"It's not like I can work while I'm in transit," Jai explained while pouring glasses of water.

"Why not? That's why they created *business class* on planes and trains," he said facetiously. "Then they created laptops, PDAs, BlackBerries, and cell phones. Some people use recorders or good old pens and paper."

"Don't be facétieux. I'm an artiste. I can't draw, hold my pad, and use a phone, laptop, and PDA."

"Join us in the present. Learn computer-aided drawing."

"What?" Jai backed away from him as if he had the plague. "That's sacrilege. Back to Hades with you, you forked-tongue devil. My art cannot be duplicated by an ill-designed graphics program on an Etch A Sketch." She clutched her chest while holding out two fingers to ward off his evil. "Oh no," she said, resting a hand on her throat. "I think you've just unaligned my fifth chakra. I don't think you should be allowed to view my work. You'll taint it with your negative chi." Her body crumpled against the counter.

He wasn't sure if his head was pounding from the blow he took or from the dramatic mishmash spewing from her mouth. "Is this your way of covering your manipulation?"

"What?" she asked, genuinely perplexed as she straightened.

"Do you or don't you have samples of your work for me to view?"

"I was getting *started.*"

"So you don't have anything?"

She raced up the two flights to retrieve her sketchbooks. Caleb remembered always being told not to run up and down those stairs, and now he knew why. It really did sound like a herd of elephants. Her bare feet echoed along the hall, warped wood protesting under the excitement of her journey. This was his third memory of the old farmhouse that Jai had triggered.

It had been years since he had come back, and he'd been forced into returning due to familial obligations. He was the oldest of the next generation to inherit the property. Each child, grandchild, and great grandchild would get a chance to own the farm. During ownership, the only two stipulations were that you couldn't destroy the house or sell the property to an outsider. So Caleb figured he'd update it. That way he'd hand it on to the next in line without it being a burden. He had every intention of making it catalogue spectacular and ready to compete with the other B and Bs popping up all over. But something about Jai moving around the kitchen, picking up things, and setting out fruit with fresh vegetables and dip made the house feel perfect in a way that he hadn't anticipated.

Upstairs, Jai took a moment to get cleaned up. She used some wet wipes she found in her bag to scrub the grime from her feet, legs, and arms. She brushed up her hair and changed into loose-fitting safari shorts and an oversized army green oxford shirt. She also needed the time to calm her insides, because Caleb, she admitted, was male decadence. The heavy-lidded look he gave her was chewing at the edges of her libido and battering down the walls she had erected to keep men out. But Caleb Vincent wasn't just any man: he was as dangerously sexy as a gunslinger and as suave as 007. He was a rogue and a gentleman, and Jai had to put all of that aside so she could take a proper breath. She forced herself to take her time going back. She didn't want to seem eager and willing, although her entire body was one exposed nerve. With clarity of mind, she solemnly walked in the kitchen.

The bag dropped to the floor with a thump. Caleb stared at the bookishly coy young woman in modest apparel. Glasses perched on her nose gave her a studious look. Her hair was pulled up in a haphazard ponytail. A naughty schoolgirl fantasy popped into his head. She was sweetly tempting, with her shirt buttoned high enough to hide her endowments, but the lightweight fabric skimming her generous bosom. She was a divine dichotomy of youthful innocence and womanly allure.

Her eyes roamed his body without censure. Caleb was helpless in hiding his reaction to her. Jai's eyes scanned the outline of the bulge in his pants, which was straining so hard against the zipper, she could swear the zipper teeth were screaming in protest at being yanked so viciously apart. She looked quizzically at him, not having expected such an overt sexual reaction. Her blood was now hissing in her ears, and the thrum that had caused his erection was being carried through the air and was hitting her in an onslaught of physical desire. Her elation was short lived, as he brusquely cleared the snack from the table, cleaned the floor, and held out his hand for her sketchbook, his face and body completely reserved. He pointed her into a seat when she didn't immediately relinquish her work.

She flipped open the small sketchbook tentatively, and peering over her shoulder, he was so blown away that he fell into his chair. He closed his eyes against the memories that engulfed him. In those eight pictures, he saw the most wondrous days of his childhood. He opened his eyes and was once more overwhelmed by the textures, tastes, and smells her drawings evoked.

He didn't see lines and shading, but feeling. He could feel the love that he had felt every time he had stepped into the house as a kid. He could feel the precious age of each of the rooms, the care that went into making the house a home, and the glow of the sunlight that flooded the entire house at noon. Jai's art enthralled him, capturing a part of him because of the unmistakable depth of reality that each drawing had. His reality, his childhood, and the hidden depths he'd forgotten about long ago. As he looked out the tiny grey door, his senses were filled with the pungent scent of nature. Out the little window, he saw the rich tapestry of leaves dappled with sunlight. Out another window, he could see the hill he used to roll down.

He wasn't prepared to go back. He wasn't ready to unleash his entire past and face the dark corners of his being. "I'm going to remodel," he said more forcefully than intended, but it was his way of closing the door to his past for good. He waited, expecting a series of protests from the volatile young woman. When none came, he continued. "I want to gut the second-floor rooms on the back side of the house so that we can have more suites like the attic."

Jai handed him a large picture of the attic, of his grandmother Siobhan Ailene Rafferty Quinlan. She was fussing over each little lacy pillow, the hand knitted spread, and a ceramic vase as shafts of sunlight filtered through the window and played in her red gold hair, lighting eyes so much like his own. She'd birthed most of her children in that room but had given it up for a time after she had the twins Seaghan and Reaghann. She'd always coveted the bright, happy space.

"The attic will stay the same," he said, with finality. He began describing the changes he wanted to make, but as they worked, he realized there were many things he truly hoped to preserve. Through Jai's eyes, he saw kids running around, sliding down the banister, slamming doors, climbing on the porch rail, and jumping off. He remembered apple pies cooling on the back porch and rocking the rocking chair so hard, he went flying backward, heels over head. And Jai saw it all. With each stroke of her pencil, he could find less and less fault with the old house.

Jai didn't like the way he snapped comments at her or the way his eyes squinted at her work, looking for errors, so that he could correct her. But the more she let herself go, the more she could hear the unspoken emotions coursing through him. Soon she was able to read the words beneath his words and sense the memories that were the essence of this home, which he was fighting to keep bottled up. She could feel the cork slipping, the emotions spilling out, and she was able to infuse the art with him.

He glanced over at Jai a few times and was taken by the speed with which she worked, altering a wrongly placed wall, adding or removing items as he spoke. He was pleased with their progress and amazed at how much they had accomplished. And he found some solace in the fact that somehow she secretly knew him. It was as if she could see past the picture he presented and into the real man that he was. Every time his eyes drifted to her or over the paper, he was compelled to tell her something. But even his silence spoke volumes. And something about watching the easy, toned-down manner in which she worked was consoling to him in some way. Her prim and proper charm was disarming, and yet it offered him solace.

"Don't you two look cozy?" Jai's head snapped up, and a crimson blush stained her cheeks. Unconsciously, she had physically gravitated toward Caleb. His presence alone was powerful, but the vulnerability she glimpsed hidden beneath that strength was the true aphrodisiac. They had moved their chairs closer together, and their thighs had touched as he spoke in dulcet tones. She told herself she had become the conduit for his visions, and their proximity enhanced the connection. James stood accusingly in the doorway, apparently waiting for an explanation as his eyes raked over the scene.

Caleb kept his arm draped across the back of Jai's chair, even though he wanted to draw her to him protectively in the face of this man. He felt the man's irate look as surely as he had felt Jai's serenity cocoon him while they worked. She had put him in a place deep within himself and outside of himself all at once. The coolness of her thigh against his, the steady rise and fall of her chest, the profound look on her face as she worked had made him aware of her demure enchantment. He'd felt his heart skip beats, and he'd had to remind himself to breathe whenever her arm brushed his chest as she changed the angle of the page. His body would tingle and his manhood would throb whenever her scent floated over him like warm honey. It was agonizing to be so close, and yet he would suffer such exquisite torture any day of the week. And this man was not going to be an obstacle in any way, shape, or form.

"James Ross, meet Caleb Vincent," Jai said, sitting up straighter in her chair, trying to put some distance between herself and Caleb while addressing the man at the door. "He's the new owner of the inn and the newest client of Creative Forces."

Jai noticed James's frame relax a fraction as he placed his camera equipment on the counter. "And here, I drove all the way back to keep you company," said James. He went to shake Caleb's hand, putting out the other hand to indicate he needn't get up. James allowed his body to cast a long, wide shadow over the lounging Caleb. A power play if she ever saw one. Caleb had no intention of letting that hand play out. Caleb slowly unwound himself from Jai and took James's hand in a fierce grip.

Jai noticed each man sizing up the other. Caleb saw James Ross as an immediate threat. James was a hulking, light-skinned African-American man about an inch taller than Caleb, was built like a tight end, and was much younger. He had amber eyes and a thuggish look to him because of his bald head and baggy, name-brand clothes.

When they released hands, James asked, "What happened to you?" nodding at Caleb's swelling nose. Jai's head dropped to her chest. She had been shaking it vigorously behind Caleb's back, but James hadn't noticed because he was locked in a staring match with Caleb.

"A run-in with Ms. Wyatt," replied Caleb.

James blinked first, and the contest was over. He shot a look at Jai, his body now taking on a more casual posture, and laughed. "No shit."

"No kidding," Caleb said, putting a propriety arm over Jai's seat.

"A girl hit you? That's bad, dude," James said.

"It was an accident," she explained, embarrassed. "He scared me. No warning, no noise, no nothing."

"I didn't know I needed to announce my arrival in my

own home," Caleb said, still staring at James. "Besides, I had other concerns. I have a flood down in the cellar."

"I'm so sorry. I forgot to ask. Is it bad?" Jai asked. James paid close attention to the answer because his next few rent checks depended on this job.

"Extremely," said Caleb. "There's about three inches of water, with a layer of sludge underneath. The plumbing's not going to hold up under another tape and bubble gum repair." James heart thudded in his chest at Caleb's words. "That's why I was in Hartford. Securing contractors, plumbers, and electricians for the renovation."

James was suddenly hopeful again. His dislike for the man dissipated, only to reveal jealousy.

"Here's what we've got so far," said Jai as she slid her sketchbook across the table, assuaging the last of James's fears. As usual, her work was astounding. Bringing life to the page, she'd depicted a house preening under the majesty of its rebirth, while marginally hinting at the revitalization.

"You did all this while I was gone?" James asked, flipping through the pages and trying to read the minute, neatly printed words in the corners.

Jai was unaccustomed to attention like this. Both men beaming at her, in awe, as if she were a five-year-old hanging a finger painting on the fridge. Lately, her work had been mediocre at best, so it was odd to hear these two handsome men giving her such high accolades. And they were both fine, gorgeous men. James was like Hercules, all blatant muscle and beauty, while Caleb was like the Marlboro man, handsome but rugged, with a trim swimmer's build. It was all too much to take in at one time. In order to fight her growing unease, she got to her feet and started puttering around the kitchen, gathering items to prepare for dinner.

Caleb had almost forgotten the tightly wound ball of energy she could be, because as they had worked, all of her exuberance had been channeled into her task. Caleb was beginning to like her both ways. He liked watching her move around the kitchen with familiarity, as if she had been doing it for years. She cut, chopped, sliced, and diced. As she heated, stirred, and added precise measurements by eye, Caleb figured her dishes probably ranked up there with those of Wolfgang Puck.

Jai was grateful for the distraction. Dolly's long, looping handwriting was easy to read from any distance, and Jai had already memorized the little cards taped to the top of each dish. Dolly had even included directions on how to shuck corn. Jai hoped she would do the food justice. She didn't really cook, but living in New York, she would never starve, not with so many eateries on her speed dial and her mother right downstairs.

Caleb stared at Jai wistfully. He couldn't decide if he wanted to help or just watch her. She reminded him so much of the days when his grandmother and aunts would prepare dinner. Everyone in the farmhouse would gather in the long kitchen, talking over the sounds of clattering pots and sizzling food, and amidst the smells, Caleb would carry dishes to the sink, rinse them, dry them, and keep an eye on stuff in the oven. Not once were his tasks considered menial, and his help was always needed and appreciated, unlike at the manor house, where a staff was hired to handle everything, from preparing meals to cleaning his room. He wasn't expected to do anything except boss the staff around. "It's their job, but they need someone to tell them how to do it," Brad used to say. The truth was the staff performed the same tasks daily and probably knew the job better than he ever would. In fact, he couldn't imagine some kid barking instructions at him.

At the farmhouse, no kid talked back to an adult, a lesson that had to be reinforced for Caleb several times out in the barn. Corporal punishment was more than okay as long as it was for a purpose. "If you won't respect me 'cause I tell you to, then I'll beat you until you do. The day you beat me back is the day I respect you more," his grandfather and father would tell him as they took a meaty hand to his soft tail, even though it was his head that was hard. The day never came. His grandfather and father respected him for being a boy in a house full of women who babied him, and for becoming a man with all those same women dictating to him. His eyes were pinned to Jai's bottom, which was swaying to music only she could hear. In two steps he was behind her. "Smells delicious."

"All I did was season and steam the vegetables, make garlic mashed potatoes, and doctor the biscuits with a honey butter glaze. I just had to heat up the lamb chops, though I added red-wine vinaigrette to cut the gamey taste. I figured they were fresh off the farm." She cut a small bite and fed it to Caleb. The tender meat broke apart in his mouth, and the tangy flavor did its job when it hit his tongue. Jai watched with delight the look of pleasure on his face. It was nice seeing the tactless and pompous Caleb take a break.

"I'd bet money you were right, and it tastes restaurant good," said Caleb.

"I think I've got a handle on where to start," James said suddenly, his nose high in the air, taking in the smells of home cooking wafting through the kitchen. "But first let's eat. It's late and I'm starved."

Chapter 13

Jai and Caleb looked at their wrists for watches that weren't there. James laughed at the two of them in a lighthearted way before telling them the late hour. James was glad he was able to penetrate their closeness. "You staying for dinner?" he asked.

"James! It is Mr. Vincent's property. What do you think?" cried Jai. "He can eat the food or throw it all out." She spoke as if she were scolding a child.

"I wouldn't toss the lamb, though. It tastes better than Dolly's," Caleb said.

"I wasn't trying to be rude," said James. "I thought Mr. Vincent had other business he might need to take care of, considering he spent the whole day here." James was trying to get an idea of exactly how much time they had spent alone together, though it didn't matter now, since he had no intention of letting it happen again. "I'm sure he's busy buying and selling stuff, building stuff, and, you know, wining and dining beautiful clients. And don't forget the broken bathrooms. The man looks more first class than backwoods. I'm sure he'd much prefer the luxury hotels at Foxwoods than this place."

"I hadn't thought of any of that. Caleb, uh, Mr. Vincent, are you staying?" said Jai.

"What?" said Caleb. "And pass on an opportunity to wine and dine a beautiful woman? And please call me Caleb." He winked at her. Caleb wouldn't have believed her eyes could have gotten any bigger, but at his unsolicited comment, they did. James's eyes, on the other hand, became slits, shooting unseen poisonous darts at him.

After setting the table, James and Caleb carried serving trays weighed down with food into the dining room. Caleb wondered for the umpteenth time in three minutes how time could have slipped so easily away. Had he been so engulfed with work or with Jai that he hadn't notice the passage of time? Most dates he went on, he would constantly sneak peeks at his watch. He didn't want to come on too strong, so he carefully timed all his moves. But even though nine out of ten times the women were more than willing to take things to the next level, he'd fall out of lust by the main course.

Jai was disturbed by the fact that every time Caleb opened his mouth, she got incredibly silly. It was as if in the face of his constant masculine brooding, she needed to bring him some childish whimsy. She couldn't help putting her yin to his yang, her peanut butter to his jelly, her hemi to his truck, her moon to his sun, her darkness to his light. He kept her grounded without seeming to pay her any mind at all.

The sound of Caleb's voice stopped her from getting too lost in herself. "Lord, thank you for this bounty and the company with which you have blessed me. Bless the hands that prepared it and all of those less fortunate. Bless my friends, family, and enemies alike. In your holy light, we are humbled. Amen." So that James could see the big picture, Caleb then told him about the manor house on the edge of the property. He was going to convert that into a businessmen's inn while leaving the farmhouse for couples.

Caleb had mentioned the manor house idea without having given it any thought. He had never considered using part of the place, not even temporarily, but it would cost about the same to update it, to accommodate his computer needs, as it would to rent space somewhere else. It also meant he'd be close to the inn and Jai and still be able to work. Although Caleb addressed James, his eyes kept drifting over to Jai. He was so glad he had made this trip, because he had gotten to meet the gorgeous voice and the sensational woman with the amazing left uppercut, which seemed to have emptied his head of all his worries and to have opened his heart to so many possibilities. Caleb thought he was being influenced by his setting. The farm was always the one place he felt himself. He hoped that it affected Jai similarly, but the looks James kept tossing her made him wonder if they were interested in each other. For the first time since meeting Jai, he wondered if she would date him. He wondered if race would be an issue for her and if she was totally unaware of the fact that he was mixed.

Caleb sat back and watched them interact, trying to gauge the dynamic between the two. It was clear by the questions James asked that he hadn't known Jai for any significant length of time. But it seemed she had an obvious fondness for him. She didn't mind indulging his questions, and they often fell into gales of laughter over some ridiculous joke that Caleb didn't get.

"That was some kinda cooking, Ms. Jai. You really put your foot in it," said James. "That's a euphemism from down South. It means it was good," James explained to Caleb. Caleb nodded, his mind elsewhere.

"Ann and Dolly stocked the place. We can eat like royalty for a coupla weeks," Jai said.

"They probably did that before the plumbing burst. I guess busted pipes mean good New England style eating for us, huh, James?" Caleb said in a goofy, exaggerated Southern accent, slapping the man hard on the shoulder. "That means we got plenty to eat."

James sat back from the table, picking his teeth. The savory dishes that had graced the table were all but gone. James rubbed his stomach like a king. "So where will you be staying? I'm sure you picked out some first-class accommodations at one of the big hotels." Jai shot James a dirty look.

"I have reservations at Mohegan Sun," said Caleb.

"Oh," Jai said. Caleb's response had caught her off guard, and now both men were looking at her. "I assumed you'd be staying here. That is the best advertising."

"You don't have to convince me. But there's only one bath, so the reservations were for all of us," replied Caleb. "I mean, I'm sure Ann asked Omar Krebs to come look at the plumbing, but it'll still be a few days, and he's more reliable than the 'definite four days, look see' commitment I got from the plumbing company in Hartford. But if you're all staying here, then I will too."

"I guess that must be harsh when you find out money doesn't make everyone jump," James retorted snidely.

"Actually, money does wonders. I need a six-man crew, and the supplies are top of the line, very expensive, made to order. It'll take about four days to get the order processed. Normally, it would take six to eight," Caleb said, meeting the challenge in James's eyes.

"You must be a mini-mogul, 'cause that ain't all that impressive. It's only a few days," James said.

"Weeks," replied Caleb. "Six to eight weeks to get the supplies, and about a month more to hire a competent crew. In four days they'll be ready to get to work."

Jai managed to shift the topic of conversation; she didn't like them going at each other. James's behavior reflected directly on her and Creative Forces, and it was her duty to protect him, just as she would any of her team. Caleb noticed that when James couldn't properly illustrate a point, she helped him out, often supplying his words. And for the second time, he found himself wondering if something was going on between them.

James droned on, but Caleb paid little to no mind. He was too busy watching Jai. Her hands were conveying stories, a cacophony of emotions was evident all over her lovely face, her effervescence was contagious, and her presence was magical. Caleb felt something stirring to life in his stomach and moving at a crawl just beneath the surface of his skin, taking possession of him like a demon. He watched as her body expressed different moods, her eyes flashing different feelings as she spoke. She was a lovely creature, with a fine bone structure; supple caramel skin; pixie jet-black curls; plump, moist lips; long, black, velvety lashes; and thick, arched brows, which highlighted her dark eyes. His attraction to her was unexplainable as well as unexpected. He always dated women who could be featured on the high-gloss pages of fashion magazines. They were tall, thin, blue-eyed, blond women who possessed too much poise and often came across as fake and untouchable. But this flesh and blood woman sent a jolt of wicked and decadent thoughts through his mind.

He wanted to see her completely naked before him so he could touch her and find out if she was as uninhibited in bed as she was the rest of the time. He wondered if she would taste as sweet as she smelled if he kissed her most secret place. He wanted to see her skin against his as he lowered her onto him. He was curious how her pliant body would be against a torrent of kisses from him. He wanted to hear her cries of passion as he licked and nipped at her full breasts and thick thighs and then delved his tongue into her, driving her up and over the brink of ecstasy and feeling her tight canal drip her feminine elixir onto his tongue. He wanted to move up her body and slide himself into her as she gripped him, arching her breasts up to his mouth so that he could savor each ripe mountain. He wanted to find out if he could make her nipples pebble hard as he moved inside of her until . . .

"Caleb? Caleb? Yo, man, you all right?" James said, waving a hand in front of his face. "She asked if you want dessert."

Through the fog of lust, Caleb tried to focus on the question, but nothing except the image of Jai wearing a whipped cream bra and swirling his tongue over her natural cherries came to mind. James's voice banished his erotic thoughts. "My mother would say if you don't finish what's on your plate, then you don't have room in your belly for dessert."

"This isn't a race. I like to take my time when savoring epicurean delights and enjoying engaging conversation. It looks like the same could be said for Ms. Wyatt," Caleb said, eyeing her plate.

"She's thick enough that she could miss a meal and still

be all that," James said. As much as Caleb was starting to appreciate that wisdom, he could see the indulgence in Jai's eyes collapse like dominos. Caleb had lived with too many female relatives to have learned nothing. First and foremost, he knew you didn't talk about a woman's hair, cooking, age, or weight, even if it was a backhanded compliment.

"James ate enough to feed the entire county," Jai said, forced tolerance liberally dousing her statement. "You didn't leave enough for me and Caleb."

"I ain't no scrawny dude. I need food," James answered.

"I could've served you rocks, and you would have put ketchup on them and swallowed them whole," said Jai. "Next time I won't bother with a dish. I'll just fling the food at you from the kitchen."

A snort escaped Caleb, and Jai gave a throaty laugh, evoking more naughty images. Jai thought it was funny that the stoic, distinguished Caleb had snorted. She found it to be an endearing quality, and she was relieved to find out he wasn't perfect. She had noticed his silence throughout the meal and had wondered if the stuck-up, superior Caleb was back. She looked into his electric aqua eyes, and an unmistakable current jumped between them. She could see him undressing her with his eyes, his intent to make love to her evident in their impassioned color.

Jai could feel the languid touch of his fingertips leisurely exploring her body, his lips effortlessly taking her mind and body to otherworldly levels while he cupped her buttocks and raised her femininity to his mouth, plunging his tongue into her in a violent motion, carrying her on a frenzied ride of unbelievable pleasure. Jai wet her lips, and Caleb's eyes turned stormy. It was as if he was turning up the heat in her body. She could envision Caleb's eyes this way when he entered her, a mix of sincere ardor, desperate thirst, and sweet agony. She imagined his body buried in hers, his eyes holding hers captive, his mouth lowering to suckle at her warm breast. . . .

"Now you've gone all la-la on me, too," said James.

It was like a fist to the stomach, and Jai jerked a little. She was so close to a release. The smile that crossed Caleb's lips was one of knowing. "I'd love to see that for real," he whispered, removing the plate from in front of her.

"I was saying, since he's got the dishes, why don't we take a walk?" said James. "Fill me in. Maybe get some night shots."

"I'm gonna help in the kitchen. We've got all day tomorrow," she said, her voice sounding scratchy and weak in her own ears. "I did hit our paycheck," she said in a whisper.

"Let me handle the kitchen. Take a seat. Relax," James said, taking over. "Have some dessert."

"If you're sure?" Caleb said, shoving the wet sponge into James's stomach like a football. "Then I'm gonna head up."

"Yeah, me and Jai got this," replied James.

"Actually, I think I'm going to turn in, too. I could afford to miss dessert," Jai said, walking out with Caleb.

"I think he's got a crush on you," Caleb whispered when they rounded the corner.

"Shut up. He does not," she said, pushing his shoulder.

"Protective. Maybe you have a crush, too?"

"My God, it's been a few hours, and you're making up stuff about me. Geez. He's my employee. And he's younger than me."

"By like what? A month? You're not Methuselah. I'm older than both of you," he said.

"So if anyone would understand, it should be you. He's like an annoying little brother."

"I'll give you annoying, but mayhap the lady doth protest too much?" Caleb said, giving her hip a push and then catching her when she lightly hit the wall. He held her in his arms, with a feral look dancing in his eyes, but self-possession kept him in check.

"I'm not protesting now," she said, lifting her face to him, her shy smile an invitation. The invitation was engraved, signed, sealed, and delivered. He allowed his hands to bring her body closer to him. His eyes closed as her plushness came into contact with his hardness, and a moan escaped him as his forehead fell forward to hers.

"You sure?" Caleb asked. "I am your boss."

"Yes. We established earlier who the boss was, and I do as you say. And if you're saying what I think you're saying, then yes."

Jai's hands went up his chest, and another moan escaped as she traced the hard contours. He used two fingers to tilt her head up to his, then used his cheek to feel his way to her mouth. She stopped breathing, trying to memorize the tempo of his heartbeat. His lips met hers, and his knees nearly buckled at the fullness he felt there. Jai's hands gripped his shirt as if she were trying to pull him farther into the kiss, determined to be infused with the feel of him. Lost in the moment, Caleb willingly surrendered himself, free-falling into the fathomless depths of the pleasure she was offering. Her tongue slid surely into his mouth. It was the first time she'd ever initiated such a move. She was rewarded with a light suckling of her tongue. Caleb then caught her lower lip between his teeth, eliciting a groan from her.

Every rapturous sensation he inflicted on her mouth flowed directly between her legs. Caleb felt the tone of the kiss change as she maneuvered her body between his legs, brushing lightly up against him while somehow putting pressure on just the right spot so that another moan escaped him. Jai could feel the moan under the hand she'd planted on his marble chest. His fingers curled up in her hair, and her body responded to something inexplicable, searching for something and somehow knowing that Caleb could give it to her. The pervasive sweep of his tongue over her tingling lips made her delirious with want.

"What are you two whispering about?" James called above the running water. "You showing him the nude you drew of me?"

Chapter 14

Jai woke up in surroundings strange to her eye but familiar to her soul. She lived on the second floor of her mother's home, and her mom had decorated it with care. It was stylish and cozy, with plenty of unique touches, sunlight, and inviting dark shadows. They had moved into the Brooklyn DuValle family brownstone after her father died. Jai had been reluctant to move out of the family's two-bedroom ranch-style home in a suburb of New Jersey. Her father had bought that house when she was ten. He had scrimped and saved to purchase it for his wife, daughter, and himself. It had been theirs lock, stock, and barrel in less than three years because Ed Wyatt didn't want anyone to take what was his.

A shiver of the sadness ran up her spine. For so many months, she'd felt so alone and so cold, and then Caleb had kissed her and the last vestiges of her misery had lifted. There had been nothing cold, sad, or scary in her during that kiss. It had been all white-hot flame and sparks of blue electricity warming every chilled crevice in her, lighting all the dark spaces. When Caleb had abruptly ended the kiss, a curtain had dropped and his aloofness had returned. She'd seen the mistrust marring his brow and the questions he wouldn't ask in his stormy eyes. He'd shaken his head ever so slightly, tugging away when she reached for him. The quizzical look on his face had demanded some sort of plausible explanation about James's statement. In Caleb's unrelenting manner he had already drawn a conclusion and had made an autocratic judgment based on his own egomaniacal view.

She hadn't been able to answer him. There was nothing to explain. But worse, in a matter of seconds, he'd cast her out and retreated back into himself. Wherever his darkness lived, it threatened to take him there again and shut him in. Jai was convinced he deserved that self-appointed hell he continued to banish himself to. But she refused to follow. She had spent too many years living her father's hell to visit someone else's.

Caleb woke with a start, hearing the door slam. He expected to hear his grandfather shout, "Stop letting the door slam! People in Ireland know you're home." This memory of his youth reminded him of Jai. She was the one who had unleashed Pandora's box, and try as he might, he wasn't able to shut it. The woman was like lava, altering the landscape of his life and forcing him to rebuild again. This time, however, it was everything that he grew up with that was now coloring his life, not just what he selected.

Caleb moved quietly through the house. It was one of the things his Aunt Bridgid had taught him. "If no one can hear you, no one can yell at you," she'd say. Yelling wasn't a bad thing on a farm. It didn't always mean you were in trouble. It was the poor man's version of an intercom system. Yells usually meant you were being summoned for meals or chores. Aunt Iona had often told him, before she left for secretarial school, to "rise early, get out the door, and get your pick of the easiest chores." He thought of all seven of his aunts with affection, but he didn't know Iona as well. She had died during childbirth, along with her child, when Caleb was still too young to question death. But he'd always remember her simple dress and quiet authority when he thought of her helping to raise her seven siblings. He could practically see her bustling past him to get into the kitchen. She'd say, "Pick up your feet. There's work to be done."

Instead, Caleb found Jai sitting at the table and was spellbound. The vice that had been squeezing his chest was released. He leaned against the doorjamb, arms folded over his chest, taking her in. She sat with one leg tucked under her, at an odd angle, her pad balanced precariously. She was surrounded by a ring of light, which made her look like a fairy. Her long shirt revealed hints of savory brown thigh, and he could see her glasses precariously perched on the end of her nose, her dark curls a mop on her head. His mouth watered as he watched her nibble a thumbnail while she studied the pad held on her lap.

Her rounded breasts hung low in the loose shirt, and his natural reaction to such a provocative sight shamelessly showed itself. The vulnerable look on her face made the moment poignant, yet her simple and scintillating attire was asking him to yank her onto the table and shower her with hot kisses until she was breathless. The bulge in his pants became a throbbing ache when she pulled her lower lip into her mouth and he heard the slight smack of her lips when she released it. She was a siren, enticing him, luring him, except that there was nothing calculated or manipulative about the unassuming gesture. She was too absorbed in her work to notice him studying her bountiful breasts and juicy thighs and full lower lip. *How is it that I can be so addicted to the sight of her?* he asked himself. *Wanting this woman has become a full-time occupation,* he thought, since he had been up all night thinking about her.

"I can hear you breathing," she said, without looking up.

"Can you hear what I'm thinking?" he asked, his crooked grin making a rare appearance.

"I'm attentive, not psychic. You blocked the breeze coming through the door. Look at the dust specks. They're falling now, instead of floating," she explained, pointing her pencil at nothing in the air.

Run! Get away from her, he said to himself, but his body was drawn to her like plants to the sunlight. He swished his hand around through the air and watched her onyx eyes dart around as if following one particular speck like a pouncing cat. "Hungry?"

"Only if you're cooking. I've got some work. My client's a real stickler for professionalism. . . ."

"Go ahead and work till your fingers fall off. Breakfast is my specialty," Caleb said.

"Mine, too," James said, moving to the oven. "Waffles, biscuits, hash browns, fresh orange juice, fried ham, and coffee. How you like your eggs?"

"Scrambled," Caleb answered, the tightness in his chest returning full force. "But I've got some things to do today, so I'll pass."

"I'm not a big egg fanatic," Jai said. She sent a blistering look at James for interrupting her moment to make up with Caleb, if only to repair the rift in their working relationship. To her surprise, Caleb caught her and sent her a wry smile.

"Although I'm in no hurry to see James naked, for

the sake of art, I'd like to check out your rendition," said Caleb.

The words struck Jai like arrows. That particular picture was personal. It wasn't meant for anyone to see, and she was pissed that James had viewed it without her permission or knowledge. She wanted to protect what was hers and walk out. No words of apology or defense. But it was Caleb's eyes that caused her unsteady hands to flip the pages. He deserved an explanation of some sort, but she wasn't sure what to say or even why she felt the need to appease his angry spirit. He was a handsome, wealthy, industrious, cultured, accomplished businessman, even if a little methodical. She was an organized mess most of the time, an unconventional bohemian, even if only by design, and she couldn't see them getting along for any length of time. So what if they'd kissed; they weren't dating or in a relationship. They were working together, but her stupid obsession with him kept getting in the way. One minute she wanted to shake him, the next make him laugh. . . .

"What's this?" Caleb, asked picking up a page that had fallen to the floor. It was a full male nude. The subject's manhood was concealed by the angle of his body, but his back, buttocks, legs, and profile were clearly visible.

"It's not finished," said Jai.

Caleb was hypnotized by the picture. It looked faded, but it had been drawn with a sure hand, as if the artist had done it with one pencil and one line in one sitting. There was something hauntingly familiar about it, as if he had seen her draw it, seen her sitting in a similar position, wearing similar clothes. She opened to another page, hastily tucking the loose sheet between the pages.

She had drawn her first nude years ago, when she was in high school. Some guy who invaded her teenage dreams. When her father found the picture, he went ballistic. He'd snatched the pad from her and set it on fire out in the yard. Later he blamed the liquor, but she knew it was because she had drawn a white man. She'd dated only black men after that in order to please him. Nice boys from school or church. During college she didn't date at all, and when she decided to date Paul, she assumed her father hated him, because he was white. It was one of the few times they had ever disagreed. As it turned out, her father had had a good reason to hate Paul: Paul was a scum bucket of the highest order.

Her father would slump his shoulders and cast his eyes down when speaking to a white person. He would say times had changed, but those were just words. His upbringing had made him subservient and inferior to white people. He once told her, "When whites pass judgment on me, I expect it, but to have other blacks put me down because I'm dark is worse. I'm trying to protect you. When people see you on the street with a white man or a light-skinned man, they gonna ask, 'How that nigger get that man? Must be she tricked him or she got money.' That's how it is with your mom and me. She light, bright, damn near white, beautiful, and smart, and me, I'm darker than a piece o' shit." So most of her private collection was filled with dark subjects, whether houses, people, animals, or still lifes.

"This is it?" Caleb asked, taking the pad from her and bringing her back to the present.

"Yep," James said, making sure it was the right picture. "That's me," he announced proudly.

Caleb could see that James's features had been reproduced, but the picture was far removed from the man in the room with him. The picture was solemn, whereas James was a raucous individual. In fact, most of the pictures reminded him of moments he'd most recently had while talking on the phone with Jai. It was him in his office or him at any number of airports, his long legs stretched out between cramped flights and crossed at the ankles, and his shirt carelessly rumpled.

The nude looked like James as well, but it evoked some deeper understanding in Caleb of himself. The man was thinking a million thoughts and nothing at all, all at once. There was superiority in the man's gaze, self-righteousness in the tilt of his head, and arrogance in the way he held his shoulders upright. That was how he had felt when speaking to Jai that first day. "This isn't James," Caleb said, more to himself than to the two people in the room.

"Sure it is. It's like she was following me around," said James.

"More like me," Caleb said in Jai's ear as he moved over to James. "Look, this man is dark skinned."

"He's the color of paper," said James.

"No. If you look closely, there's some shading, indicative of color," said Caleb. "It's like she barely brushed the side of the pencil point against the page. But it's enough to tell he's the color of a black pearl." Her startled eyes confirmed that Caleb was right.

"You're crazy man. He's tall like me . . . ," James said.

"I'm tall . . . ," Caleb answered.

"He's built like me," James said.

"Any guy willing to spend a couple of months in the gym or have three extra bowls of Cocoa Puffs could look like you."

"Look at his eyes. Dark men don't have light eyes like that," said James. He stood up, with a smirk on his face, feeling like he'd finally won.

"She doesn't know the color," Caleb whispered.

Jai felt her insides tremble. His observations were touching that part of her that she hid from people so effectively in the light of day with her off-the-wall antics. But Caleb was so astute, he was picking up on all the little nuances that made her art uniquely hers.

"She added flecks to give him pupils, but there's no shading, no color," said Caleb. "And she didn't forget or overlook the fact, because every other detail is precise. She did it on purpose. Hence, she didn't know the color."

Jai sat watching Caleb, James glared at Caleb, and Caleb looked at her. Caleb's eyes were so absolutely blue that she could see all of the Caribbean Sea in their depths. "The eyes are the windows to the soul. I don't know this man's soul, so I couldn't get the eyes right," she explained.

"Well, now you know," James said, blinking his eyes at her furiously. "So you can finish the picture."

"It isn't you," Caleb asserted in clipped but pleasant tones.

"Then who is it?" James asked, bristling.

Caleb flipped back to the other page and laid it on the table for James to see. "It's me," Caleb answered. In each vignette the artist was getting closer and closer to recreating the first picture. He was certain of it.

"Bullshit," James said, putting full plates of food on the table. He dug into his meal without pretense. "This guy may look something like you, but the other dude is a brother. A tall, big, dark black man. You said so yourself."

"I think that's the problem," replied Caleb. "The whole resembles you, but the components are me. His face is square, not round like yours, and the chin is prominent. His head isn't oval like yours, and the definition in his face is sharp, whereas you're more soft."

"I'm not soft," James said, not seeing any of what Caleb was talking about. "Besides, art is interpretive. That's why I prefer photography. Pictures don't lie." James beckoned Jai to eat.

Caleb watched as Jai's continence changed. "I've lost my appetite," she said, gathering her things. Caleb understood why. They had picked apart and debated over the most cherished and private part of her, the same way the photos in the news had exposed her and made her raw. They had served to scar her reputation, defame and demean her when she was hurting most. She came across as a lunatic and an out-of-control alcoholic, even though she had never touched the stuff before in her life and hadn't again to this day.

Jai could not relax. She hated having her art held up to such scrutiny. "I'm going to my room to work," she said, rising stiffly.

"More for us, right, Caleb?" James asked, oblivious to the undertones in the room.

"I'm right, aren't I?" Caleb asked.

"I don't know," said Jai. She left the kitchen and headed up the stairs. She couldn't stand that this bull-headed blowhard had the uncanny ability to "see" her art, understand her, and kiss her into stupidity when all he cared about was being right. Caleb Vincent was an enigma wrapped in complexities that disrupted her synapses. She stopped in a shadow on the landing, the clarity of her art reaching out to her through the dark. In that moment she knew the ever-elusive eyes were turquoise.

Chapter 15

Caleb spent the remainder of the weekend devising methods to spend more time getting to know Jai without James shadowing their every move. Since it was becoming clear to him that he wasn't going to get her out of his system easily, he figured maybe if they spent too much time together, he'd eventually get sick of her and end his self-imposed obsession.

Bright and early Monday morning, Caleb walked into Hamilton Manor House for the first time since his mother's death three years ago. The business and the house were all that was left of his inheritance, and he'd never wanted either. He was the only child of parents who had frequently traveled for business or pleasure, often leaving him with his grandparents or the household staff. At the age of six, he had run away, hiding out for three days in a barn a quarter of a day's walk from Hamilton Manor House. That was a turning point in his life, one that changed the course of so many other lives irrevocably.

He walked farther into the house, admiring the architecture with an appraising eye. The high ceilings had several skylights, and there was even a covered chandelier. The cavernous foyer was all pale marble and was large enough to host dinners and dances, which his parents had done often. The living room was off to the right, with large couches and a marble fireplace. Everything was decorated in pale colors to match the foyer and enhance the natural light. As a child Caleb had thought his home was large enough to be considered a castle, but when he'd entered school, he'd learned that his friends lived in homes twice the size, with double the staff.

A thin, young man came bustling through the door, speaking with a robust older woman. He snatched up Caleb's bag off the white and beige marble pedestal table in the middle of the foyer and glared at him. "Don't worry about the rest of the house right now," said the young man. "Get the kitchen situated the way you want, and make a list of supplies you'll need, and also make a wish list of large purchase items you want. If you have friends or family who might be looking for work, I'll interview your recommendations first. I need mostly cleaning staff and men who can handle lots of heavy lifting and moving."

"Thank you," the woman said, with a huge smile.

"And, Ms. Olive, this is Caleb," Latham said. "He's the one who rushed me to find a qualified staff in less than forty-eight hours. He's a real taskmaster, but I have to admit, I'm thrilled with this challenge. This is one amazing spot to house our headquarters."

"Hello, Caleb. It's been a long time," said Olive. "It's so good to see you. You look great. Your aunt Ann and aunt Del are always talking about how handsome and successful you are."

"Does everyone in Connecticut know everyone else?"

Latham asked, exasperated. He snatched Caleb's PDA and started up the stairs. "And from the stories this woman tells, I can't wait to meet your aunts Reaghann and Fidelma. I'll be in the office."

"Latham, I'd rather we use the den down here as the office," Caleb said before turning back to Olive. He gave her a peck on the cheek, something he felt compelled to do. She'd started working for his parents when she turned eighteen—he was about eleven then—and for years he'd harbored secret plans of them running off together. "Olive, I'm glad you're still around and able to help me out."

"Oh, I've been retired for years, but the deal your cousin called me up with was too good to pass up. I don't think I've ever had a staff this large to manage. And Latham is some kind of looker."

"I think Saoirse talks too much," said Caleb.

"Oh. It's not a managerial job?" replied Olive.

"For you, Olive, of course. I just want to know how much she's paying you. She tends to be overly generous with my money."

"I'd do it for free, just for the opportunity to mold my own staff, get them in shape. Like Hamilton Manor House used to have. Ms. Downs, now she was a terror. Even when I worked under Ms. Cook, she'd be over me all the time. And your mother, sweet woman, when Mr. Vincent was out of town but—"

"Olive, that household is gone, and I don't wish to resurrect the dead. Understand?" She looked hurt by the bluntness of his words. "Did you know Ms. Cook was really Ms. Davis? Ms. Downs was Mrs. Evers. Youngman's real name was Mark. My parents cared so little for the staff, they named them after their duties. Cook for the cook, Downs for the downstairs maid, Youngman was for the young man." Olive's face was turning a pretty shade of pink. "It made it difficult for me to find you, until I remembered you had saved the day by getting olives for my mother's party, Miss Abbot."

"Oh. You're making me feel my age. I ain't been a Miss since I was in grade school, and I ain't been Louise Abbot since I was twenty-one."

"Who's your husband?"

"Charles Owen. Works up in Hartford, for the phone company. He could retire, but then we'd have to get divorced."

"That's good to know, because I want to know the staff. First names and lasts. I want to know their families and what is going on in their lives. Like I did as a kid."

"You sure did know everyone's business. You could gossip with the best of them."

"I want this to be an enjoyable place to work. You think you can help me do that, Mrs. Owen?"

"I can do anything. Remember, I worked under the old regime. I've also worked for nice people." Louise gave him a wink. She bustled off toward the kitchen, her clipboard in hand. "And, Caleb, don't worry. You aren't your parents, and just spending time with Latham, I know it'll be a breeze working for you. You've always been one of the nice people. And, boy, I've known you most your life. It's best you call me Ms. Louise."

Elwood and Omar came in through the back atrium, waving to Louise, and shook Caleb's hand. Krebbs and Son was a decent-sized operation. They did plumbing, refrigeration, and electrical. Caleb was glad to see father and son looking good. "You know, I've never actually set foot in here before. Your parents always had there *own* people," Elwood said, touching the banister on the main staircase and knocking on the solid wood. His normally unreadable face expressed approval.

"Well then, I guess it's a good thing you're my people. When Omar told me about his work for the Ferguson spread, it seemed like you could use the extra help," said Caleb.

"You got that right," Elwood said.

"I didn't want to come into town and set up shop without letting you know my intentions. It was Omar here who said you were about ready to retire," said Caleb.

"Yep. But I like the idea of being a manager," replied Elwood.

"Good, because you'll have an entire division at your disposal," said Caleb. "But before we get to that, let me show you around and tell you what my plans are here. I want to get a crew working on this as soon as possible."

"I thought you were gonna expand the farmhouse?" Elwood said, referring to the inn.

"I was, but not like I originally planned," said Caleb. "I'm using my own crew in Hartford for that. A friend of mine suggested smaller changes, keeping as much of the original construction as possible."

"Nostalgia," Elwood said.

"Something like that," Caleb said, less apprehensive about confronting his past.

"I respect that. Lot of people around here respect that," said Elwood. "Every house, every tree, every lake reminds me of something someone did. Some place where you and Omar would ride your bikes or go fishing or steal a pie . . ."

"We didn't steal that pie," Omar said. "Caleb's aunt Gael gave it to us."

"Gael is younger than you both by eight months and

a year. She hands you a hot pie, and you don't think somethin's wrong?" said Elwood. "She was right. Boys are stupid."

"Whatever, Dad. So, Caleb, when you bringing the Hartford office here?"

"I was hoping you could help Latham take care of that as soon as possible. I'd like to stay close to town," replied Caleb.

"Doesn't have anything to do with the pretty woman staying at the inn?" said Elwood. Caleb raised an eyebrow at Elwood's question.

"Met her this morning, when we stopped over to check the damage," Omar said in a low voice.

"Of course, it does, and don't ever think I can't hear you, boy," replied Elwood. "I'm your father. I can hear your thoughts. That's how I know you and Caleb stole that pie."

"Come on, Dad. Let's see the rest of this place," said Omar. "Talking to you about girls is embarrassing."

"That wasn't a girl. That was a woman. A mighty fine woman," said Elwood. "And I hope one of you is smart enough to know that. I know that James character noticed. Didn't leave her alone with us for a second."

"Humph," Caleb said, trying not to let on how much the comment disturbed him. "Let's work top to bottom. Then we'll go out to the pool house and maybe ride out and see what kind of condition the stables are in."

"While the Vincents were alive," Omar said, "I had to go around the back and wait for you. If and when they let me see you, that is. They always made me feel like I was dirty." Caleb felt a pang of regret. He had made Jai feel that same way, and he could tell it had always bothered his childhood friend, so he could only imagine how much it would bother a grown woman.

"Aww, boy, don't be sensitive. They was just raisin' the boy as they saw fit," said Elwood. "They had money and all kinds of degrees and stuff. While we come from the other side of the tracks. It's just the way it was back then. 'Sides, sometimes you two got so dirty, I didn't want you in our house."

"I didn't know my father was a racist or how brainwashed my mother was," said Caleb. "No one told me. . . ." It had been a bitter pill for Caleb to swallow growing up. It was the part of his legacy, the part of his childhood, that constantly ate away at him. "Maybe if I'd have known, I would have been able to pick my own friends for who they were and not for where they lived. I want to apologize to you, Omar, for the way my parents treated you. It wasn't right. You were my friend."

"Thanks. I knew we were best buds no matter what your parents said," Omar said and started looking in rooms.

Elwood clapped Caleb on the back as they strolled down the second-floor corridor. "You ain't nothin' like Brad. You're just like Quinn, whether you know it or not. Quinn is a kind, fair man, with a nose for business. Smart, too, and that man can spin a yarn, I tell you."

"Not to mention handsome," Caleb said, winking an eye that looked just like his father's.

Jai was headed back to the house when she heard the commotion. She walked in the back door and found them nose to nose in the living room, with a finger in each other's chest, yelling at the top of their lungs.

"You're crass, rude, disrespectful, immature, and stubborn," yelled Caleb.

"I looked at your file, you yuppie loudmouth,"

growled James. "Just because I don't have your education or money doesn't mean you get to treat me like shit and get all in my face."

"No, but me paying *your* salary does," Caleb said.

"That's some white man entitlement bullshit you talkin'," yelled James.

"Where did you read that? On a bubble-gum wrapper?" Caleb asked.

"I'ma fuck you up . . . ," James said, moving menacingly toward Caleb.

"What in the hell is going on here?" Jai asked, ready to jump into the fray.

"This idiot almost blew a deal for me," Caleb growled. Jai was ready to pounce on James.

"I did not. We were just talking," James said, ignoring Caleb, silently imploring Jai to believe him.

"You were talking about her, and not in a flattering way. You don't talk to people like that," Caleb said, getting in James's face and redirecting his attention.

"Why not? They regular people, ain't they?" said James.

"You do not make those decisions in my home, at my job, or anywhere that I have dominion," said Caleb.

"Woo hoo. Still in the room. My employee. Please let him have his say," Jai said, not certain of which side to take until she heard more.

"Where I'm from, a phat booty is a good thing," James explained, sending a wink at Jai.

"I know what p-h-a-t means, and I'm not disputing the description," said Caleb. "I have a problem with the fact that you said it to people you don't even know. Those are my clients, just like I'm yours. You have undermined my authority and made yourself and me look like ignorant fools."

"You guys think I have a nice butt?" Jai asked, color rising on her face.

"I do. Junk in the trunk and all, but white boys like them skin and bones things . . . ," James said carelessly.

"White boy?" cried Caleb. "Who the hell do you think you're talking to, you—"

"You what? You jiggaboo, nigga, coon, sambo, pickaninny? I ain't light enough to talk to your honky-tonk, white trash friends?" yelled James. "Or is it that you don't want anyone to know you used to hang around with broke white folks? You think I'm some uneducated thug nigger from the ghetto that you can look your thin, snobby, white-boy nose down at? And that you can just toss your old friends away because you got a little money, you fuckin' hypocrite?"

Jai squinted her eyes, ready to kill James. She suspected that James was way off track with his assessment. She didn't think this had anything to do with color but was almost certain it had to do with James's lack of refinement.

Then Caleb said, "That's it. I've had it with your ignorant mouth." He was preparing to beat James down. "You want to be a nigga, then let's take this shit outside. I'll fuck you up like a runaway slave."

Jai's eyes shot to Caleb; she didn't want to believe what she'd heard. She couldn't imagine that the mouth that had kissed her so righteously could speak such racist words. In order to keep her own mouth in check, she said, "That's a lawsuit. I'd let him beat me up if I were you, James. You saw how much he's worth."

Jai plopped down on an overstuffed, worn, and comfy chair and began doodling in her book, her mind still swirling with the possibility of Caleb being prejudiced. She had allowed his hands to roam her body. She had marveled at how beautiful his skin looked against hers. She'd even let herself dream of what their children might look like. But, of course, she had let her imagination get the better of her. He was a man just like all the others she knew, and sex was probably the only thing he wanted from the big, thick black girl. He probably wanted to satisfy his craving for dark meat. Cure his jungle fever.

It was sad that even though she knew Caleb was a white man, she still felt as if he was different, and not in the romantic sense. She felt like a part of him understood being ostracized by society, being held to an impossible standard, and being forced to fight or hide who and what you were. For her, it was always her photographic memory. For her father, it had been his glossy black skin. For her mother, it was trying to break away from expectations of a mulatto woman of superior background. For Caleb, she didn't know. But she was sure it was there.

"I ain't no punk, so don't worry, Mr. Vincent. I'm gonna fight. I don't need your money. And if I did, I'd sue you for being a fucking Aryan supporter with your blond hair, blue-eyed racist shit."

Caleb gave the lawsuit possibility some thought. With his company in on so many big projects, a charge of attempted murder was not something he needed. "How about we race? My Jaguar against your white box."

"My Miata is souped," James said confidently. "You're on."

"I can attest to that. I looked at the engine myself," Jai added. "It's a top-of-the-line sports car, accessorized and drag race capable."

"Then let's do this," Caleb said.

"Loser leaves," James added. And they shook.

* * *

Jai stood out on the lawn, waiting impatiently for Caleb to change out of his work clothes and for James to find his keys. The silent grudge match was bad enough, but challenging each other to a drag race was absurd. And to top it off, they expected her to stand in the middle of the road, like a 1950s Betty Sue, to start the race.

"Will you two hurry up?" called Jai. "I can run faster barefoot than both of you."

James came out first, his keys jingling in his hand. Youth and brawn propelled him over the banister and to her side. Caleb was all lean muscle. He moved with purpose, suppressed power radiating all around them.

"I don't know how you can determine which of you is better as a man. I mean, the cars are doing the work, and don't get me wrong, but the Jaguar against the Miata would be cool to see, but it only proves one of you has a superior car and you drive it well," Jai said, with a smirk.

"So what do you propose, Ms. Wyatt?" Caleb asked, his arms folded over his chest and his face wearing the same smirk.

"A foot race. To the trees, 'round the big oak, and back," she answered.

James looked at Caleb. James had him by about two, possibly three, inches, giving him the longer stride. "Sounds cool. I run all the time on the court. The Jag might be a challenge for my Miata, but I can beat anyone on foot."

"You ready?" Caleb asked, hunkering down like an Olympic racer. James bent at the waist, digging his feet in.

Jai stood up straight and looked at them like they were crazy. "You're gonna race in those? You two look stupid." James's sneakers looked like they weighed five pounds easy, while Caleb's sneakers didn't look as if they offered any support or protection whatsoever.

"These are the new Mike Jordans. I use them on the court all the time," said James. "But those sissy sandals might need a layer of cow when I'm done with old dude."

"Don't worry about me, young buck. These are Barcelona Cross Trainers. Rubber sole, lightweight, durable. They're made for distance," Caleb said.

"Probably expensive as hell," James muttered.

"One hundred seventy-five dollars," Caleb said.

"Two hundred ten bucks," James said not to be outdone.

"Nine ninety-nine, on sale at Wal-Mart," Jai said, rocking back on her no-name, beat-up tennis shoes. "Okay. On your mark, get set, go!"

All three took off at a sprint. Jai fell behind and paced the runners ahead of her. She kicked off her sneakers and gained speed. James was burning energy fast. His feet were so low to the ground that he kept catching tufts of grass.

Caleb was familiar with the terrain and hoped that would be to his advantage. He remembered the slight rises and drops and was able to avoid the pitfalls. He made the turn at the tree with ease. Halfway back to the house, he heard James closing the distance and almost felt the man's sweat on his heels. But there was nothing more that he could do, since he'd been going full throttle since the beginning of the race. Just as he was about to taste victory and see the last of James, he caught a glimpse of two brown arms swinging wildly in his peripheral vision. He saw James struggling about ten seconds behind him, but there, right next to him, was Jai.

"Tie!" she screamed, with her last breath. She fell to

the ground as gracefully as possible, which resembled a Muppet tripping.

"You okay?" Caleb asked.

"This is a big ole smile of triumph. That man there is the agony of defeat," she said, watching a lumbering James walk off the pain of his exertion and catch his breath.

Caleb sat down on the grass, next to Jai, who was leaning back on her elbows. Both of them were waiting to see if the big man was going to collapse. "If I didn't know any better, I'd think he was a smoker," Caleb whispered in her ear, sneaking a sniff of her hair.

"Nope, he just got smoked is all. Chokin' on my dust," said Jai.

"I gotta get me some of those Wal-Mart specials for the next blacktop b-ball game," said James. Jai wiggled her toes at James and pointed to her sneakers, which lay in the grass about a yard away from them.

"You gotta be shitting me," said James. "I lost to a white boy in sissy sneakers and a girl with none. I swear, I'll never tell my boys this story."

Jai hated James's casual white boy remark, but Caleb seemed unfazed. He immediately volleyed jokes back. It was the most relaxed and fun time the trio had had since arriving and having to deal with each other.

"You better start packing now, or I'll tell all of Brooklyn about your loss on a billboard on the Belt Parkway," said Caleb.

"Best two out of three, and I get to drive the Jaguar," James said.

"And then what? Rock, paper, scissors?" Caleb came back.

"No one is going anywhere," declared Jai. "It was a tie, so James stays, but he has to be extra nice and respectful.

James, it's time you learned not everyone is your boy and can be treated as such. We'll talk more about it later."

"Yes, ma'am," James said.

"And the same goes for you, Mr. Vincent," said Jai.

"What? What did I do?" said Caleb.

"You pick at him, and you know it. Ah . . . ah . . . ah . . . ," she said, wagging a finger to keep him from talking. "In the future, if you have a problem with James, don't incite him. Instead, find me and take it up with me." Jai got up off the ground and stretched her well-exercised muscles. "Now if that's all, I'm going in."

"Shouldn't the winners at least go out to dinner?" Caleb asked.

"A gracious winner would take the loser out. And since this is really between you two, hope you have a good time," Jai said, going into the house.

"What time should I be ready, boss?" James asked, putting an arm around Caleb.

Chapter 16

The three temporary residents of the inn settled into an easy existence. Each morning at eight thirty, Caleb went to the manor house to work, and by four o'clock Latham and Louise started throwing everyone out. Caleb usually arrived at the inn around five, as James and Jai were getting the table set and dinner ready. It was a lovely little scene, except for the fact that James was playing man of the house. His house.

Caleb tried to rationalize his interest in Jai, telling himself that she was a novelty and he wasn't really attracted to her. So whenever he saw her, he took her full measure. She lacked the detached polish of the mannequin women his parents had paraded in front of him, and she had more personality than the women who sought him out. He liked that she wasn't vain and wore her glasses when required. She pulled her hair up if it was in her face and kicked off her shoes when she liked. The reality was he liked her and so many things about her. He envied that she was comfortable in her own skin, and he wanted that to rub off on him.

Jai spent most afternoons alone. James did his

requisite picture taking in the morning, following her around, asking questions, examining her work, studying and improving his own. He was eager to please and easy to teach. At around ten or so, he would run out to meet with Ann and Dolly, joining them in whatever they spent the day doing and dropping the film to be developed. Jai would then take to the outdoors. At first, it was because Elwood and his crew were running pumps and cleaning out sludge, and the sounds and smells drove her out, but after four days, the outings became a welcome part of her routine. They also made it harder for James to find her when he came in. He was a sweetheart who lived for the minute, as she did, but he rarely thought about the future, and that, in some infinitesimal way, she saw as a weakness, his fatal flaw.

Caleb, on the other hand, had maturity, sophistication, masculinity, and a sharp, dry wit—wrapped in a sexy and humble package. She didn't think Caleb had any idea how gorgeous he really was, and although she often caught him looking at her like a chocolate wonderland, she was sure he had a slew of women back in New York who were more elegant than she. But the one delectable kiss they had shared was hers forever. The supple feel of his lips gently teasing hers, the provocative movement of his strong hands shamelessly exploring her attention-deprived body had made her feel again. She could not forget the keen interest in his cyan eyes, which had feverishly raked over her with unconcealed yearning.

She growled in frustration as she pulled open the back door and stormed inside. Her composure was threatening to shatter and strike anyone in her way. It was too much to fend off one man and want another, especially when the man you wanted did nothing to make his feelings known. Caleb saw the slash of hostility on her face as she entered the dining room.

"Who's that for? We expecting company?" she asked, irritation in her voice.

Caleb couldn't help but smile. He found her anger as enticing as the rest of her. She was cute with her lips poked out, her hips cocked forward, red tinting her rich cocoa skin, her dark eyes trained on him. Her anger was as palpable as the Furies, and he knew she'd be a viable opponent.

"No one ever brought you flowers before?"

Her lips formed a big O as her eyes took in the simple setting for two. The "good" dishes sparkled on the off-white linen tablecloth and the matching cloth napkins were folded in some intricate pattern. He held out her chair and took her pad and charcoals. Her sharp eyes collided with his smoldering eyes. Dressed in olive pants and a forest green shirt, he was radiant, like a lantern in the night, and Jailyn felt grimy and dirty.

"Let me get cleaned up while we wait for James."

"James is skipping dinner tonight. He left a message. Something about his car not starting."

"Yeah, right," Jai said, her raspy voice still laced with venom. She was thinking he probably met some fast-ass girl. It didn't matter, though. She wasn't interested in James like that, but she was used to him showering her with attention.

She didn't take long changing into a fresh T-shirt and washing up. She returned to the table, with a sour look on her face, and Caleb didn't want to believe that she might prefer James's company to his, especially since he had rushed back to the inn to get dinner on the table and spend some time wooing her. He put the food down harder than he intended.

"I don't know who pissed you off today, but I hope it ain't me and that we can have at least a civil meal, if not a nice one," he said. "Latham reamed me out for missing a phone conference, my father called and cursed me out for not having called all week, and Louise sent me off with a tongue-lashing for leaving my coffee cup out all night. She claimed it was a mold experiment."

Her lips curled into an affectionate smile. "It takes longer than a night for mold to form."

"Yeah, like I was gonna admit to leaving it out all week."

Dinner was an epicurean delight, and the conversation engrossing. Caleb found Jai's observations on every topic they explored to be astute and comical. She thought Caleb was knowledgeable, worldly, and remarkably entertaining. He loved looking at her as much as she loved to look at him. His eyes were so clear and absolute in their oceanic color that she thought she could smell the sea air. Caleb never lit the candles he set out, because the sparkling onyx of her eyes caught the setting sun through the windows and hypnotized him throughout the meal.

He followed her onto the porch, carrying out two slices of warmed peach cobbler with a dollop of whipped cream on hers and ice cream on his. He sat on the top step, and she on the swing, eating in companionable silence, watching the night settle in. Caleb found his mind wandering as he watched her sensually lick the dessert from the spoon. The blood rushing from his head to his groin and the cooling of the night air made him light-headed. He was attracted to more than her voice and her body: he envied her passion for life, he admired her work, and he was intrigued with her mind. She had childlike powers of perception and didn't miss anything, the proverbial question *why* always at the forefront of her mind, but she had this intuitiveness—some sort of sixth sense—that helped her find the answers. He wanted more of her, and he didn't know why she wasn't picking up on it, but he knew just how he'd get her.

Caleb cleared the dishes and took a shower before he went to the attic and tapped on the door to her room.

"Come in," she called.

He swore she hardly slept. He often heard the pitter-patter of her feet as she roamed the house late at night or early in the morning. At first, he had suspected she was paying visits to James, but James's snoring proved his sleep went uninterrupted. So one night when he couldn't sleep, Caleb went down to make warm milk, like his grandmother would make, and there she was, sitting in the living room, holding a cup of something and talking to ghosts. Not in an eerie, creepy "I see dead people" kind of way, but in an "I wish you were here to help me; I miss you" type of way. It reminded him of his grandmother. She had lived for a year after his grandfather passed on, but everyone said Siobhan Quinlan died of a broken heart.

He opened the door to see Jai sitting up in bed and James's huge body dominating the foot of the bed. Photos were spread out on a poster board next to her drawings, and a half-completed storyboard sat on the nightstand. It was apparent that they were hard at work, but it still irked Caleb that James was back. "You two look cozy."

"Just work," James said, with a wink to Caleb. "When the car mysteriously broke down, I was buggin', 'cause I had the bad boy checked the day before we left. Jai, I mean Ms. Wyatt, was with me. But the guy at the casino ain't never seen nothing like my car. So when Ann came in from gamblin', she had a go at it. That woman knows her cars. She had it on the road in no time. She said the insides get all jarred on these roads, wires get loosened, small animals eat away at stuff, and sometimes they even die in there. I tried to call, but Ms. Wyatt's phone wasn't on."

"I keep forgetting to recharge it," Jai said, making a quick show of looking for her bag. "But Caleb passed on the message."

"Ann told me to call so you wouldn't hold dinner. She didn't know how long it'd take, and she didn't want you to worry," explained James.

"Yeah, we were real worried about you, James. I'll let you get back to work," Caleb said tersely.

"See ya," James called out.

"No disruption," Jai said at the same time. "Seriously, stay. It's the campaign for the inn. James isn't seeing my vision, and I don't think his is working. Your input would be valuable."

"I'm burnt tonight. I can't wrap my mind around work," Caleb answered.

"So what are you here for, if not work?" James asked, with a sly smile that said, "Go on, buddy. Get out of that one."

"I was here to ask Ms. Wyatt if she'd go to the upcoming party with me," Caleb said in a quiet voice.

Jai picked up on Caleb's reluctance to say anything in front of James, but she also felt the sincerity of the invitation, because his eyes were pleading with her. The look changed into raw sexual tension and nearly burned the clothing from her body. She didn't hear her own answer, because the blood roaring in her ears was blocking out all sound. He was still standing in the door when she tapped the space on the bed, next to her. Her answer and actions met with his approval, because he climbed in the bed, next to her, scooping her under his arm as if they did this every night.

"I hope you don't mind me taking your boss out, James," said Caleb. "We get out every day, so she should, too."

"A hoedown is not getting out," James replied, jealousy coloring his statement.

"It's a party, like any other. Food, live music, dancing, and people having a good time," said Caleb. "And don't fret, James. You're invited, too. You'll just have to get your own date, though." Before James or Jai could respond, Caleb pulled the storyboard closer to him and began offering advice, suggestions, and constructive criticism. He explained how he didn't feel as though James was seeing *their* vision, putting James on the defensive and clearly on the outside of the team.

"How about you two map out some specifics for me, and I'll take some shots in the morning? As cozy as this is, it's too weird for me," James announced, getting to his feet.

And as much as Jai liked the feel of Caleb's body so close to hers, she had to admit James was right: two men and one girl in a house in the middle of nowhere, in one bed, made for interesting headlines. Caleb was also feeling changes taking place. His body was on high alert because of the delectable woman next to him and the imminent possibility of them being alone in bed together. The effect was more than he could hide.

"I guess we'll pick this up in the morning," Caleb said, readjusting himself and getting up from the bed.

Both guys were out the door in a flash. She could hear the Miata growl and speed off. Jai sat there, confused and curious as to how she had managed to repulse them both without so much as moving a muscle. She let the emotion go as quickly as it came.

It took her all of three cleansing breaths for her mind to "see" the campaign clearly. She rearranged the pictures and started working on the captions. When she was satisfied with her progress, she put the storyboard and the poster board aside. Somewhere in the big bed, she could hear the faint melody of some familiar song. After five seconds it started again, and it continued until she pulled back the pillow and found a cell phone. She figured Caleb must have dropped it. When she looked at the screen, it had a picture of her on it.

Chapter 17

"Hello?" Jai asked cautiously.

"Hey."

"Caleb?"

"Yup." Jai giggled until her giggle turned into full-blown laughter. "What's so funny, Miss?"

"The fact that the only way you could call me was to give me a phone," she said in between a few hiccup coughs.

"I'm sure you'll misplace it in no time," Caleb said, a huge smile on his face. He was sitting in his grandfather's big chair. Jai's energy was so dynamic, he could hear her through the wall and feel her vibrations through the floor.

"I don't misplace things. Usually, I break them, or in the case of cell phones, I forget to recharge them." She wandered in a huge circle in the room until her feet carried her into the hall. As they talked about nothing and everything, she examined all the details in the hallway, then she plopped down on the floor.

Hearing Caleb's voice on the phone was like finding an old friend. The tranquility in his voice was like sitting on the edge of a brook. It was steady and reassuring, but mellow, musical. The conversation didn't match their first turbulent phone calls, when he spit fire and ice at her. But now that she'd seen him, she knew that his body was a temple, harboring the secrets of a primitive barbarian and the lightness of being. He was the origin of man; God had created in Caleb some of his finest workmanship.

"So, since you're still up, how about I meet you somewhere for a drink?" said Caleb.

"Like where?" she asked as he opened his door and stared down at her. "As much as I like you guarding my door and protecting me from James, I think there's some hot cocoa in the kitchen calling my name."

Caleb held out a lean, strong hand, a feral look in his turquoise eyes. "I promise I won't bite you," he said, bringing her scantily clad body up close to his. "Unless you *beg* me." The words skimmed over her like a fantasy, and a quivering began low in her stomach.

Caleb couldn't help but dive into the wide black abyss of her eyes, which were now open so wide, she reminded him of a doll. *Slow down,* he admonished himself, *or she'll take to the wind like a scared deer.* He moved his body away from her, but his eyes were drawn to her rounded breasts, which pressed against the white fabric of her nightshirt, leaving little to the imagination. As his eyes savored her dimensions, her nipples peaked and hardened under his gaze, and his own body responded to that glorious sight.

Jai stood timidly, pleased to see Caleb had no control over his carnal thoughts, either. She blatantly perused the contours of his body with her eyes, wanting to touch the buttery soft skin of his arms; his chest, which was covered by a thin T-shirt; and his nipples, which had puckered to hard pebbles. Jai felt the hallway sway, and she took a step toward him, the warmth of his body beckoning her. They embraced, and she felt his erection pressing eagerly against her stomach and knew she couldn't turn back. She wanted him, and she wanted to surrender to the promises his body was making. She raised a hand and tangled it in his liquid gold hair. The heavy locks twined around her fingers as she brought his lips to hers.

Caleb let out a low moan that made him sound more beast than man. His body wanted to possess her. He ached to pull her closer, to shower her with kisses. Holding the potency within him in check was making his knees weak. It was as if she were Delilah, sapping all of his strength in that one kiss. The muscles of his chest were expanding and contracting with each elated breath. She could feel his heartbeats between her own. His hands traced her generous curves so lightly, it was like a whisper caressing her skin. He was in awe of her and wanted to give her due reverence, but the animal inside him wanted to pin her to the closest surface and bury himself within the warm, wet confines of her body.

He slowly lifted her off her feet, Jai's tongue curled expertly around his, and she nearly unmanned him right there. Caleb thought she was sin incarnate as her body moved seductively against him, her tongue darting in and out of his mouth. Then she slowly devoured his senses whole by sucking his tongue into her hot mouth. She was uninhibited in his arms. Caleb had created a cocoon for her where nothing but this moment, these needs, existed. She felt safe and weightless in his arms as he carried her on a sea of eroticism. It was a miracle he stayed upright long enough to maneuver into her room, but finally he set her down. She made a tantalizing sight standing there before him, her eyes glinting with hedonistic intentions, her lips puffy from kissing, her body tempting him with its smell, her heat and passion making their way into his bloodstream, making his heart beat double time. He kissed her one last time before walking to the door.

"Why?" she muttered. She knew how desperate she sounded, she knew she was setting herself up for rejection, she knew she didn't want to be used, but more than anything, she didn't want him to just walk away. She was tired of being afraid of rejection, of being afraid to feel, and now that she had some hope, she wasn't willing not to ask why.

Caleb had known the answer all along; he didn't even need to turn around. "I have a lot of feelings I'm dealing with right now. Being back home, dealing with my childhood, facing some demons in my past. I hadn't expected it, but being here with you made it that much easier for me to see myself and not judge myself so harshly. I don't want to give you any reason to leave prematurely."

Caleb started shuffling to the door. It seemed like the longest walk of his life. He was waiting to see what she would do. Even if she could promise him she wouldn't leave, he would walk out the door, anyway.

"Don't go," Jai said. Her voice was stronger owing to the honesty in his confession. "Stay with me tonight. Make love to me."

Caleb turned slowly to her. Elation stormed through him like a dam bursting. He hadn't realized how on edge he had been until that moment when it all lifted from him. "Are you sure?"

She nodded, her dancing blue-black curls the only visible sign. "Stop being so cynical."

"Practical," he countered.

"Stubborn."

"Cautious."

"S l o o ow."

"Very," he answered, his eyes roaming her body. "I've got to go get something from my room."

All of her senses came alive when he reentered the room. He filled the threshold before easing the door closed and locking it. She closed her eyes, letting her mind take over. She could smell his aquatic blue eyes devouring her, his desire traveling on his masculine scent, which was just below the pungent smell of Ivory soap. No fancy oatmeal or apricot scrubs for him. No expensive cologne to hide behind. He smelled of the fresh outdoors after a rain. She heard the gentle rustle of his too-long hair as he made his way across the room. Like wheat fields blowing in the wind, it, too, changed color, from pale sand to molten honey gold. She felt his presence linger on the air, his energy engulfing her and something even more intangible suffusing her, raising her temperature. He had an aristocratic swagger, a notch below conceit, settling at confident.

When Caleb touched her skin, an inferno erupted between them, the sensual haze taking him higher and higher and out of control within minutes. He laid her on the bed, his emotions driving him, as well as his body and hers. He found a dimple in her back, which he massaged, and as her body arched up to his, he buried his nose in her fragrant hair while raining hot kisses on the supple skin of her neck. Jai was trembling with every touch, his kisses branding her with his desperate desire. With each kiss, her body sizzled beneath his lips and her hips rose up to him, silently inviting him in. He removed her nightshirt in one ruthless motion, exposing the full mounds to his burning gaze.

Jai's nipple tightened even more as he pulled the tip into his warm mouth. He covered the other with his hand, allowing the weight to settle in his fingers.

The pressing of her sleek body against his sent a fresh wave of desire to his groin. The ache almost unbearable, he reared up, snatching off his few nightclothes and ripping the pretty women's boxers off of her. They both gasped simultaneously. Caleb thought she was the most picturesque woman, more than his dreams could ever have conceived. He touched the silky curls between her legs reverently. They were as dark as her eyes and as soft as the hair on her head. They were glistening with moisture, and the earthy smell of her staggered him.

Jailyn saw the size of his member and chided herself for believing in stereotypes. His phallus stood out from his body like a divining rod, and all those corny phrases she'd read in romance novels popped into her mind: endowed with a platinum pipe, rod of the Gods, wand of wishes. The man was endowed, to say the least. He looked deep into her eyes and brought the hand that had been playing between her legs to his tongue. He moistened his thumb, parted the lips, and found her hardened clit. All of her thoughts became focused on that one spot as she went careening to the edge of a deep precipice, but she couldn't get over.

When Caleb felt her body ooze more cream onto his fingers, he removed them from her and licked her off of each digit. He sheathed himself, and then he rubbed his phallus between her lips, getting himself fully coated with her juices. No longer able to control himself, Caleb entered her in one stabbing stroke, impaling himself to the hilt, bliss coating his face and being as nothing else. He pulled back and entered her a second time, feeling the confines of her body tighten around him. A blinding explosion rocketed through Jai, centered in her womanhood. At first, she thought she was climaxing, but in truth, she felt like she was being sliced in two. There was nothing pleasant about it. Caleb thought she'd climaxed when her peeling scream pierced the air and ricocheted back to him. Her nails, which had been clutching his back, were now digging trenches in his flesh. He looked into her face to see pain contorting her features.

"Oh my . . . God . . . I'm sorry, Jai . . . why didn't you . . . I didn't know. . . ." He attempted to withdraw with a grace he could not manage. He could feel her hot, slick walls gripping him tighter, as if the latex didn't exist, making him loathe to pull out, but he was a fool for allowing his manhood to run the show. He should have asked her if she was a virgin. But it seemed so unlikely. He started his agonizing retreat.

"No!" she shouted, her nails threatening to dig more trenches. "Give my body a few more minutes to adjust. It's been a . . . long time."

"More like never," he grumbled.

"Are you crazy?" she asked, moving around below him.

"Stop that, or you'll own my manhood," he ground out. He was trying to calm down, and she wasn't helping by having her clinging, soaking wet walls contracting against him.

"I'm not a virgin . . . It's just . . . that . . . it's . . . been a long time. . . ."

"What's a long time?" he muttered through clenched teeth.

"Three years," she mumbled. "Plus, you're . . . exceedingly . . . blessed. . . ."

Finally, he looked into her flushed face. Her embarrassment had given her a beautiful, angelic glow.

"Thank you. But know that some of it is backlog." He slowly rolled them so his weight wasn't fully on her. Her walls clutched him, causing him to groan with frustration.

"Backlog?"

"Yeah, let's just say, it's been a while for me, too. And don't ask. Men don't like to tell when it's over a month."

"A month is nothing!" she screeched, moving and making him stiff all over again.

"Stop wiggling, or they'll find us like this in the morning. And I agree a month is nothing, but when you start talking in terms of years, for a man, it's like asking a woman her weight."

She didn't respond. Instead, she watched the color creep up his neck and into his face. She wasn't sure if he was embarrassed or angry.

"I'm picky, and I've been looking for the wrong thing in the wrong places, and then I meet you and kablowie! You blow all my preconceived notions to hell." He took a deep breath before going on. "Since that first phone call, you've been plaguing my thoughts. You take me outside of myself, you take my mind places, you make me want things, good things, and I'm not afraid."

As he spoke, Jai began stroking his hair and running her hand over the marble surface of his chest and stomach, tugging at the hairs there. He held her in a way that made her feel treasured. There was no Spidey sense tingling the back of her neck; there were no second thoughts floating through her head. She looked at him and felt like if this was all she ever got, she'd be okay. It was love, and she would be satisfied even if it was for one night. In a brazen move, she rocked her hips against him and felt his manhood thicken.

"I'm no Casanova, but I think you're taking advantage of me," he said and smiled.

He allowed her to set the pace. A growl came from deep within the stone wall of his chest as she turned them so that she sat astride him. Her body melting at his kiss, and she completely gave herself over to his touches, as if starved for them. But she moved like she was a master at the art of seduction.

"Baby, if you keep it up, you're gonna get more than you can handle sooner than you expect," murmured Caleb.

"You can't mean to say it gets bigger."

"Much." He winked up at her.

Jai's body clamped down in a moment of panic, and a fresh wave of pleasure conquered Caleb, sending another groan into the air. He clutched the generous flesh of her rear, trying to steady her, but her churning hips. The bouncing of her breasts above him, the swinging of her curls, the feel of her luscious bottom in his hands, and the wetness from her womanhood glossing his erection was more than he could take.

"Baby, seriously," he whispered. "Slow down, honey. Please, I'm about to make a fool of . . . oh . . . ohhh . . ."

Jai somehow managed to open her legs a bit wider and arch her body so that she was pulling his thick, hot manhood into her silky heat. He rolled her over and pressed her into the bed, pulling all the way out of her to make sure he had her attention and to give himself a quick respite.

"Relax, or you'll make me come before you can enjoy it," he said. He kissed the protest from her lips, smoothing all worry from her brow, then slid into her and stilled himself. Heaven wasn't nearly as decadent as this.

He slowly sank all of himself farther into her warmth. "That's it, Jai. Let me in. Open, oh, yeah, ohhh yes . . ."

She moved, and he moved with her, until their bodies moved in tandem. He slid easily into her, touching the spot that had blinded her with pain only moments ago. Now it was the source of her pleasure as he pounded relentlessly against it. She was recklessly driving him toward the rising tide of desire, sweeping him into a tidal wave beyond his control. Jai didn't care. The feel of Caleb buried deep within her was comparable to nothing she'd ever experienced before, and as her body headed for its zenith, she knew there was plenty of him for her to enjoy. As the cascade of sensations threatened to drown her, she bucked again and again as it plunged over the precipice, into the rapturous place that it so longed to be. Her mind went blank with the profoundness of such absolute pleasure. She clung to the smells and sounds of Caleb as his sublime kisses and words of ardor brought her back to him—mind, body, and soul.

"I missed you . . . ," he whispered. "Where you been?"

"Heaven," she giggled.

After he came back to bed from cleaning up, she curled up next to him, her face alight with excitement. "I told you it's been a long time," she said.

"I'm glad you waited until you met me."

"I told you, I'm not a vir—"

"Shh. Let's not ruin this for me." And they giggled themselves into a deep sleep.

Chapter 18

Caleb walked out of the hobby shop, satisfied that his purchase was going to have the desired effect. It had been two days since the night he and Jai had made love, and he wanted to show her in as many ways as possible how much she meant to him. He was grinning from ear to ear like the town fool by the time he reached the top of the hill. He looked through the binoculars he had unearthed. They were a gift from his pop a lifetime ago, to remind Caleb that he was never far away.

He spotted her easily. Her head was rolling from side to side as if an invisible lover were pleasuring her. Jai's shapely mocha-colored leg bounced in a quick staccato to a drummer only she could hear. He opened his other two gifts and scribbled a quick note.

Jai had more than a few fully formed ideas in her head, and it wouldn't take her long to get them down on paper. But she wasn't quite ready to leave the farm-house and go back to the same old grind. Her mind was free again. The dark images were now fleeting. She loved hanging out with James, whose mind was like a sponge. He was so eager to learn, and she'd always wanted a sibling. And as it turned out, Caleb was the man of her dreams. Although they would continue to work together, it wouldn't be nearly as romantic as this.

The beat in Jai's head changed. The bass was growing more forceful, like a dive-bombing bug. She scrambled up, screaming and waving her hands around her head when she saw the big blue and white remote-control plane coming toward her. And it was big. It sailed lower, then landed smoothly next to her without a putter. She shielded her eyes against the spring sun and bright sky but couldn't see anything in the immediate distance. The wing of the plane nudged her leg, and she heard a static crackling, which made her jump back.

"Houston? Come in, Houston. Houston, do we have a problem?"

Jai dropped to her knees and fished out the ancient walkie-talkie strapped in the pilot's seat. She depressed the TALK button. "Houston here. Come back . . . Ra."

"Ra?"

"Sun god."

"Apollo," he countered.

"Apollo, Greek. Ra, Egyptian," she explained. "Sol in Norse mythology, depending on who you ask."

"Niiiiice," he said, drawing the word out.

He watched as she lay back down in the cool grass. He sat with his legs stretched out, glorying in the feel of the sun. All his life he'd been cautious about spending too much time outdoors, about getting darker and revealing his true color, so to speak. Bradley had accused him of flaunting his mixed heritage in his face, of having people question if Caleb was his son. Behind closed doors, Bradley had referred to him as that "bastard nigger." He would say, 'You know the Irish are Europe's niggers, so since you are part Black and part Irish, you're a full nigger." Caleb shook off the memories of growing up ashamed of such a significant part of himself. Once he had told a woman he cared for about his mulatto roots, and she said that it didn't matter and that they never had to talk about it again. She wanted to ignore it, just like Brad. But not Jai. He enjoyed the fact that Jai accepted him as is. She thought he was attractive, sweet, funny, and smart. She wasn't concerned about his wealth, his career, or his future goals, although she paid close attention whenever he spoke about his aspirations.

They talked on the walkie-talkie about their morning, and he told her all about the hobby shop. She exacted a promise that he'd take her there one day soon so that they could buy a kite kit. Kites were another throwback to his childhood, to summers with Quinn and Omar, when they would build their own kites, planes, go-carts, and bikes. After forty-five minutes, the phone on his hip vibrated. "Work calls," he said.

"Oh," she said, forgetting it was a regular workday. Out in the country, time seemed to slip away.

"Where's the cell I gave you? I'll call you," he said.

"It's still in the hallway. Battery's probably dead. Charge it for me when you get home. . . ."

Home. Such a simple word. It brought so many feelings crashing down around him. Home with Jai. Jai standing on the porch, waiting for him. Waiting for him to come home. He was beginning to appreciate the appeal and magic of the house. It had been home to so many, and for years, it had been his home. He had returned and had found out that that had never changed. It was still his home, and Jai was there in it.

"Will dinner be ready when I get there, June?"

"Sure, Ward, but only if I can talk to Ra again tomorrow."

"It's a date. Over and out."

"Ghost."

"Ten-four."

The plane eased around and took off into the air, giving Jai the sweetest sight. A little banner unfurled in the wind. It read MISS YOU ALREADY -C.'

Jai skipped her way back to the inn, her heart pumping extra beats. She stopped suddenly, her sixth sense jumping into high gear. James came sailing down an overhang like Superman, but with a lot less finesse. He wore oversized jeans, construction boots, and his adorable smile, and he had no shirt to cover his ripped chest and six-pack abs. She couldn't help admire his Adonis build, considering he was standing there, flexing like a body builder. But the way he looked her over like a sirloin sent a creepy feeling over her skin.

"I bet you got tan lines on your thighs from always wearing them long shorts," he commented.

He was right. Because she wasn't a stick figure of a woman, she didn't wear tight clothes or anything too revealing. She hated the little paunch she had and the jiggle in her thighs. "So what?"

"Whoa. No need to get all defensive. I was thinking maybe you want to go take a dip in the pond with me. I been up there in the hot sun, taking some photos. I could use a cool down."

"I don't own a swimsuit, but don't let me stop you," she said as pleasantly as she could manage.

"You don't need one. Promise I won't look."

"I don't swim."

"I bet you float," James said, his eyes dropping to her breasts.

She turned and marched in the house, waiting for the door to slam behind her. When it didn't, she turned around and fell right into his waiting arms. James held her firmly, and evidence of him wanting her pressed between them. The coldness in her eyes wilted him, his arousal dissipating. The evil smile on her lips was frightening. The next thing he knew, she had snaked her arms out of his grasp and had begun tickling him. In seconds he was rolling on the floor, trying to catch his breath.

"Girl . . . chill . . . You gonna make me pee on myself," he said, letting her go. Her body had felt good against him, and the tickling had released a stream of energy, realigning the cosmic forces for her. It reinforced his belief that she was special.

Jai picked up her pad and walked off, head high. "Choose your fights more carefully next time," she said, with a playful wink.

"I had you just where I wanted you."

"Yeah? And what about now?" she asked, floating away from him.

James didn't know how to respond. He didn't understand women. Especially this one.

Jai threw her dead cell phone back into her bag. She wanted to talk to Eva right now. Eva was a hard-nosed bitch when it came to guys. She could eat them like nails and spit out diamonds. All of her exes had turned into real sweethearts, and Eva hated them all. She liked them rough and tough. Diamonds were not Eva's best friends; she'd much rather chew nails. She'd definitely know how to handle the likes of James Ross. Jai didn't want to emasculate him, but she did want him to back off. Eva would give her the perfect advice. The walkie-talkie flared to life in her pocket.

"Hey, Ace. How was the return flight?" she asked.

"Disappointing. Fat guy on one side kept snoring, and an old lady threatened to cut me over the armrest. I gave her my peanuts in exchange for protection," Caleb said. "You find the phone yet?"

"Yeah. In the hall, on the floor."

"Well, go get it, and I'll call you on it."

"No. This is way more fun," she said, with a giggle.

They carried on more silly conversation while Jai got dinner prepared. James came in, offering help.

"About the kiss . . ." mumbled James.

Jai's finger was off the button too late. "What kiss?" said Caleb.

"What the fuck? You gotta be shitting me! Even when he's not here, he's here," said James.

"I'm here now," Caleb announced from the doorway. "What? No kisses for me?" he asked, holding out his arms to James.

"Why you playing with my mac?" James asked.

"I'm not playing anything. I'm *courting*," Caleb said, leaning against the doorjamb, resembling the picture Jai had drawn.

James was surprised by the comment and struck by the stance. Jai was blown away by the statement and leveled by Caleb's casual good looks. With the flexing muscles of his arms, which he'd crossed over his broad chest, he was raw male. His tousled hair was way too long for business standards, but it was perfect for enhancing the color of his eyes. It was turning a red blond color, which reminded her of the aged single malt whiskey her father used to drink. His skin was bronzed from hanging out in the country sun. Jai stood staring.

"No one *courts*, unless we're talking basketball days," James said.

"You're macking. He's courting. And I didn't kiss James," said Jai.

"No, but you were all over me," James bragged.

"I tickled you, brought you to your knees, and made you beg for mercy like a girl. I think you squirted me with a little—"

"The man doesn't need to be regaled with what we do," James said, cutting her off.

"Then stop trying to make it more than it is," Jai admonished. "I'm flattered by the attention. But we're here to work."

"Easy for you. For the first time in my memory, the men outnumber the females," James said, carrying food out to the dining room.

Despite Jai's protests, neither man heeded her words. James used any excuse to get close to her and engage her in seemingly innocent physical contact. Caleb took her to the hobby shop, helped her pick out and build her kite, and then taught her to fly it. He also called every day on the walkie-talkie.

One night Caleb walked in carrying a three-liter bottle of blue soda. Jai was lost to him in a fit of snorting laughter. James didn't get it and right after dinner headed back to the casino.

"You ready for our date?" Caleb asked on the walkie-talkie later that night. He was sitting in bed, staring at the ceiling.

"It's not a date . . . It's a hoedown," said Jai.

"Do you have a dress? Shoes? Did you get your hair done?" he asked playfully. Jai hadn't done any of those things. "Don't get all quiet on me now."

"Now I'm nervous."

"How about a practice run?"

"What you got in mind?"

"Meet me in the kitchen for hot apple cider."

"Cool," she said eagerly.

Caleb opened the door to find her sitting on the floor. "Your butt's gonna get pneumonia."

"I have on jeans," she said into the walkie-talkie as she fell into his arms, lips first.

"I still think I should have a closer look," he said, diving into her soft mouth and taking a handful of her rear in each palm.

"Ten-four, good buddy," she said, dropping the walkie-talkie to the floor and greedily stealing kisses.

Chapter 19

Jailyn felt the quickening between her thighs and the pool of hot liquid in her panties, which was threatening to seep through her jeans. There was no denying she wanted this, that she wanted this with this man. In her life she could count her lovers on one hand, not for lack of wanting, but for lack of inspiration. Caleb inspired her body to relish the sumptuous sensations he created in her. She was no longer shy, inept, or unsure of herself. She didn't have to hide behind false bravado. Caleb's body responded to her in every way, as if she could do no wrong.

Caleb was addicted to her. He couldn't believe how many days had passed where they hadn't shared a kiss or a touch, because now that he held her in his arms, he felt complete. He was lost in the delicate lines and soft textures of her body. He was heady with the fragrance of her hair and skin. He was hungry for her taste. The realization chilled him, but she immediately warmed him with her tentative touch, her refreshing kisses, shooing away any doubts that he had gotten caught up too quickly. She didn't push, she wasn't needy, and she didn't issue ultimatums. They didn't commit with words, and yet he knew he wanted her. He didn't want to be without her. Waiting for her to come to him, ready, had been the hardest part.

Slowly, he unwound himself from her body and pulled her into the room with him, only to cover her again with his passion. She looked at him through lust-filled eyes as she peeled away his shirt. He swayed and teetered on shaking legs when her heart-shaped lips pulled at his nipple and her hand snaked up his stomach. Jai felt emboldened by the languorous sounds Caleb was making. She removed his pants with help from him and found he was a masterpiece coated in a layer of molten gold. As she stood staring, he tugged her up against him, eyes glowing. A cavalier smile was on his face.

"You see something you like?" he asked.

"Are you that color all . . . over?" she asked, worried that he would think she was juvenile or, worse, a virgin. "I mean, did you go and tan at a nude beach?" The idea of him lying nude on stark white sand sent a wild frenzy of erotic pictures through her mind.

He let his boxers slide to the ground, and her eyes dropped with them. "So?" he asked. "Do you still think it's a tan?"

All the gold hairs covering his arms, chest, and legs were like corn silk. The hairs surrounding his crowning glory were thick tight curls the color of a smooth scotch. His huge, thick erection pointed at her almost accusingly and continued growing before her eyes. All of his body was the color of honey, as if the sun was radiating from beneath his skin.

"Now let's divest you of your clothing, shall we?" he said.

A storm was brewing inside of him, stirred up by the innocent fascination in her eyes and her blatant perusal. He could see her controlling her fear, but he still needed to calm down. He needed to take his time and clear some of the lust that was fogging up his brain. He moved around her like a phantom, dropping silent kisses on spots of skin that he revealed as he took off her shirt. On bended knee, he removed her jeans, loving the feel of the taut denim against her fullness. Her heady scent wafted into the air, and his reaction was immediate. His appendage was ramrod stiff. He could see her wet, swollen lips through the damp satin fabric of her underwear as he slid them over her ample hips, and he rested one of her legs on his shoulder so that he could better see her delights through the blanket of dark velvet fur.

Jai shivered as he exposed her to the chill air, but it was the sensual way his eyes raked over her that made her entire being tremble. Caleb's tongue thrust between her legs, opening her moist lips and tasting her sweet nectar. He massaged the soft mounds of her bottom while pressing her fully against his lips. She moaned with pleasure while his mouth explored her body at a sedate pace. With his hot mouth ravaging her most sensitive spot, she ran her fingers through his hair, allowing his creative tongue to deftly penetrate her core. At the juncture of her lips, he coaxed her clitoris to show itself. He blew on it before allowing his tongue to circle it and hungrily draw it into his mouth, where he suckled and nipped at it until he felt her fingers curl in his hair and her body buck against him. He was spellbound by her fragrance and lost in her succulent juices. He swept his tongue in wide, swirling circles before pushing up into her and stroking her with his mouth to ecstasy.

Jai looked down at his golden mane of hair, which brushed against her sensitive thighs like raw silk. His long, thick lashes rose so that his crystal cyan eyes locked with hers, her tenuous hold slipping away. Her breathing became shallow as she took great sips of air, reminding her uncooperative lungs what to do. But watching the flicker of his pink tongue into the dark, crispy hair snapped at her senses. His soft tongue, traveling deep into her valley, unraveled the last vestiges of control in her. She could feel the earthquake in her bones, the eruption about to occur. Her body undulated with each enticing sweep of his tongue, her mind giving itself over to the sultry assault as she reached her fulfillment. Her mind reeling, she felt a tightening beginning low in her abdomen. A charge from his electrifying tongue surged through her, sending her flying over the crest. A yell from deep in her chest bounced off the walls.

He watched her eyes close, her head fall back, and her leg tighten over his shoulder as his tongue slid easily between her wet, parted folds. He was able to seduce every corner of her as she opened for him her pink center, preening for him. Forging ahead, he lapped at her cream as her raging release gripped her. Her sublime liquid oozed down his face, onto his chin. He was determined to drink his fill and to ride out the last tremors between the velvety softness of her thighs with his tongue buried deep in her womanhood. In his exuberance, he dipped his head lower, and her body experienced another orgasm as he buried his tongue in her hot hole, his face cushioned between her quivering rear and his hands filled with the juicy mounds, which tightened in his palms.

Jai had never had an orgasm quite like that. Caleb seemed to know her body like no other, and to have her first experience with him made her certain that it had nothing to do with color or stereotypes, but just a man and a woman truly finding one another.

Holding her steady in the circle of his arms, he rose, lifted her like she weighed nothing, and carried her to the bed. He pulled the covers over them and settled her in the curve of his arm. Within minutes he felt her heated kisses in the crook of his neck. His fingers were tangled in her hair. "I thought you were sleeping," he said.

"Not sleepy. Just winded."

"Then does that mean if I let you catch your breath, I can do that again?" Caleb asked, licking his lips.

"No, that means it's my turn," she said, stroking his body and wrapping her hand around his elongated member. Her robust sexual appetite was exciting him. The way she was caressing him and the suggestive way her body was rubbing against him were causing his manhood to ache painfully with want. Her husky laughter held him captive, and her spontaneity sent him flying. She had thoroughly invaded his senses; his mind was completely derailed from rational thought. An earthy, primal groan escaped him when she began moving down his body. She had removed her bra, allowing her breasts to brush against him as she placed scorching kisses along his collarbone and down his chest, to his stomach. Her kisses lingered the lower she went. She gave a flirtatious wink before really creating havoc. . . .

Jai took her time getting to his phallus, which stood out of the nest of thick golden hair. When she took it in her hand, the weight alone made her body flush all over. Looking at it close up, she found the length daunting. She tried to be playful and coy, to build up her confidence, but it didn't help that Caleb lay there all cool, not moving a muscle, except to watch her.

"That's it. You're killing me with all your teasing," he said. In one savage motion, he pulled her up and pressed her body beneath his. "I surrender. Uncle. I give. You've seduced me enough. Another minute of that and I'd have lost control." The hunger and longing in his narrowed blue eyes penetrated her defenses.

"Where's the condom?" she asked. He sat back and fished one out of the drawer. She took it from him and rolled it on him with both hands and mouth.

Caleb let out a sound that was more a growl than a moan. He flung her back onto the bed and thrust into her hard, deep, and fast. The storm she'd created in him was now taking over. Her nails tore down his back without mercy. He could hear nothing but his own labored breathing as he drove in and out of her like a piston. His hunger was eating her alive. She found herself being swept along in the intensity of his desire. Her cream coated him in burning heat as he plundered farther into her, only to find himself lost in the maelstrom of sensation her body was dishing out.

Their bodies had molded together, each driving the other one higher and higher. His teeth rubbed against the exposed skin of her shoulder as she placed dizzying kisses wherever her lips landed. He put her legs up on his shoulders, and she opened to him, encasing him in her moist confines. His mind reeled with the feel of her tightness, which continued to pull at him whenever he withdrew. She gyrated against him, her hips meeting every arduous thrust, until he impaled himself so deeply in her that her body gripped him like a vice. Her body wrested the lethal climax from him. His orgasm was so intense he gave a primal yell, as if his soul was being ripped from his body. She yielded to her own release and felt each tremor of his body. The turbulent storm finally subsided, and they road out the last waves. Her pulsating walls milked the last of his juices, leaving him light-headed, the pent-up ache he'd been suffering now abated.

He slid out of her, disposed of the condom, returned with a washcloth to clean her, then climbed back into bed. She snuck a cursory peek at him under the covers before exhaling and snuggling against him.

"What was that all about?"he asked.

"I didn't know if you came or if you had an orgasm," she said.

"They're one in the same."

"Nope. When you come, you can go again usually. When you climax, you're down for the count. I wanted to make sure you were down for the count."

"If you keep looking at it, I won't be," he said, with an intent look on his face.

"Then you didn't orgasm."

"You're kidding, right?" His engorged member started stiffening.

"You'll never need Viagra."

"Not with you around." They laughed, and his hands sought out her sensitive nipples. His head dipped to take a taste. Her breath caught in her throat, and her heart fluttered in her chest. His intent was all too evident. She pushed him back on the bed and climbed on top of him, looking deviously devilish, with her black curls tangled about her head, her dark eyes dancing, and her body undulating against him. She lowered herself, and there was nothing he could do to stop her. With a triumphant smile on her lips, she took his entire thickness into her sweet, juicy mouth. He didn't think she could do more to turn his world upside down, but as she sucked on his hard phallus, her big black eyes staring up at him, his world became unhinged. The bed rocked and tilted as he lifted himself to meet her mouth when she sat up. She rapidly and shallowly suckled the head. It took every ounce of control not to grab her and jam his manhood to the back of her throat and release his hot cum into her slick mouth and drip from her heart-shaped lips. The image sent another wave of blood into his shaft, making him growl in need. The saliva from her mouth dripped down the veins that were now showing themselves, and her hand began working the lower part while her mouth continued it's torture on the upper part of his rod.

"Oh God. Yeah, stroke me, baby. Tighter, harder . . . ummm, yeah, that's it right there," he cried. As she stroked him with precision, her mouth went down to his balls, taking one in, releasing it, and then taking the other. His eyes rolled up into his head as he gripped the bed, enjoying the fleeting warmth of her tongue no matter where it went. She sat back and started playing with her breasts. She traced her fingers over the swollen tips as they puckered and hardened.

"Show me how to make you come," she said in a siren's voice.

He started stroking himself as he watched her shake and jiggle her breasts in front of him. He watched, fascinated, as she opened her legs and showed him the curly black hairs shining with her moisture. He stroked faster and faster, watching his own live porno when she leaned forward, put his manhood between her breasts, and started sucking the head. The sight was more than he could take, and soon he spouted his seed all over her chin and chest, his body still jerking as she milked the last of his cream from him and then kissed the head. She grabbed the washcloth and cleaned them up as his body still shook and shivered.

"I think I just had my first orgasm," Caleb said on a weak breath.

"Are you sleepy?"

"Yes."

"Weak?"

"Hell, yes."

"Does it feel like you wanna cry?" Caleb looked at her like she was crazy. "Because it felt so good and you're sorry it's over?"

"Oh, most definitely," he said, yawning, too exhausted to do more than snuggle closer to her.

She lifted the cover and took a look at his long, hard, bronzed body. Not a muscle moved. She looked up at his face. His eyes were closed, his dark gold lashes fanned against the aristocratic lines of his face. His long hair was damp and wavy, and sweat still clung to his brow. His breathing was heavy and even. Even in repose the man was gorgeous.

"Yeah. You've had an orgasm," she whispered.

Chapter 20

Jai heard the beep of the horn and made her way outside. She stepped out into the balmy night, looking at her date. Caleb stood by his car, dressed like a cowboy. He wore faded black jeans, which hugged his thighs as he walked around to open her door. His starched white shirt was buttoned to the neck, where he had affixed a black string tie with a beautiful silver clasp. The shirt was tailor-made early cowboy and fit his broad shoulders and muscled chest to perfection. He wore a faded brown Stetson, which matched the black and brown piping on his shirt. He held out a hand for her, kissed her cheek, and helped her into the car, where she found a dozen multicolored roses.

Caleb took a slow stroll around the car to get his bearings. She was dazzling in the soft pink dress. It was simple in design and yet flattered her figure in every way. It was cut to just below the knee and gave a clear view of her silky calves. It hugged her hips and dipped in at the waist. The V-neck was low enough to showcase her creamy brown cleavage without being vulgar. The demure color of her dress set her skin aglow in the bright moonlight. Her hair was styled in long, glamorous waves that reached below her neck, the curled ends brushing her exposed shoulders. He'd been bewitched from the moment she stepped outside. How was he expected to get through a night of being amicable when all he wanted to do was ravish her body?

"Are the flowers for me?" she asked, her husky voice seeping into his bones and further beating at his resolve.

"Yes. I didn't know what your favorite color was, so I got them all."

"Thank you."

They fell silent for a few minutes before she cleared her throat and spoke again. "I hope I look all right. I mean, I did wait until the last minute before I went and picked something out."

"You look fine," he said. But *fine* was an understatement. He saw the dress had tiny silver threading, which made it shimmer even in the dark interior. It kept catching his eye with the rise and fall of her breasts. "I didn't peg you for a pink kind of woman."

"You don't think it looks good on me, do you?"

"I said you look fine."

"They say black is slimming. I should have worn black. I look like an ice cream cone. But the store I went to had all these prairie skirts and petticoats out front, mostly blue and red. I thought I'd fallen into a time warp. Everything was denim and flannel in one section, and then the church stuff was all dark colors. The rest of the place had weekend warrior wear. Bright-colored shirts, sweatpants, and cutesy patterned shorts sets. But the girl, Tammy, showed me some stuff she had in back. And let me tell you, the clothes were something else, all hand made. I ended up getting this and a skort set."

Caleb had a hard time keeping his eyes on the road,

because every time he looked at her, he noticed some other little adorable accent she'd added. Her lips were covered in a pink gloss, and when she talked, he could smell the sticky sweet smell of bubble gum. Her eyes were large and luminous, with a faint brush of pink over the eyelids. The prim way she sat, with her hands clasped shyly in her lap, was making him itch to pull her close to him and taste her lip gloss. She wore pink gemstones in her ears and had a similar color painted on her nails.

"What's that?" he asked, lifting her hand to let the little gold figure dangle from her pinky. He allowed his thumb to travel a slow course over the back of her hand before she snatched it away.

"It's nail jewelry."

"You can draw with that on?" He saw her nod, her embarrassment growing. "Who is it?" he said, squinting at her.

"Taz. You know, the Tasmanian devil."

"Yeah," he said, mulling it over. "I could see that being an appropriate choice for you. A little wild, a little untamed, and all over the place." She punched him lightly in the arm. "We've all got a little devil in us. At least yours is cute."

Caleb parked by the other cars, off to the side of the barn. He was grateful for the cool breeze that was blowing. He smiled and waved at people mulling around outside as he helped Jai from the car. Her soft, full curves brushing up against him made his eyes close and his body go weak. He took in a ragged breath and was assaulted by the delicate fragrance of her skin.

"You okay?" she asked. When he opened his eyes, she was smiling up at him like a wood nymph.

"I'm trying to be a gentleman and court you the proper way. But if you keep looking at me like that, you're gonna walk in there with grass stains on your dress, and you'll sully my sterling reputation." He pressed her against the car to drive his point home, then captured her mouth in a long, drugging kiss before releasing her.

It took her a moment to catch her breath and recover from the kiss. She shivered now that his hard frame stood away from her and the breeze blew over her. She pulled her lip in her mouth, tasting him, feeling him on her. Someone caught Caleb's attention for a brief second, and Jai scurried past him, toward the humongous barn. The music could be heard battling with laughter and raucous voices. Everyone she passed said hello, with a curious look in their eyes. She turned the corner and immediately understood why.

The huge doors were thrown wide open. Streamers hung from the rafters, and balloons floated lazily by. Near one wall women in aprons spooned out heaping portions of home-cooked food. Tables had been set around the perimeter without rhyme or reason. The bandstand was opposite the doors, and hay was scattered on the wooden floor. Couples danced, people ate and drank, the band played, and Jai was mortified. All the men wore denim pants and garishly colored shirts of flannel, and all the women and girls wore some variation of a prairie skirt and petticoats with brightly colored tops. She turned to run before the remainder of the town saw her, but she felt Caleb's hand at her back, pressing her onward. He gave her shoulder a tight squeeze as he moved her into the room.

"You look fine," he said.

"You said that in the car. You were wrong then, and

you're wrong now. I'm overdressed," she whispered harshly through a deranged smile. "Why didn't you tell me? I'm leaving."

"No, you're not, and what did you expect me to say? Go take off that form-fitting, sexy pink number and put on a bulky getup." She put her hand over her mouth to stifle a laugh. "And, no, you are not leaving. Just make sure you tell everyone you're not from around here, and they'll understand."

"I'm *not* from around here. I'm from New York."

"Tell them that, and they'll think you're crazy."

Chapter 21

Jai plunked herself down at a table near the door in order to catch the light breeze teasing the night air. James brought her a cold glass of lemonade. He nursed a beer. She could see Caleb socializing with the men and playfully flirting with the women. This Caleb was a departure from the man who dressed for work in collared, button-down shirts and pressed slacks; walked with his cell phone pasted to his ear, using curt tones and a direct manner; and shared smiles as if he was only given three a day.

Caleb was a head taller than most men, his body was country-boy buff, and he moved with a confident swagger, giving a nod to anyone who caught his eye. He was suave and charming, and he fit right in. The women fawned over him, the children laughed with him, the boys tried to imitate him, the single ladies tried to entice him, and the men wanted a moment of his time. But from every corner of the room, he winked at her. His pretty blue green eyes made her stomach do somersaults, and her nipples tighten against the linen dress.

He scowled more than he smiled, his brow in a

permanent arch, which gave him a dangerous, virile edge. But he was open and approachable. Unguarded. He was a far cry from the industrious, ostentatious, insulting guy who she'd first spoken to on the phone. Although he was quieter and more thoughtful, he wasn't melancholy. He watched her with expressive eyes, often revealing more than he intended with a look.

"Mr. Vincent's been busy all night. I overheard him talking, and it sounds like business. Must be a boring date for you, huh?" James said, swigging his beer and frowning in Caleb's direction.

"I hadn't really noticed," Jai said truthfully. When she'd gotten only three feet in the door, women had begun approaching her; introducing themselves with a hug, a kiss, or a nudge to the ribs; and complimenting her either on her outfit or her date. She was regaled with stories of how she'd caught the most eligible man around and was told that they seemed like a matched couple. She tried to dispel the rumor, but it was fruitless.

Latham was introduced to her by Omar, who then took her out on the floor for her very first square dance. Ann joined them and shouted instructions as they spun around. Dolly and some of her bingo friends came over to ask about her dress. Elwood introduced her to Emily and then taught Jai how to waltz. Right after that, Latham invited her on the floor, where they did a fair but incredibly fun Lindy Hop. She and James did the twist together and four or five other dances. When she sat down to eat, Tammy came over to thank her for sending so many orders her way and wearing her design so well. Word of mouth and small-town gossip had already made them both famous. She hadn't had a moment alone, and whenever Caleb was near, he made sure he came over and gave her a kiss, or slid his hand under her hair to massage the sensitive skin at the nape. Not for a moment did she feel neglected. At one point Caleb winked at her from the drink table, and Jai could feel the flush on her cheeks and heat coursing up her thighs.

"I noticed. I think everyone has," said James. "He hasn't even danced with you."

She wanted to tell James he sounded jealous and drunk, but she knew he was harmless. "I guess it doesn't matter. I've been having a great time. Lots of friendly people to talk to, good music, and I love the food. I don't go out when I'm home, because whenever I do, it's always a bunch of people trying to hook up."

James turned a crooked smile on her. "Yeah. I'm tired of all that myself. I want to find one woman I can be cool with. But ya'll be killin' a brotha. Ya feel me?"

"Maybe if a brotha wasn't always trying to get ova."

"But look at cha boy. He's awight lookin'. He's got money, education, a good job, and the girls are feignin' for him. Then you got me, a strugglin' artist. . . ."

"Yeah. Good-looking, built like a gladiator, funny, cool. With a decent job that will probably make you famous, not to mention rich, by the time you're thirty. And you messin' up. You sittin' here, flirtin' with me, when you got all those numbers in your pocket. Like I didn't see that." She playfully rolled her eyes.

His beer hit the table hard, and he jammed his meaty fist into his pocket. "I don't care 'bout none of them. Here. Get rid of them. Throw them out if you want. . . ."

Jai had heard that line often enough. Guys were always trying to make a big show of stuff that they really didn't want to do. "I don't care, James. Like I said, I'm here to have a good time. Aren't you?"

"I'd have more fun if you'd dance with me again."

"Cool," Jai said, getting to her feet. She heard a slow

song playing and didn't like the idea of getting caught beneath a drunken James if he tripped over his feet. Her feet wouldn't move as her brain furiously searched for an excuse. Then a large shadow blocked the light. She looked up into Caleb's handsome face. "I didn't shit, shower, shave, and drive all this way not to get a dance with the finest woman in here," he said, taking her hand in his.

"It wasn't even a five-minute drive. You get the next one, buddy. This is my dance," James said, grabbing her arm.

"James, didn't you accuse my date of ignoring me?" Jai said, rubbing his hand until it dropped to his side. "I've danced with you all night, and we've been having all the fun. Sheesh, give the guy a chance, would you?"

"Yeah. Me and Miss Jai have been having a nice time. Don't think you can mess with that kind of chemistry, kid," James said as Caleb led her away.

"Thank you. I didn't think I could take his breath, let alone hold him up," said Jai.

"Don't thank me yet." Caleb tugged her to the middle of the floor and signaled to the band. The thumping strains of "Achy Breaky Heart" filled the barn to the rafters. Men and women were vying for space on the dance floor. Jai looked around at the lines forming.

"Oh no," she said, shaking her head and holding up her hands. "This is not for me."

"C'mon. Follow me," Caleb shouted. He moved in jerky, kicking motions. He was awful, which made her awkward attempts less embarrassing and highly entertaining. Two little girls had glued themselves to his side, and he bumped hips with them, making them laugh. He winked at the teenaged girls admiring him, and they scrambled off in gales of giggles. By the end of the song, Jai had got the hang of the basic steps, while Caleb was doing his thing like a pro. His thumbs were hooked in the belt loops of his pants, his hat was tilted at an angle, his butt was firm as it shook and squatted, and his thighs were suggestive in his black jeans, making her hot and sweaty from watching him.

Caleb pulled her close for the slow dance that followed. "You've done that dance before, haven't you?" she asked.

"Yeah. My specialty. That was for my fans," he said, eyeing the crowd. "This is for you."

He spun her around the floor in sweeping, ever-expanding circles. He threw her out and pulled her back in again with ease, leading her through a series of intricate steps she didn't know she knew. When they finished, she was balanced in the crook of his arm, her hair brushing the floor in the most amazing dip.

He lifted her back into his strong embrace and gathered her already heated body to his fiery one. He looked into her face, and his brilliant aquamarine eyes scorched her with the force of the emotions she could see there. He spun her around with flourish and then brought her to him so that even the wind couldn't pass between them. With one hand, he caressed her cheek, with something akin to devotion swimming in his eyes, and with the other, he worshiped her back.

"Excuse me, partner. But song's over. My turn now," James said, bullying his way in. His steel arm wrapped around her, yanking her up on tiptoe so that her breasts were mashed against his chest. "A real magical night for us, isn't it?" James asked, his beer breath making her eyes water as he swung her around like a rag doll. For Jai, the magic was moving across the floor, looking like a lost puppy. Seconds later the tempo changed, and James squinted at the stage. "That bastard," he murmured.

Jai craned her neck to see Caleb by the stage. He shrugged as if he'd heard James's words. It didn't take long before James was herded away by every single woman within spitting distance, his dance card full. It was obvious that Caleb Vincent was smitten. Caleb made his way across the floor, declining several offers as he met up with a smiling Jai.

"I think I've shown my beautiful date a good, wholesome time," said Caleb. "And I've watched while other men danced with her, flirted with her, propositioned her, and drooled on her shoes. I've danced with her like a gentleman, and now I want to be alone with her and do some not so gentlemanly things to her body in that sinfully pink dress. So I think it's time we said our good-byes."

She placed her arm through the arm he offered. Despite all the compliments and adoration she'd received tonight, Caleb had spoken the nicest words she had heard in a long time. "You speak very well with that Blarney Stone in your mouth," she told him.

Chapter 22

He drove the darkening road, keenly aware of the radiant beauty next to him. Her skin was like burnished copper in the moonlight. Her long, gleaming black waves of hair had turned back into the tight, frizzy curls he'd come to adore, owing to her dancing all night in a stuffy barn. He brushed a finger over the gentle slope of her neck and pulled at one soft, wooly curl, which snapped back into place. She peeked over at him, her eyes as dark as the night, and looked out from behind a bounty of lashes.

Jai tried to remember the last date she had had that made her feel this good, and the only thing she could come up with was her high school prom. She and Eva and three of their friends had rented tuxes and a limo and had gone stag. It had been Eva's idea, since every boy in school had asked her out, except the one she wanted. No one had bothered to ask Jai out since she was built like a boy. But she'd had the time of her life asking every boy in the senior class to dance, and not being turned down was a bonus she hadn't expected.

She'd felt like a princess all night long, and tonight she felt the same.

Caleb watched the flashes of a smile pull at her saucy pink lips. She might have been in her own world, but he had her and her world all to himself. He watched her cross and uncross her shapely legs, making his mouth water with each movement that allowed a provocative hint of coffee-colored thigh to show. The fragrance she wore mingled with the scent of the flowers and became an aphrodisiac that was messing with his mind. He watched her slip out of her thin pink leather shoes and noticed her toes had been painted to match her dress and fingernails. He was distracted just enough to hit a large hole in the road and send them skidding. The car puttered as it came to a stop.

Caleb checked the car. "We have a flat," he said, poking his head in her window.

"Need help changing it?"

"No. I don't want your dress to get mussed up, unless I do it."

Even with her dark complexion, he could see her blush. "And what about you? That's an awful pristine white Panhandle Slim shirt you got on, cowboy," she said, raising a question in Caleb's eye.

"What do you know about Panhandle Slim?"

"Nothing. But he seems to be all over Tammy's store," she said, with a sheepish grin.

"I'm going to call someone," he said, getting back into the car. "That way we can both keep our good clothes good."

"It would be faster if we did it ourselves," Jai said, putting on her shoes.

"I don't have a jack," he said, checking his pockets.

"Nor do I have my cell phone. I think you're rubbing off on me."

"I guess we should start walking," she said, leaning down to remove her shoes. Her rounded cleavage straining against the pink fabric made his blood boil, the small shimmy of her ample hips in his car made him hard, and the fall of her hair . . .

"You're temptation from the devil. Forgive me," he whispered as he took her face into his hands and claimed her mouth in a long, drugging kiss.

His tongue swept over her lips, hungry to taste more. In his urgency, he pulled her onto his lap, quelling her squeal by deepening the kiss. His hands traveled up her thighs, while his mouth plundered hers, seeking its mate. He groaned when her lips parted and her tongue came out to dance with his. As he fed from the sweetness of her mouth, his hand massaged the hot flesh of her thighs. Jailyn was twisting on his lap, and he felt the plump cheeks of her rear writhing on his hard rod, causing an insatiable ache to course through him like water smashing through a dam.

His hand found her moistness, and he groaned as he touched the silken heat of her panties, pushing them to one side in a quest to feel all of her. He sunk two fingers into the tightness between her legs. Simultaneously, he plunged his tongue into her mouth, setting a rhythm that had her rocking to match the pace.

She groaned as his tongue darted inside of her mouth. Her hips swayed fiercely, and her hands became tangled in his hair, as she was swallowed whole by the delicious sensations, the cataclysmic event a breath away, just over the horizon. The pad of his thumb found the hard nub at the apex of her womanhood and swirled in circles, applying just the right amount of pressure. His tongue swept into her mouth, and his other hand squeezed the soft flesh of her buttocks. The friction she created as she arched into his hand made fresh blood rush to the head of his manhood. Her purring made him light-headed, and he begged with his mouth and hands for her to come. Jai's legs opened farther of their own volition to accommodate the addition of a third finger into her narrow sheath. The strokes gained in momentum, driving her faster and faster in an agonizingly teasing fashion, while his tongue fucked her mouth to ecstasy. Caleb could feel her grip his fingers, her gulp of air against his mouth, her hips humping his fingers so that he could touch the core of her.

Jai felt her body jerk and shudder as she impaled herself deeper on his thick fingers, now coated in her nectar. Her body screamed as it plunged thankfully into the abyss of an orgasm and smashed against the far reaches of pleasure. She became boneless in her skin and floated on the final waves, while clutching his shoulders so hard, the fabric gave way. She slumped against his chest. His breath was hot in her hair as he mumbled words of caring while cuddling her like a baby.

Caleb shifted her slightly on his lap. His balls had become like rocks as he watched her climax and then saw the thick, glossy film of her excitement spilling between his fingers. He snuck a taste of the shiniest digit when her head fell limply to his chest. He would have a serious case of blue balls if he didn't find someplace for them to stretch out so he could love her body some more.

"We should get a move on," he said. Her smell filled the tiny space, wiping away the scent of the flowers. He'd never smelled anything quite like her, and he lifted his hand again to take a whiff.

"Stop moving," she said, putting his hand back against her hip and snuggling against it.

"You're moving," he whined as she drew lazy circles around his chest, causing his nipples to pucker. The tender nubs rubbed against the starched cotton of his shirt, and the sensation added to the messages being sent to his testicles, making his cock dance around uncontrollably beneath her.

"I said stop moving."

"I can't. That, my dear, is what you do to me," he said. She looked up at him, and her mouth formed a beautiful O. He leaned down and sipped on her bottom lip and then feasted on the top one. "We really should go." Jai looked into his eyes, which were shrouded with lust.

"I'm in no condition to fix a flat, let alone walk," she said, letting her head fall back onto his chest.

"What, and you think I am? I am as hard as the man of steel just from touching you. It's so bad that I may have to let you drive."

"You'll ruin the rim if you try driving on it."

"Oh that. I lied," he admitted, holding her tighter so she couldn't swing at him once his words hit home.

"What? You found your cell?"

"No . . . We don't have a flat." She glared up at him, and he understood that hell hath no fury like a woman. "I couldn't wait to get to the house. I'd been waiting all night long. . . ."

She scrambled off of his lap and out of the car before he could pull her back. Her dress was riding high on her hips to easily accommodate her racing off into the night. A moonbeam settled over the bouncing globes of her rear, which hung succulently out of the hot pink panties with lace edges. Befuddled by the sight of her Rubenesque beauty, he forgot to go after her.

She had put plenty of distance between them by the time he started the Jag and pulled across the road. He came to a stop at a cluster of trees, worried he'd get stuck. His old sky blue pickup was used to on and off road. His Jag was used to road period. Cement, concrete, tar. He jumped out and followed her on foot.

"Jai, wait up. I'm sorry . . . I wanted you so . . ."

Jai stopped suddenly and turned on him like a rabid dog, and he was really sorry he had allowed himself to get within striking distance. With a shove and a kick of her leg, he fell to the ground like a brick off of the Empire State Building. Then all of her weight was pinning him to the cool grass.

"My turn," she growled with a wicked smile on her face and a playful gleam in her eye. "I owe you this for lying to me."

She slid her ample bosom down the length of his body. She opened his shirt to the elements, and he felt the caress of the tepid air over his chest. Her touch ignited an inferno from the outside in. It was the most pleasure-filled tug-of-war he'd ever endured, and he wondered if it was possible to spontaneously combust. Each hair on his chest became a tiny exposed nerve ending as her tongue curled around each one. She sat back, and his body let out a shiver from her missing heat, but she worked quickly, getting his belt off before leaning over him, her breasts swinging just beyond his mouth. In very swift motions, she pulled his arms over his head and secured his hands with the belt. He started to protest, but she stopped him with the persuasive lick of her tongue over his nipples. She suckled them until they were hard enough to cut glass.

"You can get out anytime you want," she said, nodding toward his hands, with a sultry look in her eye. "But I think you'll enjoy this payback . . . ," she added, lowering herself to drop a plethora of feathery kisses down the center of his chest to his stomach.

Jai jerked his pants and boxers down over his slim hips, enjoying the sight of him almost helpless beneath her. She pulled his pants off and then put them under his head so she was sure he could see her. Then she positioned herself between his legs and pushed back her curls. Caleb had a clear view of her plump lips, which were even more enticing while hovering over the swollen tip of his manhood. The fleshy valley of her cleavage pushed over the top of her dress, creating a delightful backdrop for his reddening shaft.

The explicit I'm-about-to-put-it-on-you look in her eye was a voracious invitation to sit back and be a willing victim to his own demise. Her bottom was up in the air—the hot pink against her smooth, round behind—eye candy in the highest order. His phallus was getting harder due to the picture she presented, and he knew she was doing it on purpose. *If this is punishment for a little white lie,* he thought, *I'll have to consider lying more often.*

The sound that escaped him was animalistic in nature. It erupted from somewhere down by his knees when she wet her lips with her tongue and allowed her mouth to generously lubricate the head, mixing with his own preseminal juices. She moved her hand the length of him, spreading the sticky film over him, and then lowered her head to sweep over the sensitive hair of his balls. She then slipped each one into her mouth while running her hand over him in slow, tantalizing strokes.

Caleb felt the world fall away as her mouth continued its sweet invasion of areas of him that rarely saw the light of day. She pulled back for a moment, and he couldn't open his eyes, because her body was keeping him warm. It was all he could do not to thrust when her mouth made its slow descent down the entire length of his manhood. He could feel the swirling motions of her tongue, the way her lips pulled back over her teeth and she clamped on. The suction she was creating was almost the same as being buried inside of her. His body shuddered as a new sensation entered the picture, and he nearly strangled her when he thrust hard into her mouth, and the intense ripples of an orgasm gripped him. She milked every last drop from him with her mouth, his body responding to her intimate theft of his most prized possession.

"You have a fucking tongue ring?" he said when his head thumped the ground.

She sat back, and he marveled when he watched her throat work overtime, swallowing his essence. Then she stuck out her tongue, and the silver barbell caught every piece of moonlight filtering through the trees.

"I've been kissing you all night. When the hell?" he said. "What the f . . . You swallowed. You cheated."

"I told you it was my turn."

He yanked the belt from his hands and savagely pulled her to him, ripping off her panties with one hand and exposing a breast with the other, laying siege to her puffy lips with a torrent of exploratory kisses. Caleb was trying to find that spot on her that made her melt in his arms. He kissed behind her dainty ears and was rewarded with a groan. He placed kisses on her long neck, and she vibrated against him. He dropped sweet kisses on the bridge of her petite nose, and she giggled. He nuzzled the dark valley of her breasts until she squirmed breathlessly against him, but when he licked at her collarbone, that's when she melted into him.

"Ow!" she screeched.

"What? What? I hurt you?" he asked, holding up his hands.

"My foot is tingling."

"Okay, that's a new one. Let's see if I can get the rest of you there," he said, dipping his head back to her neck.

"No, you clown. It hurts," she said, swatting his chest.

He sat her down in the grass and checked her right leg and then her left until she howled at the moon and punched the ground. *Thank goodness for small favors,* he thought as he watched her pummel the grass until he released her. "For all your histrionics, it's clear it isn't broken. It's more like a strain."

"A sprain? You sure it isn't broken? It hurts like all hell."

"I've never been to hell, but I'm sure it's much worse than a little tingling in your foot. And I don't think it's as serious as a sprain, because there's no swelling, discoloration, or even tension."

"It's broken. Call the National Guard."

He couldn't help laughing at her silliness. "C'mon. Let me get you home." He dressed swiftly.

Jai was stunned into silence when he lifted off the ground like she was a wounded animal. Caleb carried her to the car as if she was a little more than nothing, and when they arrived back at the inn, he hoisted her up the gravel drive and into the house. The freshman ten had settled around her middle, the sophomore five have landed on her thighs, the junior fifteen had balanced it out, and postgrad had added twenty depressing pounds, and there wasn't a man around willing to try and lift her without fear of putting out his back.

"Put me down before you strain something we might need at a later date," she said.

Caleb's heart caught at the idea that there was something beyond the present, and his manhood leapt at the concept of more. She jumped from his arms and lowered herself gingerly into her favorite cushy armchair. It was a sight to see since she usually plopped, flung herself, or fell into the chair like a jubilant child hopped up on sugar. He brought a bag of ice from the kitchen and an Ace bandage from the first aid kit. He took a moment to pull himself together, reprimanding himself for being at the ready despite the exhaustive ejaculation he'd had just moments ago.

He bent down in front of her, her eyes burning a hole through his pants. More precisely, he was burning a hole out of his pants with his fierce hard-on. *Ignore it, and it'll go away*, he told himself. But he knew it wouldn't as long as he was touching some part of her body.

Jai hid her smile behind her hand. Her eyes bulged at the unexpected sight of the huge lump straining against his jeans. She could tell he was embarrassed by the way he avoided eye contact.

"Tell me if I'm hurting you," he said.

"I don't feel anything at all. It feels normal."

"I told you. But let's ice it for a few minutes more, then wrap it up."

Leaning forward, she tilted his face to hers. "And after that let's take care of your problem. It seems you have a piece of wood trapped in your pants."

He fell back and pulled her with him, agreeing to work on his problem first.

Chapter 23

Jai was insatiable when it came to Caleb. She was thrilled that the feeling seemed mutual. His long fingers deftly massaged every spot they touched; his lips worshiped the flawless skin of her neck and shoulders. Her eyelids fluttered like butterfly wings until they closed, and she gave a self-satisfying sigh, which became an inward groan and an outward plea to release the building pressure. Caleb tightly clasped Jai's statuesque frame. She pressed her mound against his growing need, feeling it lengthen between their bodies. Her body hummed when his hand slid lower, cupping the hill of her cheek, kneading it, plumping it, and tapping it lightly until she gasped with pleasure.

With her lips parted, her tongue darted out to moisten parched lips and steal his breath. Below her, she caught Caleb watching her mouth, his eyes mere slits. She leaned back, showing off the provocative slope of her mountainous brown breasts, which spilled out of the soft pink dress. Caleb's fingers danced an intricate pattern on her back as he cursed silently because he wanted more hands. His erection, asserting itself more urgently now, had to be like a spear in her leg. He was shifting their positions when she shimmied and peeled the upper half of the dress down over smooth brown shoulders as she rested on her ample hip, showing off the lacy pink panties. He couldn't believe he was drooling as he eyed the deep hazelnut color of her lavish breasts.

Some unknown need was driving her to be uninhibited, unashamed, and bold with Caleb. She forgot all about propriety, and for a split second she hesitated, wondering if this was destined to end badly, like all of her other relationships. But she felt Caleb's hands moving over her with care, treasuring her body, encouraging her to feel the passion and reach for that something beyond. She wanted to bury herself within him, get into his clothes, burrow into his skin, and course through his veins in the same way he invaded the essence of her. She saw Caleb as a beacon visible when the fog clears for a split second, the light calling to you, directing you away from jagged rocks and certain death in murky seas. A beacon that leads you to calm waters and the safe harbor of home. He was her home; the hole left by her father's death was now filled.

Caleb held on to her while she traveled in her mind, but he knew instantly when she saw nothing but him. "Nice to have you back," he said, his voice dripping with desire.

"Thanks for waiting," she said, the quirky smile on her face more reassurance than her words. Then she lowered her body to him until her chest burned through his shirt, and she opened each button with the aid of her teeth.

His world spun from the heat of her. He was dizzy from the smell of her hair, lost in the silky feel of her skin, and entranced by the sultry movement of her hips.

His clothes were falling off of his body as she slipped out of her dress. The entire moment was scintillating, as if she were a meal presented on a silver platter. She pulled a condom from his pants pocket and sheathed him with a tight grip, causing little moans to jump from his lips, his fingers to dig into her thighs, and his body to convulse. She balanced herself above him as she teased the head with her tight, wetness, just barely past the outer lips, her inner labia making a sweet kissing sound and clutching at his erection, trying to suck it in deeper. He pumped his hips upward just as Jai brought her weight down, and he felt himself slide into her to the hilt. Both of them were now wide eyed. Caleb's climax surged forth and triggered hers. Her body seized him. He filled her completely, his size massaging her interior walls. His body was covered in sweat, the sinewy muscles stretching still, and his eyes held hers in surrender as his spray drowned her in one thick, heavy coat.

Jai's mouth hung open, trying to replace the air he'd stolen from her lungs. She trembled at the massive width and length of him now contentedly embedded in her luscious cave. In that nanosecond, time stood still, and their bodies were suspended somewhere outside of them and still touching the deepest parts. From head to heart, they had just merged and become a single thing. Her body screamed for more when this had yet to end. His mind tried to prolong the moment for eternity. They didn't understand that a deal had just been made with their souls.

Jai collapsed onto him, and the abrupt change of position caused a yell to erupt from him. A second set of intense earthquakes shook him to the core, and his body practically separated from the vibration. He felt dazed and in a place of extreme chaos. Emotions slammed into physical sensation and drove over his internal organs, overriding his brain, until in the middle of things there was Jai. Her entire being surrounded him and carried him off to a blissful state. He closed his eyes and just let himself . . . feel.

Chapter 24

Caleb scoured the kitchen for ingredients and threw together a salad. He found one of the bottles of mulled white cider his aunt had stashed around the house and heated it on the stove. With a mug of the cider in his hand, he raced upstairs and tapped on the attic-room door. When he got no answer, he pushed it open with his foot. He almost dropped everything when he saw her sound asleep in his grandmother's bed.

She looked so . . . right spread out on the big bed. There was something pure and almost mythical about her, from her unique jet-black eyes to the silken little corkscrew curls wildly fluffed out on the frilly pillow. She was lying there like a dream. He wasn't sure if he should touch her, but he was aware of the lascivious thoughts in his head. He placed the cider on the dresser so she'd have something for breakfast.

He looked at her snuggled beneath the pale blue sheets with the pink roses. The roses had faded to a dusky pink, and it looked like petals had been sprinkled across the bed. The nightshirt she'd changed into was a simple cotton crewneck, the outline enhancing all of her curves. He could only imagine that it barely covered her generous rear, making his cock riot at the thought. He never wanted a woman so much in his life, and somehow that made him feel inadequate. He wanted to give her more than just a physical relationship; he wanted her to open up to him. But then again, she really was an open book: she spoke and laughed and lived like no one was watching. He wanted that in his life. He wanted some of it to rub off on him. Yeah, he was courting her and all, showing her how much fun he could be, but he had yet to show her him.

He took one last look at her, with his hand on the doorknob. Her features were so angelic in sleep; it was as if she was lit from within. Her innocence was like a candle, her skin was aglow like that of a cherub, and her tangle of black curls framed her slumbering face. The bed looked so big, and she looked so small curled up to one side, leaving plenty of room for him to climb in and spoon with her.

"Could you bring me some water when you come to bed?" she said, her voice muffled by the sheets and sleep.

"I brought you hot mulled white apple cider," he said, his voice too eager.

"Sounds alcoholic."

"Yeah. Like a lager."

"I don't drink. It's what aided in killing my father."

"Sorry," he said. When she tried to talk to him about something as personal as her father, he shut her down, told her he didn't want to hear it. And now he wanted to know it all. There were things he wanted her to share with him and stuff he wanted to share with her.

"Not your fault. Forget the water," she said on a yawn, flipping the covers down. He was right. The shirt barely covered the bubble of her butt. "Come to bed. I'm gonna be sore in all kinds of places, and not just from dancing all night."

"Running through the dark and beating up the grass wasn't smart," he said, climbing in the bed and spooning her just like he'd imagined.

"Oh, and making love on that hard living-room floor was a stroke of genius?" She snuggled against him, using him as a sheet to warm and cover her.

"No, just fast," he answered, with a gasp, feeling the crack of her rear cradling his hardening phallus.

"There's nothing fast about the way you do the things you do to me."

"If good looks were made . . . You know you coulda been some honey . . . The way you stole my heart, you know you coulda been a cro-ook and, baby, you're so smar-art, you know you coulda been a schoolbook. Well, you coulda been anything that you wanted to, and I can tell, el, el the way you do the things you do, aight, the way you do the things you do. . . ."

"At least you look good trying to carry that tune. Don't quit your day job."

And just like that she nodded off to his off-key humming, her body cocooned by his, his nose buried in her hair, inhaling the scent of sweat, grass, and the outdoors. The perfect end to a perfect date.

Jai slept like the dead, her body feeling all melty inside, as if her bones had been sucked out. She made it a habit of releasing all stress, but this feeling was better than a massage, smoothie, power walk, and therapy session rolled into one. She woke to the smell of wood, sweat, and musk, a lethal combination that sent her pheromones raging and her body into overdrive.

"Where'd you go?" she asked, looking at his dusty, faded blue jeans and his boots, which were caked with all kinds of sawdust and mud.

"Barn raising," he said proudly, flexing a muscle covered with sweat-streaked dirt.

"Barn raising?"

"Yep," he said. "We were supposed to do it before the dance, but we didn't have a barn to raise."

"And suddenly you found one."

"Naw. But the principal of the elementary school was telling me that they needed some work done and that the school yard needed to be expanded."

"That doesn't sound like a barn."

"The idea is to help your fellow man. Back in the old days, all the men went to each farm to help with the big projects, such as fixing the buildings that had fallen into disrepair during the winter season. Any new farmer could get a barn erected with the help of the town. It saved time and money and gave them an excuse to have a big ol' dance every year."

"I can't imagine that being good for a construction company."

"Why not? Think of it as a tax write-off when I donate materials. Now if ya don't mind, I need a shower." He pushed back his long hair, which was plastered to his head like a helmet. "I need to get back to town and get to the barber." He jumped on the bed and rubbed his rough cheek against hers as she squealed and pushed at the hard muscles of his sculpted chest.

"Uncle, I'll do it. I'll do it," she shrieked as he tickled her.

"Oh no. I'm not letting you get near me with any sharp objects."

"Hey, I went through some pretty awkward teenage

years. The only time boys would look at me was when I was cutting their hair. Face it. I have a knack for anything aesthetic." She lifted her hair at the nape of her neck and showed him the neat little lines she'd designed.

"Okay," he said, kissing her neck until she moaned.

"Get away from me. You smell like a barn. . . ."

His shower was quick and cold. Just those few minutes playing in the bed with her had given him a hard-on. How was he going to sit through a haircut with her body pressed up against his? He'd slept fitfully with her body against him all night, his cock fully aware of each movement. The way her body molded to his was a good sign in his book. In fact, everything about her seemed designed for his enjoyment. Jai was the first woman he'd met who wasn't interested in any one thing. She spoke and listened with the same intensity. She was damn near indecipherable in her exuberance over something as minor as a spider "sneaking" into the bathroom with her, as she put it. She was untouchable as she worked on some invisible plane between this world and the one her mind created. And she was thoughtful and considerate when someone else spoke, never interrupting and taking a moment to weigh her response. She reminded him of her father's sweetheart Doe. Doe was a beautiful mulatto woman full of jokes, stories, fun, and wisdom. She was the first person he was able to tell about his mulatto blood, the blood his mother denied and his stepfather despised.

He shuddered, wondering how Jai would react. Perhaps she would go tearing off into James's arms for solace, because James was a true black man, a real brother, and not a mutt like himself. He couldn't really see that. She wasn't into stereotyping, and he was hardly a stereotype. He was darker than James, his nose was wider, and his lips were fuller. He'd processed the kink out of his hair so often that without Pierre and a huge bottle of Vidal Sassoon conditioner every week, he'd wake up looking like a scarecrow. He stepped from the shower, critical of the curly mop on his head. Other than his cyan eyes and reddish gold hair, he was very ethnic in his looks. Jai, on the other hand, looked like no one at all. Her eyes were black, her face was round, her hair was a mop of silky, riotous curls, and her body was full, but her features were European, and her color was like nothing he could describe. She wasn't to be compared to the mysterious secrets of Africa, nor was she a queen of nations to be conquered. No, she was his compliment. As different as they were, he felt most himself with her . . . most at home. James Ross, Bradley Vincent, and society could not keep him from going home.

Jai swung around him as he sat in the chair, her eyebrows shooting up and down, the corner of her mouth twisting, and her eyes squinting at him from fifteen angles. She moved behind him, and he got his first look in the mirror. She had buzz cut the sides and back of his hair, then had trimmed all the jagged edges his hairdresser, Pierre, always complained about. She'd given him a fine-lined goatee and mustache. The overall effect left him somewhere between a lion and a pirate.

She squirted a dime-sized blob of lotion into her palm and vigorously rubbed it into his scalp. The massage made his toes curl. He watched the second half of the transformation with less trepidation and more fascination as his curls slowly smoothed out without the aid of a one-hundred-thirty-five-dollar visit with Pierre. When she was done, he looked like a traditional businessman. She had even managed to temper the stark white highlights that plagued his hair by blending them with the red patches, making his hair look all one color without three bottles of dye.

"They're called sun streaks, and they aren't white. They're honey blond. It comes from the sun stealing the color from your hair. This stuff is a ninety-nine-cent store staple," she said, holding up the bottle. "Hair lotion, with like 101 SPF sunblock and vitamins. Use as directed, and it won't cake, weigh your hair down, or take on that oily look."

"You sound like a commercial."

"Advertising is in my blood. Right now you've got what I call the Pat Riley, but if you leave the gel out, brush it up. Get yourself a manly scrunchie. . . ."

"Oxymoron. You cannot have a manly scrunchie."

"Okay, get a beige stretchy. Better?"

"Much more masculine, like a wifey . . ."

"Rubber band?"

"Rubber." He let it roll on his tongue. "I like. It's manly. Steal it from the paper. It's dirty . . . grrr."

"Anyway," she said, uncomfortable with the playful commitment word, "if you go natural, pull it back and wear the fluffy ponytail. . . ."

"Fluff is for Nutter Butters and poodles."

"Not manly?"

"Not hardly."

"Then when you get out of the shower, use a little lotion, rubber, and you got the Steven Segal thing. If you leave it out, you've got sort of a George Clooney. *ER*, not *Ocean's Eleven.* You can cease with the overprocessing."

Caleb made a face, and she stuck out her tongue. He wasn't comfortable with his secret being aired so nonchalantly. His thick, curly Afro, a sign of his African-American ethnicity, and the red color, an indicator of his Irish heritage, were things his stepfather constantly berated him for. And on top of everything, the word *wife* was still stuck in his brain. "All this hair talk is not so manly."

"Then go make a quiche," she said. Caleb watched her drop her hair supplies into her bag as if she was preparing to leave any day now. Caleb tugged Jai onto his lap so she could feel his "manliness" and he could prolong their time together.

"You do know that James is back in the building?" she asked.

"So be quiet when you come." She slapped his shoulder while scrambling off of his lap.

"The boy is seriously hung over."

"Then we should go out and give him some time to himself."

"And what shall we do on a Sunday morning? Because I don't know nothing about raising no barn."

Chapter 25

Although they slept in separate rooms, Jai felt Caleb all around her. She also had a dreamless, sound sleep. Now Caleb removed the silk tie he had used to blindfold her. She blinked twice, the smile spreading from her eyes and waking up all of her childlike playfulness. She clapped her hands and threw back her head in raucous laughter as tears streamed down her face. "You know, you really can stop courtin' me now."

"This isn't for you. It's for me." he said, pushing past her to load their plates. "I haven't had a good, hearty breakfast since I've been home. These are all the things my family used to cook. My grandparents, my father, my aunts, and I would all help." He heaped spoonfuls of scrambled eggs onto their plates.

"Were there a lot of you? Because this is a meal for like twenty people, not two."

He placed flapjacks on each plate and pushed the three types of homemade syrup within arms' reach, along with the two types of jam, whipped butter, and fresh fruit preserves.

"Counting my grandfather Rory, Grandma Siobhan,

and me, there were ten of us." Caleb saw the questions forming in her head. He passed her a bowl of cinnamon raisin oatmeal and put a plate loaded with bacon, sausage, and ham in front of her, hoping to stave off the third degree.

She gave him a quick hug over the table before pouring fresh orange juice for the two of them and taking her seat.

"What was that for? It's just breakfast," he said, feeling a smile break through on his face. He bowed his head for a quick prayer. His fork was hovering over his plate when he saw her staring at him. "What's wrong? Dig in before it gets cold, or James gets up and eats it all."

"I don't have a big family. I mean, I do, but I don't see them. Dad's drinking kept everyone at bay. I think I met his sisters a few times, but they could pass me on the street and I wouldn't know them, and most of my mother's family is in France."

"Really? Is that how you learned French?"

"When I was a kid, Mom would make me spend some of my summer vacation there. That way she and Dad could deal with his problem. But that stopped when I was young."

"Why? You didn't like going?"

"Naw. Her family thought my dad was a lost cause. They didn't think she should have married him, let alone have kids with him. I couldn't stand the way they talked about him, as if I didn't understand. They were always trying to get her to leave him and join the family business."

"Obviously, she didn't." He smiled at her. "Your mother chose to follow her heart."

"Yeah. She was studying to be a social worker when they met. She wanted to help people. Dad always felt like he was her personal crusade. He thought if he was sober, she might not want him."

"I used to know a guy like that. His wife loved him, but he couldn't believe it. He felt unworthy of her love."

"Of any love. Dad grew up in Lynchburg, Mississippi, during Jim Crow. His father went up to New Jersey when Dad was about eleven. When my grandfather had enough money, he sent for his wife and my dad's three sisters. Dad moved around alone back in Lynchburg, working when he could, sleeping anywhere, keeping such a low profile that sometimes he didn't eat for weeks. He worked nights, walked during the day, slept occasionally. He felt like he blended into the night, and even though he could hear the dogs chasing down men, women, and children, he felt safe. During the day, he was harassed, threatened, chased, and publicly beaten.

"Finally, he managed to get word to his family. His father sent for him, but it was too late. My dad had already been psychologically damaged so bad, he no longer knew how to trust people or love his family. His family didn't know him, either, which made it even harder. His father understood what is was like to be a black man living with such indignities as being forced to shit on yourself in the street while a crowd laughed, because they wouldn't let you use the toilet. Or going through garbage bins because certain restaurants won't even let you purchase food from them, but his sisters couldn't relate."

"That's . . . ," Caleb said, not exactly sure what words would help. But he definitely understood being on the outside of your family.

"My mom was a passenger in his cab one night. She was crying. Her family wanted her to join the family business. They felt she didn't need the Master's degree, and they wouldn't pay. She had one shot at a scholarship, but she was too emotional to focus, so she fell behind. My dad said he could help. He had a sketchy education, but with a photographic memory, he'd spend his down time reading her work. He'd pick her up after class and recite the stuff back to her while he drove."

"Your dad had a photographic memory?"

"Yeah. Me, too."

He studied her for long moments, and things fell into place, including her ability to speak three languages flawlessly, her realistic art, and the tons of clearly defined ideas spilling out of her like waterfalls. It was because she never forgot anything; it was etched in her brain.

She went on. "When my father died, I went completely numb. I didn't hear, see, or eat. I stopped living." Caleb had felt nothing when his stepfather and mother passed. He thought he would run wild with his newfound freedom, become a beatnik or hippy, but he essentially was already what they had made him, and somewhere inside he had become complacent. "When the first handful of dirt was thrown on the coffin, his reality brutally slammed into me, knocking me to the ground. His entire life flashed before my eyes, searing itself into every recess of my brain.

"Every grotesque atrocity he saw, every gruesome experience, every putrid odor, all his hellish nightmares from a time before I was born pelted me like fire and brimstone. And no matter what I did, it wouldn't stop. No matter how much I drank or danced or ate or drew, it was there in my deliriums and haunting my blackouts. I was hunted." She spoke faster now, short of breath, as if she was trying to escape those nightmares again. Jai broke out in a sweat, her body trembling, evidence that she was still capable of seeing those things.

She continued. "Three days of loud music, alcohol, sleeping pills, scalding showers, ice-cold baths, and round-the-clock partying did nothing to get the rank smells out of my nose, or the crawling feeling off my skin, or the screams echoing in my head—"

"How did it end?" Caleb asked, hoping to end it now for her.

"I saw a rainbow." Caleb stared at her, holding his breath as she went on. "Late one night I had this dream about my dad finding peace and me being rescued." "'By you," she wanted to add but thought better of it. "Then when I woke up in the dark, I could see a rainbow out my window, even though it hadn't rained that night. Over time these nightmares have faded."

Caleb couldn't believe his ears, and yet it seemed so fitting. He had found the one woman who wasn't related to him who believed in Irish rainbows. Caleb's family all believed and always tried to get him to have faith, but in his entire life, he'd never seen one. It was like a wild goose chase for him, so at some point he just stopped. Now here it was again.

"How could they fade if you have a photographic memory?" he asked.

She thought about his question before answering. "I figure because they're dreams. Not many people recall their dreams, let alone with sharp distinction, and eventually, they're forgotten altogether. I figure the same happened with me."

"I can see the logic in that. But these weren't your dreams, so linear thinking doesn't apply."

"Nope. So why shouldn't I forget them? My dad and

I shared a bond that for a moment transcended life and death."

"Death? I can understand time and distance, but death? And why his nightmares, and not his aspirations or hopes? And why for days? Why not the rest of your life, like him?"

"Hey, Maury, I don't have the answers. I do know I couldn't have lived with those visions any longer. I was on the brink of suicide. It was to the point that they blocked out all else. I dreaded going to sleep. I didn't want to wake up. There was nothing that these nightmares hadn't infiltrated and destroyed. And maybe that was the point. He spent his life dealing with that while living for himself, my mother, and me. He tried to live the best way he could in order to give the finger to those who had tried to thwart him. He proved to be a strong man. A warrior. And I love him."

"If only you could have told him that."

"What, are you crazy? Of course, I told him that. He was my hero, my savior, and I suppose I was his."

Savior. The interesting term struck a familiar chord with Caleb.

"Even after the nightmares were gone, it took me months to shake the feeling, to get warm again, but I'll never be the same," said Jai. "For awhile I was serious, withdrawn, and cautious, because I was afraid and alone. His mind had turned against him, had eaten away at him, and what little he had to alleviate it, he gave to me so I'd never know his pain. But then I did, and I couldn't handle it. I'm only just finding a balance."

"Well, your dad had your mother to help him."

"Mom always said a man who can paint the world for you with his words was a blessing. He was her world. He made it so she had the job she wanted, a husband she adored, and a baby she loved. He bought her a home and gave her freedom to live without the yoke of her family. She was always upset that she couldn't free him." Jai quietly ate. She picked up her juice and looked at the pulp swirling in the glass.

"I didn't get freedom until my parents died," he admitted, with sadness. Her eyes flickered over his face and then returned to her glass. She picked up her fork and resumed eating without comment. He cleared his throat and went on. "My mother got pregnant at sixteen, but she wasn't married, and my dad wasn't accepted in her circle. Like your parents, her family didn't think he was good enough. My mom is Corrine Elizabeth Hamilton."

The name sounded familiar to Jai, but she couldn't place it.

"The Hamiltons have a prestigious fishing history, which followed them from the South up to Maine. Crabbing mostly. Lots of money. My great-grandmother had an affair with Mr. Hamilton. She was a black domestic in their house, and they fell in love. They even had a daughter, and when his wife died, he moved my great-grandmother and grandmother up to Maine and claimed my grandmother as his legal daughter and introduced her into proper society. When he died, he left everything to his daughter, so my great-grandmother found her a good husband with breeding and class. With all the Hamilton money to help her along, she married well, and my mom lived the perfect princess lifestyle. They weren't about to let her make 'a mistake' and ruin the future they had planned for her."

"So her parents looked for the right suitor. They wanted someone who wouldn't ask too many questions. Bradley Vincent entered stage right. He had the pedigree and a shaky family business. He was more than willing to marry the rich beauty my mother had grown into, and he didn't realize I showed up seven months later, or at least he didn't care."

Jai was watching him in earnest now, and he closed his mouth around two pieces of ham that were dripping with fat and syrup. The comments he had made to James weren't racist; they were angry. He'd been angry about the assumptions concerning his identity. He'd lashed out because he had been raised to hide his identity. But just as he had not offered her words of empty sentiment when she told him her father had passed, she did not try to empathize about something she could only understand as a third party. She had been raised to be the best person she could be. Her mother had enjoyed cornrowing Jai's thick hair when she was young because her mother's own hair was more like Caleb's and tended to curl and frizz easily. Her mother had to douse herself in sunscreen to keep from looking like a lobster, while her dad had hated the sun, because it made him darker. Jai was the ideal mix, she had been told. She was light enough to go anywhere and be friends with anyone, and yet she was dark enough to appreciate her culture. Jai continued to eat, and Caleb resumed his story.

"I met my biological father when I ran away at seven." He fell quiet and Jai stole a look at him. This time he spoke to her. "Landed here, in the barn. My aunt Reaghann found me. You know, Ann. Said from the minute she saw me, she knew I was my father's son. My father insisted that whenever my parents traveled, they were to leave me with them. So I spent summers, holidays, and plenty of weekends here with my grandparents, my aunts Iona, Fidelma, and Reaghann, who's my father's twin, and my aunts Bridgid, Maeve, and Gael, who's a few months younger than me.

"They never blinked an eye at me. I walked in the door, and I was family. I'd forgotten how much I loved being here, because my mother had let my stepfather send me to boarding school for high school, and my stepfather rarely let me come home after that, and when I did, he made me work with him. He'd torment me and my mother about my black, Irish, and white characteristics. He'd say I was a 'ghastly anomaly. A one of a kind bastard' . . ."

"A unique mosaic," she instinctively said. He was quiet so long, Jai thought she'd blown it. "When I see you, I should see art. You're like this perfectly blended human being. A sign of the times, a product of what the American melting pot is brewing these days. There are so many cross-cultural, biracial children, and my God, they are so beautiful. Midnight black children with grey eyes, and children the color of sand with thick, knotty Afros and cornrows. And white children with dreadlocks and slanted, almond-shaped eyes, owing to their Chinese and Jamaican roots. My mother is one mixed heritage. Her great-great-great-great-grandmother was an octoroon woman from Louisiana who by happenstance ended up in England and who married a duke, who was utterly in love with her. Her father was a Frenchman. But now you don't hear terms like mulatto, Os Rouge, or octoroon. Instead, we say biracial, mixed, or multicultural. You are one of many, and it's sad that you weren't given the opportunity to learn that and perhaps enjoy it. God, I am so babbling. . . ."

"I'm enjoying it," he said, taking her hand across the table. "When you look at me, I feel like a man. There's no qualifier, no color, because of that picture you drew.

I saw all of the intricacies that make me, me in black and white. So all this time I was trying to become someone else, and it was futile, because people saw what they wanted. My Irish family saw me as Irish, my stepfather saw me as black, and my mother saw me as a threat to her status and her marriage. My real father tried to help me come to terms with everything, but I wanted no parts of it. I was who my parents shaped me to be. I wanted a wife they would have approved of. I wanted to make the business a success and have two point five kids. I don't know if it was in spite of them, to spite them, or because of them. But I didn't want to remember anything from my past. I couldn't separate the good from the bad, so I shut them all away."

"I can't imagine ever wanting to forget all this great food," she said, with a smile and a wink, breaking through the melancholy that had seated itself at the table with them. "My goodness. How is it you aren't the size of a house, growing up on this stuff?"

"It's a farm. There's always something to be done. Look at all the walking we did yesterday, and all you saw was the barn, the orchard, the pond, and the stables. There's still the field, the gardens, the meadow, the hill, and the valley. Not to mention Hamilton House and all of its outbuildings."

"Another day. I'm still sore from all of our outside activity and indoor gymnastics," she said. He was about to grab her when James entered the room, holding out a ringing cell phone.

"G'mornin'. Yo, man, put this thing on vibrate so a brother can sleep in," mumbled James.

"Sorry," Caleb said, taking the phone and noting Latham's missed call. "What time is it?"

"Too early o'clock a.m.," James answered sarcastically.

"It's about eight forty," Jailyn said.

"I've got a nine o'clock conference call," Caleb said, snatching up his tie and dropping a couple of biscuits into a napkin. He patted James's shoulder and kissed Jai on the head and ran out the door. "I'll see you guys later. We need to work on the plans. The crew is ready to get started."

Chapter 26

"Good morning, Mr. Vincent. I suppose late is a time," Latham said. Caleb swung his chair around to see Elwood, Omar, and Latham coming through the office door.

"I'm surprised to see you at all. Saw Jai leaving on her jog, and she had a special type of glow to her," Elwood said, making Caleb get up out of his seat.

"Dad, stop bothering the man. This isn't a high school locker room," Omar said.

"It most certainly is not," Latham said in his most stringent voice. "However, let me just say that is one foine woman."

"Smart, funny, and creative as all get out," Caleb added.

"Loves to dance and moves pretty good," Latham said.

"Made friends, dresses like she's from here, playful, too," Omar noted.

She's comfortable in her own skin. Pretty skin, too, Caleb said to himself.

"So like I said, what are you doing here, boy? You could use a little R & R," said Elwood.

"I'm gonna have to agree with Dad on that," Omar said.

"I've got too many eggs up in the air," Caleb said.

"Actually, sir, now is the perfect time," Latham said, holding up his PDA, which had more empty space than he'd seen in years. "I spoke with Saoirse this morning. You'll be getting a package from Hawaii later this week. She also said to tell you she's hired on two new people. One by the name of Allen. She said he loves Hawaii, and he's already got them moving into the next phase without a hitch. The other is Gael."

Caleb couldn't believe his ears. He only hoped Allen wanted the work and didn't need it. And his aunt, too.

Latham continued. "Now Omar and I have successfully moved the Hartford office here, and Elwood is just about done restructuring the divisions and hiring more guys."

"Clive has two crew ready to do the outbuildings here. In a week I'll have a crew ready to start on the inn," Omar added helpfully.

"Looks like you've given me a new life but made yourself obsolete," Elwood said, putting his feet up on the desk. "Let me and these two hold down the office for a few days. Hell, boy, take a week. You deserve it. We'll shoot over if we need you. Go court that girl some more."

Caleb looked at the men, who had been his closest friends over the last few weeks. He had hired the most competent people around, people who believed in looking out for one another. If he wanted, he could go back to New York, but even there he wasn't needed. Saoirse was having a fine time running the office, just like his father had said. Now that her twin boys were in school, she needed a chance to spread her wings, and she was soaring now. This would be his first non-working vacation since his summers at the farm. He could go to the islands or even back to Hawaii. Take a tour of Europe, and hit up France, England, and Greece. But what he really wanted was to be at the inn with Jailyn Wyatt, on his farm, in his home.

"You might want to stop thinking it to death and go tell the woman," Omar said once the two of them were alone in the room. Caleb hadn't even seen the other two leave, a fact that Omar picked up on. "They went in the other room to take the conference call. Wanted to show you you're in good hands here. Your father wouldn't let it be no other way. Now get going before she finds something else to do today."

Caleb didn't move. Elwood walked in and smiled knowingly. "Uh, there is this message from New York. Latham took it. Seems urgent. Personal. Might want to hand-deliver it."

Caleb took the note, put it in his back pocket, and headed for the door, leaving his PDA, briefcase, cell phone, laptop, and BlackBerry in the office.

Jai stood beneath the scalding spray, massaging all of her muscles. Her early morning jog had turned into an agonizing trot. She felt a breeze skirt the front of her thighs. She pulled back a corner of the shower curtain and saw James's back. "Hey, buddy, this is not a coed bathroom at the moment."

"I had to go," he said, holding the wall and wobbling just a bit. Jai could smell the beer coming off his skin like heat waves off tar.

"Go outside! I'm your boss, not your boy!" she raged.

She couldn't believe he'd gotten this comfortable with her. Usually, she dated a guy before he took her for granted. But this was her employee. She'd been so caught up with the house, the project, and Caleb, she'd totally let James run wild. The boy needed more guidance and training. He needed structure. "James, please meet me in the kitchen. . . ."

He flushed the toilet, and she screamed as the ice-cold water pierced her skin. She jumped out of the tub with no regard for modesty. James was ogling her without censure, his morning stiffy rearing its head. He loved her full figure, which had muscle tone and was slim in the right places, giving her that hourglass shape all sistahs should have.

She snatched a huge bath towel and robe before pointing a finger in his face. "You're fired."

"You're kidding me, right?"

"No," she said, watching the obnoxious smile melt off his face.

She couldn't deny James his good looks. He wore no shirt, and curly dark hairs littered his chest in a T shape, all the way down to his low-slung flannel pajama bottoms, which looked like they were being held up by his erection. She wasn't impressed. Her eyes snapped back up to his face. He reached for her, and she backed away.

"Let's stop playing games," said James. "You make me hard, you're so fucking hot. And now that I'm fired, we got nothin' to stop us."

"Get out or get out of my way, because murder by Lady Bic isn't going to be pretty."

"What?" he asked. Jai didn't like the look in his eye. He seemed drunk, as opposed to hungover.

"James, I'm not interested in you that way," she said, calmly hoping he was more reasonable than horny.

He moved closer, sniffing her like a dog. "How can you say that? We connected. We like the same stuff. I met your mother. We danced all night. Oh, and the picture. Don't forget the picture you drew of me. . . ." He leaned forward to kiss her, and she put her hand up to his face as she retched at the smell. This was way more than beer.

"Caleb was right."

That comment had him reeling back. It was like a splash of cold water. "What's that white boy got to do with us?"

"The pictures are him. I drew them after talking to him on the phone. And the only us includes Caleb. We work for him."

"Not no more. You fired me. Without cause. I'll sue you for leading me on and making passes at me."

"You're not drunk. You're crazy. Your photography skills are mediocre. You been gambling at the casinos every day, drinking every night, sleeping with gosh knows who. Not to mention that you've been rude and crass to your direct employer and the client. You lack technique. You would need to develop more discipline before we'd take you on, even in an apprenticeship. That's why you're going back to New York ASAP."

"I got that. I saw it," James said, almost in tears. "You got his hair, his stance, his eyes, even his soul. . . ."

James then leaned over the toilet and vomited his guts out. She helped clean him up while he profusely apologized and let go of some more of the gin and juice he'd overindulged in. She held on to him, trying with all her might to keep the man on his feet.

"No bullshit, homey. If you need a friend, you call," said James. "That bastard hurts you, and I'm back with a disposable Gillette."

"Fair enough," she said. "When you get back to New

York, report to Toiji." She was feeling like his big sister again. "He's got a computer gaming account that could use your precision work."

They stood in the bathroom, laughing and whispering. A half-nude James leaned on Jai, who was clad in her bathrobe. The steam from the shower surrounded them like dream smoke. Caleb turned on his heels and headed out the door, fighting the urge to burn the house to the ground and kill them both. His rage was unfathomable, welling up from a deep pit of despair inside him, like bile. He flung the bottle of blue soda high and wide.

It was worse than the day his stepdad had called him an Irish nigger, on his fifth birthday, in front of friends and family. Or the day Bradley Vincent beat his mother until she confessed to her biracial roots. It was worse than learning at seventeen that his stepfather was willing to sacrifice Caleb's life to save his own.

Caleb settled behind the wheel of the Jaguar. The solitude of the car calmed him, the white leather pushing at the darkness threatening his world. He should have known this would happen. She had been nothing but drama since their first phone call. His father must have known how crazy she was. All that crazy in such a beautiful package was making Caleb nuts. Her taupe-colored skin, her jet-black eyes always twinkling with mischief, hinting at mystery and exuding intelligence. Her kinky hair, which managed to accentuate her big eyes. Dark brows; long, glossy lashes; high cheekbones; pert nose; and luscious lips, all framed by the dark locks.

Each morning he'd watch her leave for her jog. She was sculpted muscle housed beneath a layer of pillow-soft plushness. The effect she had on him, even now, was arousing. How could she have chosen that crass playboy over him? He had finally taken a woman seriously and taken her to bed, in his home, and now . . . Caleb started the Jag, his anger coming at him full force from all directions as James exited the house and headed toward the Miata. Caleb jumped out and stormed toward him. "You ready?"

"What?" James asked. But before he could focus on the question, he was headed to the ground. The world turned mute colors as darkness hovered at the edges of his consciousness. "Motherfucker," James muttered, bringing his hand to his jaw.

"More like Jailyn fucker," Caleb said, shaking his fist. It had been like hitting granite, but it was well worth it to see James laid out on his behind. "I hope you know you got my sloppy seconds."

"You picked the white boy over me? Figures," James said, watching Jai jog to his side.

"You've got to be kidding me," said Jai. "James, you got the worst luck. You don't get the girl, you get fired, and then you get into a fight."

"It wasn't a fight. He attacked me," James whispered from the ground.

"That's convenient, Ms. Wyatt," Caleb spat. "First fire him and then fuck him."

"I wish she had fucked me. Instead, all I got was fucked up," James said. "I should sue."

Caleb pulled a check from his pocket. "No need," he said, flinging it at her. "That should cover his medical costs and your fees for all your services rendered."

Jai looked down at the figure on the check and then peered up into his eyes, noting the hatred, which manifested itself in a deep cerulean blue. His whole being was closed to her. He thought she was a whore. "There aren't enough zeros to include me sleeping with you."

"You really did pick the white boy over me," James said as she helped him up. She wished she could storm off and get away from Caleb.

"He's no more white than me or you, James. He's got coffee in his cream, and he and his mother suffered for it. She was sold to his stepfather like a modern-day slave, and he was thrown in for good measure."

"I'm not above slappin' a bitch," Caleb snarled.

"You must have forgotten how much it hurt to watch your mother being treated that way," said Jai. "No doubt he called her a bitch and slapped her around. I thought, if anyone, you would have learned how to treat people better than that, seeing it first hand. Experiencing it."

"I did. I don't degrade people unless they deserve it," growled Caleb.

"And you are judge and jury and have come back with a verdict to treat me like dirt," said Jai. "I'm not the one. Those who cannot learn from history are doomed to repeat it." Jailyn dropped the check and kicked dirt on it. "Come on, James. No matter how much he puts on that check, he'll never afford a woman like me."

James looked back over his shoulder. "Guess I get the girl, after all."

Chapter 27

A light mist started to come down as Jai sat in the parked car next to the house. After getting James a flight back to New York, she'd driven to Foxwoods and walked around the casino. She then had an early dinner in town and stopped and drew pictures of the newly constructed barn that Caleb said he had helped to erect. She noticed that all the lights in the inn were out and hoped that Caleb was nowhere around. She wasn't sure she was ready to face him. She could hear the deep sound of Caleb's voice pleasantly tossing around in her head. She could feel the thick, corded muscles of his chest on her fingertips. She could taste his kiss on her lips. His behind was tight and round, and she imagined you could bounce quarters off of it. His thighs were all sinewy muscle and were coated in a deep mustard color. His chest and stomach were ripples of gorgeous, chiseled flesh that made her mouth water. Every time her pencil touched paper, some part of her art was infused with a part of him. All the images her father had seen were completely gone now, and all she could see was the lightness of Caleb's being.

Jai got out of the car, slipped off her shoes, and scaled her favorite hill. She lay on the slope, which seemed designed for her body, and tilted her face up to the sky. Her legs were crossed and bouncing to a beat all their own.

Caleb watched from the window as she made her way to her spot on the hill. He went out on the porch and watched from the shadows until the rain became huge drops, bouncing in the puddles beginning to form in the grass. "You know, it's raining," he called out.

"Uh-huh."

"Most folks try to get out of the rain," he said, strolling over to her.

"I'm not sugar. I won't melt."

Caleb looked into the sky, blinking as cool drops splattered his face. "Are we looking for something in particular?"

"Yeah."

He lay down beside her. They lay together like that until his hair was dripping and his clothes were plastered to his body. "What are we looking for?"

"Rainbows."

"You need sun for rainbows."

"Not always. Sometimes you just need a little bit of light, the rain, a comfortable place to watch, and good company."

"If that was the case, we should have seen one twenty minutes ago."

"Sometimes you have to chase a rainbow in order to catch it."

He stood up and held out a soggy hand to her. "You won't catch a rainbow lying around like that."

Jai trained her eyes on Caleb. It was the first movement she'd made, other than her bouncing legs, since he'd joined her. Even with his hair a wet, matted mess, he was a god outlined in red gold against the smoke grey clouds on a velvet sky. She got up with his help, her clothes clingy and transparent, his eyes raking over her with lust. Her nipples puckered until she thought they'd tear through her bra and a diffused ache settled over her.

"Tag. You're it," he said, tapping her arm and running off. The man was playing! And she was suddenly even more turned on. He was usually so stoic and stodgy, but now he was playing. She took off after him. He dodged and circled while she swung her arms at him haphazardly, trying to get him. They played in the rain, chasing one another and tackling each other, then rolling down the hill in the squishy grass. Soon they lay naked under the stars.

Caleb licked at the raindrops that had pooled in her belly button and dropped kisses on her body, lingering more the lower he went. He loved the taste of the rain mixed with the salt on her skin and the way she moved beneath his hands. When he reached her mound, he inhaled her heady, natural scent. He dipped his tongue into her honey and watched the expression of rapture morph her into a goddess. Her body was so ready for him, it took both his hands to hold her as she pumped his face. His own blood was thrumming through his veins as he opened his mouth wider to taste all she was offering. He ran his tongue flatly over her opening, causing another climax to tear through her, raining her juices on him.

Jai was shutting her eyes and turning her face up to the rain when the second orgasm jolted through her, splintering the darkness behind her lids with a bright golden haze. She shouted her completion to the heavens.

Caleb was searching the ground for items thrown from his pockets when Jai's panting caught his attention.

Her eyes were so big and bright as they bore into him, clearing his mind of all thoughts but her. She pulled him to her and kissed him with raw sensuality. He slowly felt himself sinking into her as she opened to him like the spring flowers she lay on. The knowing way her body moved beneath him sent him cresting after just a few slow strokes in her heat. The tips of her nipples grazed the hairs on his chest, her tongue worked wonders on his mouth, her hands squeezed his rear, and her legs wrapped around his as she deepened each stroke. She rode him from the ground, and his body flew apart as his cum surged inside of her like a geyser. His body shuddered sporadically, and he thrust farther into her sheath until he felt the tremors mount within her. She was systematically draining him of every last fluid. Even his mouth went dry. With his last bit of energy, he ground into her until she was launched like a rocket into space, shooting out of the atmosphere, past the clouds, the rainbows, the sun, and the stars. Her body arched against an unknown force and then hurtled back toward the earth like a boomerang. A chute opened in the nick of time, and she glided into Caleb's open arms.

Minutes later in a place time forgot, Caleb collapsed against her in a heap. He pulled back so that he wasn't pressed against the far back wall of her canal and readjusted his weight so she could breathe easier. When she groaned and arched onto him, he growled back, "If you're ready, I am, too."

"How about we take this inside so I don't catch pneumonia?"

"How about you let me worry about you?" he said, scooping her up into his arms and carrying her into the house.

Chapter 28

The door crashed open so hard that the house shook. Caleb sprung from bed, looking for something to grab, while Jai threw on a shirt and panties. "Don't make me come up there, or all three of us gonna be embarrassed," Ann's voice boomed. She wasn't making an idle threat, Jai thought as she ran down the stairs, leaving Caleb behind her, struggling into a pair of jeans.

Ann was hunched over, hands on her knees, when Jai entered the foyer. "Girl, get your clothes on and get on a plane. I got two guys outside waiting to take you back." Jai looked over Ann's shoulder and saw Kevin and Toiji on the porch. She went out on the porch and took in the grim looks on their faces. She was back inside in seconds, flying up the stairs, past Caleb, who looked confused.

"Aunt Ann, what's going on?" said Caleb.

"I don't know much. Them two ain't talking. Something about hindering a case," said Ann." But James told me that when he went back to the office,it was closed. Then he saw on the news that Jai was reported missing and was in possession of stolen money. James went to the two guys, and now here they are. That's all

I got. They said they left messages with your office, but no one got back to them. Started makin' them think she might be guilty."

"Ah shit," Caleb cursed as he took the stairs three at a time and caught Jai in the bathroom. It had gotten so intimate between them that she often left the bathroom door open so they could talk if one of them felt the need. This time the door was shut tight. "Jai, baby, what's going on?"

The door flew open, and Caleb moved out of her way as she barreled out, tossing things randomly into her bag. She went back in and spit before speaking. "One of my partners filed Chapter Eleven."

"That's not unusual when someone mismanages their funds."

"Uh-huh," was all she said as she grabbed her bag and portfolio and ran back out. Caleb was right on her behind her.

"Give me a sec, and I'll go with you."

"Can't. I got three other partners who need me, not to mention a staff who's real worried right now. I gotta go be the boss, and really, you'd be a wonderful distraction that I don't need. Give me a few days, and I'll be back. If you're here, then I can make it up to you. If not, then I'll have my office contact yours to finish the project." Jai turned to Ann. "I left my clothes. Send them to this address." Jailyn pressed a couple of pieces of paper into Ann's hand. "There's also a traveler's check to cover the expense. Pocket the rest to settle my bill."

Ann gave her the check back and gave her a big hug. She whispered in her ear, "You have done so much for my brother and my nephew. You were there for them when no one else could reach them. You're good for the family." Ann released her but held her face in her palm.

"You've even managed to put a smile on my face. James said he misses me. I think he's gonna be my second husband. Now you keep this money and go with those other two sexy men. We'll be here when you need us, and don't worry. I'll keep an eye on that one. Oh, and take my keys. I'll ride in the matchbox car, but only for you."

Jai gave Ann a tight hug before running out the door. "Give me your damn cell phone before they find your body in a wheat field," Jai yelled to Kevin, just as the truck ground to life. It faded into the distance.

Ann listened to the deafening silence and went to find Caleb. He was packing a bag. "Let her go for now."

"Don't tell me if you love someone, set them free. She's not a fucking bird," Caleb said, throwing clothes and shoes haphazardly into the overnighter. Ann never thought she'd see the day that meticulous little Caleb would be so passionate about someone that he forgot himself.

"Listen, little boy. You don't contradict your elders, and you don't tell a loose woman no. So pay attention. She'll call you. When she needs your help, you be ready to give it, but for now, stay home and keep an old woman company. It took you a long time to come back. Let's enjoy it."

Caleb felt hollow inside, but his aunt was already filling the void with forgiveness and love. "You're not an old woman."

"Sure ain't. I was talking about Dolly. You remember tellin' me if you ever met that woman, Doretha's daughter, you'd marry her right off?"

"Yeah."

"Then I guess you best be getting a tux. That there girl is Ed and Doretha Wyatt's daughter." Caleb dropped everything he had been holding and fell onto the bed.

"Yep. Figured you didn't figure it out yet. After I fill you in, I suspect you'll have some words for my brother and my daughter."

"Saoirse was in on this?" Caleb asked, dumbfounded.

"How the hell else do you stage a coup?" Ann asked, putting his clothes away, a smile lighting her old face. "Your office fits her just right."

"It fits me perfectly."

Ann stopped folding his clothes and looked him square in the eye. "So does this house and that girl. Question is, which you want more?"

On the ride to the airport, Jai spoke with Eva, Ros, and Judith, who each gave their account of events in a succinct manner, leaving all editorials for another time. However, Judith was still abroad and felt the need to gossip just a bit. "What did you do to this James Ross guy?"

"Nothing. Why? What did you hear?" Jai said suspiciously.

"Eva said he talked about you nonstop when she picked him up from the airport yesterday. She said, he said he'd finally met a woman who 'got him' and who wasn't so hard to get. Did you two . . . ?"

"Did we . . . Noooooo. Ill. You need to stop listening to he say, she say shit," Jai said like a twelve year old, garnering stares from Kevin and Toiji.

"Then you got some mighty powerful Vulcan mind trick, because Eva said the boy was glowing like a lightbulb. Said he may even be ready to settle down. He had Eva fork over his paycheck, then take him to cash it. Then he asked her if women preferred sentiment to pricey, 'cause all he could afford was sentiment."

"Eva said pricey sentiments, right?"

"Sentimentally pricey. So you're gonna get something very sweet and as expensive as the man can afford."

"That ain't much," Jai confided.

"Do I need an ugly froufrou dress, with petticoats and garish colors that will null and void my tan and bring out my freckles, and that I will never wear again, despite the mint I'll be spending on it?"

"Let's not get crazy."

"You better not tell the boy no. You may never get another offer. Besides, you could turn him into a womanizer like Christian, a user like Reynolds, or a monk like DeAngelo. None of them had a stable woman, and you see what happened to their minds."

"James Ross is fine, and we have more pressing matters than a wedding or my sex life."

"I'm going to get a flight back sometime this week. My husband will take care of the kids."

"No. I want you to stay right there. I don't want you any more involved than absolutely necessary. If your adoption gets stopped because of the mess over here, I'll never forgive myself. Take care of you first, Judith."

"You sure?" Judith asked, the mothering in her voice.

"As long as you have the papers from Eva, we should be all right. Don't worry."

"If you need me . . ."

"I'll call. Just hang on to all the stuff you've been faxed over the last few months. I think it's what will clear us."

Jai hung up the phone. Kevin and Toiji stared at her as they hauled her into the terminal and checked in. They didn't let her go until she was ensconced between them in first class.

"You had sex?" Toiji asked.

"With Ross?" Kevin asked.

"We don't approve," they both said, handing her paper bags as the first wave of nausea hit.

"It's very hot in here. Can I get some ice water?" Jai asked as her stomach did somersaults.

"He isn't much of a photographer," Toiji noted.

"Fast learner. Needs a strong mentor," she said. "I hate planes."

"He can barely pay his rent," Kevin mumbled.

"He lives in the East Village. You can barely pay rent there," Jai said into the bag as the stewardess offered her the water.

Toiji took the cup and waited for her to sit back. "He doesn't have a five-year plan."

"He's too pretty to be a real thug. He's more Kanye West than Method Man," Kevin spat. "Reminds me of Reynolds."

"Tobin," Toiji corrected.

"Uh-huh," Kevin agreed, wiping spittle from her lip. She spent the rest of the short flight with her head hunched between her knees, listening to the two of them tell, tennis match style, the story of their business over her head.

Jai ran out into the terminal, never in her life so thrilled to see Eva and James. "James, be a sweetheart and go and find Doe and Quinn," Eva said, rushing Jai out the door and to the curb.

When everyone was in the parking lot and Jai had sufficient color back in her face, she started talking. "I've got bits and pieces of a plan. Eva call Ros and get her over to my mom's brownstone. Have her pick up all the files I have there. Quinn, if you'll donate the bar?"

"What's mine is yours, lass," he said, holding tight to her mother's hand.

"Wondered if you were ever gonna ask her out," Jai said.

"I wondered if she was going to say yes," Quinn said, looking at Doe with love in his eyes.

"Nice. Okay, I need Kevin and Toiji to get the staff together at the bar tomorrow for dinner," said Jai. "We should have some answers by then. Then I want Eva and Ros to get all our clients together at the bar the following night. I want them to know as much as we do by the time we have a press conference. I'm gonna work on scraping up as much money as I can. . . ."

Her mother piped in unexpectedly. "You can have your dad's insurance money. Don't you even look at me like that. It's what he would want us to do. And DuValle Winery has already supplied you with four lawyers. And don't bother thinking that I'm making them do it. They know how much you loved your father, and they're just stepping up now that he's gone."

"My patrons have been helping out by watching the news, clipping articles, following the stock, and keeping your staff laughing," said Quinn. "Everyone wants to help."

"What about you, James? Are you in?" Jai said as she looked at him.

"Long as I get paid," replied James. The group looked at him through squinted eyes. "What? I'm trying to buy a ring. Geez, you're all a bunch of nuts. What a way to get volunteers."

"You're no longer a volunteer, James. You're officially a member of the nuthouse," Quinn said, slapping him hard on the back. They all headed off in different cars, with purpose in hand, and James had the distinct feeling he'd met that man before.

Chapter 29

Caleb drove the Jaguar up the road to Hamilton Manor House, thinking for the millionth time in four days that he should turn around and head to the airport. He looked into the rearview to see the little Miata hot on his tail. And for the millionth time in four days, he knew he wouldn't be able to outrun his aunt and her team of guards. Omar was probably the only one on his side, but since he'd been spending his free time with Tammy, he wasn't around to help Caleb plead his case. But at least twice a day, Omar would manage to sneak him away from prying eyes so he could make a call to Jai. Her cell phone was no longer in service, and the answering machine at the office was a pleasant prerecorded message that was pissing him off. If Jai was dismissing him and their time together as insignificant, then, he told himself, he would as well. But he could no more forget their time together than he could forget to breathe.

Sometimes he was sullen, and other times outright surly. He'd gotten so riled the night before, he'd almost walked out the door and driven to New York to demand an explanation from Jai. But his aunt had sat at the door, speaking words of reason, while Dolly had made them all tall glasses of lemonade spiked with something to help him sleep. The only problem was he had dreamt of Jai.

During working hours, Elwood was constantly trying to get Caleb absorbed in a game of chess, while Latham gave him hourly updates on every move everyone made in the company. Louise and Dolly would bring in scads of food, which his stomach wasn't feeling, but Elwood and all the workers had no problem polishing it off on his behalf. His aunt would drop some pearl of wisdom in his ear before heading off, wielding a hammer, with one of the construction crews.

Caleb knew they were trying to distract him as well as keep him away from any news sources. Omar had Caleb's laptop, Latham had all his other electronics, and Elwood's job was to keep him away from the television, newspapers, and phones.

"Stop moping, boy. Is it that bad hangin' 'round us?" Elwood asked, handing him some contracts for review.

"It isn't you. . . ."

"Well, I sure as hell hope it ain't me," Ann said, coming in the office, tool belt tight around her waist. "Because I'm having the time of my life."

"Caleb misses his woman," Elwood said. "We ain't no substitute for that."

Latham came in and started giving them the morning updates. Ann listened but could barely hear anything over the sound of her nephew's heart breaking. She had taken one look at Jailyn Wyatt and had known she was the one. She was the one who would bring life back to the farmhouse and the one to make a home with her nephew.

He had dated too many "perfect women" who were

perfect for someone else. Caleb would indulge the women through dinner, listen to their insipid conversation, and take them home without one improper overture. They thought him shy or polite and eagerly awaited calls that ceased to come. It had been that way since he was a young man, and not much had changed. Ann might not see her nephew as often as she liked to, but she knew exactly what was going on in his life, and the man had become way too complacent with women stopping the planet for him. It was about time he got one that was a loving challenge. Caleb Hamilton Vincent was as picky as his father, Seaghan Quinlan, when it came to women, but this time he had picked the right one.

She'd accepted that he took to bed the pushy, loose women who threw themselves at him. Yet somehow he had managed to avoid being a womanizer. But most of the time he was indifferent; he hadn't found anyone who made him stop and do a double take. Until now. Jai had solved that dilemma, and now Caleb couldn't keep his head straight.

The office phone rang, drawing everyone's attention. Caleb looked over to see if it was his private line. In four days that line had not once rung. "Okay, fellas. Let's clear out. The man has business," said Ann. She hustled the two out the door, handed Caleb his laptop, and turned back to her nephew. "You better get that. Could be for you."

Caleb turned on the laptop, picked up the receiver, and listened for a good minute. It was his father, and Seaghan Quinlan did not mince words when he had something to say, but Caleb was his father's child.

"Quinn, I'm not turning Tobin over to the feds. I'll do what I can, but I can't do that."

"He used your company to launder money. He unsuspectingly used your money in his loan-sharking deals."

"You may not understand this, but he gave up having a normal life so that I could keep mine. What we did is between us. The scorecard will never be even, no matter what he asks of me or I ask of him. We'll always be there for each other. . . ."

"Caleb. Son. I think it's time you talked to someone. . . ."

"Pop, I don't need a psychiatrist."

"I'm not talking about one of them. I got someone here a lot more special. Someone who could use your help, and I think you might wanna do some talking, too."

He heard the phone being shuffled around on the other end and then a steady silence, which was broken by the sound he'd been waiting for. "Hey, Ra. When's the next flight?"

Her voice was as sultry as ever in his ear, enveloping his soul with a smile. He could hear the tired, defeated undercurrent hidden in the falsely cheery greeting. He could see her looking strong and stoic, as well as small and forlorn. It was ripping into his heart like jagged teeth. He couldn't help himself. "You may not need me, but I need you," he said. "I need to be with you and near you."

"Good, because I want you here with me," she replied. Her words staggered him as he sagged with relief against the chair.

Even though Jai stood in the quiet brownstone, with her mother and Quinn in the next room, she felt Caleb all around her. His devastatingly handsome face, his penetrating bluish green eyes, the smallest hint of a New England accent coming to fruition, his piercing smile, and the lingering warmth of his touch were all achingly real. His well-articulated words were nothing compared to the song in his heart, which he sang out for her. The one that he sang to her over hundreds of miles. The song that kept her ears listening every night and woke her up every morning and that she heard all through the day. The only thing in life that made her forget art and want to live again.

"I've always had my father to lean on," she said. "He always understood exactly what I was going through. And even though my family and friends are here, I feel like I'm carrying the burden alone, and I don't want to give you my problems. I want to give you me."

He understood that she was opening herself up to him, and he would take her, problems and all. For the first time, they would exist outside of the sanctity of the farmhouse and the niche they had carved for themselves in the Connecticut countryside. He understood it was now and forever. "I'll be there on the next flight," he said. He could hear her smile beaming through the line. It warmed him from the inside out. They said their good-byes, and he hung up.

As Caleb grabbed some papers, the feed from CNN on his laptop caught his attention. He heard the faintest words drift to him. "Creative Forces." "Chapter Eleven." "Charges filed." Caleb saw the faces and images of people he knew. He was stunned by the report as he listened to the details. But one face in particular caused him to make a call other than to the airline.

"Hello." In that one word, Caleb heard the thick Brooklyn accent.

"Hello, Tony," Caleb said.

"Gary. Gary Tobin. You must have the wrong number."

"Well, if you hear from Anthony Binetti, tell him to call me."

"Straight to the point. I've always liked that about you, Caleb." A nervous laugh came over the line, and there was a moment of silence before he continued. "Keep in mind, this is an unsecured line."

"Sorry about that. That was rude of me, but I need you to understand the seriousness of the matter. Do you need to call me back?"

"We haven't spoken in a long time. First, let me hear what you're up to," said Tobin.

"Creative Forces. DeAngelo. Familiar?"

"Vaguely."

"If I figured it out, they will, too," said Caleb.

"That's because we go way back. You know enough about me to get me sent up for twenty years to camp Fed, or to wipe me from the face of the map completely."

"I don't know anything of the sort, unless you want to count that time on spring break in Montego Bay. Someone should have shot you for those lame pickup lines." The two men shared a respectable laugh. "Oh, and let's not forget how you recently undercut me in Hawaii. Now that was criminal." This time they both felt the old competitive streak rear up, and the camaraderie they had always shared surfaced, as they enjoyed a heartfelt laugh. "It seems we will continue to cross competitive paths. This is one of those times, since Creative has taken me on as a client."

"So now we get to the crux of the matter. How can I help you, friend?"

"What can you tell me?"

"Not much. Let's call it a business investment gone awry, shall we? Reynolds was in deep. They got him the job and the arrangement to meet the Winston woman.

But Daddy Winston was smarter than that, and a prenup ended that payday. So Reynolds went to Christian Meyer and decided to go a different way. But Meyer got greedy, and Reynolds got stupid. Decided why pay when they can take it all and disappear. DeAngelo was a facilitator, nothing more."

"I'll be discreet."

"Let me ask around first."

"You have the Hawaii deal to protect. If any of this gets out and you're found out, at the very least you can kiss Hawaii good-bye and anything else you've got, and the worst is you could end up dead," Caleb said, like a parent reprimanding a child.

"Why do you want to get involved and unearth corpses?"

"I know the woman intimately," Caleb said in hushed tones.

"Your grandfather, my grandfather, your stepfather, my father, my uncles, even the women are all gone," Tobin said, without a hint of sadness. "We've paid back all those old debts and then some."

"It's about time. This sins of the father shit was getting on my nerves."

"Visiting iniquities of the Father's upon the children unto the third and fourth generation of them. Exodus Twenty, Five. We stuck it out. Have a pretty good friendship to boot. After this I can focus on Hawaii. I'll get you Reynolds."

Caleb closed his eyes and ran his hands through his hair harshly before taking a few deep breaths. He and Gary Tobin, alias Anthony Binetti, had been through a lot and were best friends despite everything, and Caleb wanted to protect Tobin as much as Tobin wanted to help Caleb. And all Caleb wanted right now was to be with the woman he loved. His father's words kept coming back to him. *You need friends, family, and most of all, love.* He did need them, whether it was his father, Gary, or this woman. He knew he needed all three to make his world complete. "What about Meyer?"

"Fell off the radar. Even DeAngelo lost the trail, and he never loses anyone. But by the time you and I get together, I should—"

"Don't get involved."

"Since when are you the boss of me?"

"We promised your father," Caleb said, his voice exact.

"And for the most part, we have honored his wishes. Besides, if something goes wrong, I know you'll bail me out."

"Don't I always?" Caleb asked.

"Indeed, you do," Tobin answered. "You're the best friend a man could have. I want to do this, okay? My choice."

"I'll see you when I get to New York."

"And bring the woman disrupting our lives," Tobin instructed.

"Not on your life." With that Caleb clicked off the phone, closed up his laptop, and, with a smile, headed out the door to the airport.

Chapter 30

Jai walked into the cozy brownstone, with her last bit of energy propelling her forward. "Eww!" she said as the two bodies popped apart in the romantic lighting.

"Oh, sorry, me love. Don't mean to be upsetting you," Quinn apologized, getting to his feet and wiping his mouth.

"What are you apologizing for? I'm the grown-up here. In fact, we're all grown-ups," Doe said, looking at her new boyfriend with indignation.

"She doesn't need to be seeing what we do," he mumbled for Doe's ears only.

"She can close her eyes. We both live here, you know. I can have male company if I want," Doe said defiantly.

"You best be having only one male keeping company with ye, woman," Quinn said, kicking her crossed foot, his Irish accent thickening.

"Before I cause an all-out war, how about I just go up to my apartment?" Jai offered, rubbing her stomach.

"Not before you get some hot food in ye. I bet you missed lunch today," Quinn said, heading for the kitchen.

"And breakfast and dinner," Jai whined, allowing herself to be babied.

"Oh, no, you don't, Mister. You're not stuffing her with junk," her mother tsk-tsked, going after Quinn.

"Think of it as comfort food. Caleb will be leaving for Hawaii," Quinn said in his defense.

"Not for another day. At least let him get on the plane before you start making excuses for her," said Doe.

"It won't be enough to wreck her diet," Quinn added.

"I'm not worried about her weight. It's her health . . . ," Doe said, getting in the last word on the matter as they moved out of earshot, playfully continuing their faux fight.

Jai slumped awkwardly in her favorite chair, her legs dangling over the arm. The mention of Caleb's name had made her melancholy. He had swooped in and had started sprinkling magic all over and making things easier to handle, but their personal relationship had suffered. Since his arrival in New York, they had continued to drift further apart. When they spoke, his tone was abrupt, his words exacting and direct, his personality frigid and aloof. He was constantly in meetings, rarely having time to be civil, let alone social. Although she was more than grateful for his assistance, she much preferred the old Caleb.

She must have dozed off for a moment, because she awoke to a shake and a "psst, psst," from James, who was holding out a banana chocolate smoothie from his perch on the ottoman. His knees practically covered his face, the way he sat there, hunched forward. She smiled at the irresistible playfulness they shared. She had become dependant on it to get her through the days. If they had met a year ago, she would have admitted he was perfect for her. They both shared the same brand of humor and had so much unbridled fun together, it was amazing. No one understood them the way they understood each other. But James was like a Rockwell painting. He evoked one feeling in his perfectness and told one story, the one he painted precisely to show what he wanted, no interpretation allowed. It made Jai miss her days in the country with Caleb. James and the smoothie would definitely help her forget Caleb's upcoming trip to Hawaii and the rift that they could not seem to mend. She would allow James to once again be her knight and her comforter.

"Did they see you?" she asked, reaching for the huge cup, which he pulled away.

"No. I move in the shadows, ducking in and out of crevices, clinging to the ceiling, fighting the bad guys in order to get you the gold."

"My hero," she said, batting her long lashes.

"That's all I wanted to hear," he said, kissing her forehead and slipping the cup into her hand. "So how was work today?" he asked, removing her shoes from her swollen feet.

"I could have finished if I hadn't spent more than half the morning in the bathroom and the afternoon dozing," she complained pleasantly.

"See? I should have been there with you to keep you up."

"Yeah, but we would've fooled around so much, I still wouldn't be done. Besides, you had class. How is that, anyway?"

"It's cool. I blew through the indoor technical stuff. Now we're getting into the more creative stuff," he said, shifting on the cushiony little hassock.

"That's what you need to pay attention to."

"I know, I know. So who was there today? Besides my baby," he asked.

"The regulars. Tyrell, Ros, Mickey, and Akiba."

"No Kevin or Toiji?" James asked, throwing his long legs out to one side in a quest to find comfort on the small square.

"No, I don't need the two of them hovering over me. I can get through tomorrow without them," she answered.

"And that's it? All the accounts are on maintenance?"

"Yep. All the contracts have been fulfilled. So you, my friend, better start looking for a real job. We gotta be out of the offices by the end of the month. Playtime is over," she said, taking a deep slurp.

"What? I'm not leaving you. I'm in this till the end," James said, with bravado.

"This is the end. 'Sides, there's no money left to pay you. . . ."

"Okay. Well, nice knowing ya. Don't forget to write me a glowing recommendation for my unfailing dedication," he said, with a smile.

"Punk," she said.

"I'm kidding. I'm kidding."

"I'm not. My Dad's insurance covered the back taxes, fines, and penalties. Whatever was left, plus my own chump change, covered the severance packages, and I'm scraping the bare bottom to contract out these last eight accounts. Your classes and Tyrell's college are the last of the Creative Forces pennies." Jai shook the thick concoction.

"Don't worry. My fiancée always has a plan."

"You better talk to her first. Girl seems fresh out of ideas if you ask me."

"She can't be. She has a big wedding to plan," he said, trying to fold his long legs Indian style on the footrest. "Fancy invites, frilly bridesmaids' gowns, chicken or steak, who sits where, flower arrangements, photographer, church, band versus DJ, reception hall, family fights, and cake selection."

"Not all women want big weddings."

"Why not? All girls dream of their Cinderella gown, the handsome prince, the happily ever after. I swear, it's written somewhere that each married couple must start out destitute. So why not go for broke on the nuptials and the honeymoon? Besides, all mothers want to browbeat their daughters over the choice of napkins and appetizers, right, Mom? All moms love this stuff. They need it to feel complete, right, Doe? Tell your daughter to stop being selfish." Doe had come into the room. James spent so much of his time in their home that Doretha had invited him to move into one of the extra rooms to save money. He was now, in Doretha's eyes, one of the family.

"Don't go dragging me into a conversation I only heard half of. Now go lock up. Jai, your food's on the table. There's enough for both of you."

"Thanks, Mom."

"My male company and I are turning in for the night, so keep it down. You two laugh like hyenas," Doe said, giving her daughter a brief hug and kiss as she retired to her bedroom.

After a few minutes passed, Jai decided James was taking too long, so she turned off the lights in the living room and hall and started a slow trek to the kitchen. She felt his magnetic presence before she saw the figure leaning against the door as if this was an everyday occurrence. "Are you here to rob me, have dinner with me, or have your way with me?"

"Number three," the voice answered in a low tenor.

"How is it you always know when I enter a room?" he asked in a seductive whisper.

"You change the current in the air," she said, her voice husky.

"Someone told me that once before." He moved swiftly and took her into his arms. "Did you feel the air change just now? Because, for me, the world moved."

"I'm going to be getting married soon," she said coyly.

"Yeah, so I've heard," he said, trailing hot kisses down her neck.

"My future husband is a big, tall, strong man who is crazed with jealousy."

"Yeah, so I've heard. I'm not worried," he said, sweeping her off of her feet and into his arms. "Let me make love to you before you take that walk down the aisle."

"And after?" she asked as his tongue danced around the whorls of her ear.

"I'll love you every night we're together," he said, biting her earlobe and carrying her up the steps. He held her body closely nestled against his so that she barely noticed the little bumps along the way. But each time her plump body shifted infinitesimally in his arms, his body had a resounding and immediate reaction. "Stay still," he growled in her ear.

"I don't want you to drop me," she squealed as he kicked closed the studio apartment door like a barbarian. "Shh! You're going to wake the whole house."

She scrambled out of his arms. Caleb held on to her waist and stared into her face as if he hadn't seen her in years instead of hours. For the first time in her life, Jai saw her true self reflected in those eyes. She saw herself as worthy of a grounded, realistic love, his love. There was no question about giving herself to him as she felt his love overpowering her senses. Her love for him was like a forceful winter wind, stealing over summer even before fall had settled in. He looked at her with those eyes, and she didn't have to paint a picture of what she imagined true love to be. She didn't have to make up a story in her mind of what type of man she wanted, and she didn't have to pretend to be a special kind of woman. His eyes told her she was a special woman. He kissed her in such a way that she could feel the nails on her toes curl. Her body reveled in the latent sensuality of his touch, and her mind reassured her that she was with the right man.

"Now get in the bed while I go back down and get your dinner. This isn't going to be like those other times where we never get to the kitchen," he said.

"I know that," she answered, a look of love and trust painted on her features, as he went to the door. "But there was nothing wrong with them," she said in a sultry voice, freezing his hand midway to the doorknob. The smile that bloomed on her face undid him like no other. She was in his arms before he realized his true intent. He loved her, and he needed to show her how he felt as love flowed through their kiss. Each touch of his hand to her skin was a testament to how she moved the heavens for him. Each fiery caress was proof that he could never let her go, and each heated stroke of her hand across his chest dragged him deeper into that love.

She took her time removing each article of his clothing until he stood stock-still beneath her quaint appraisal. When she took a step back, he moved forward. "Stop. Stay right where you are," she said. Her voice was heavy with lust, and he savored the raspy sound.

"Why are you torturing me?" he asked, watching her

remove all her garments except the sedate, oversized men's button-down dress shirt. He admired the view of her powerful legs, rounded behind, and regal feet. Each demure motion made his mouth water. He asked again, "Why torture us both?"

"Because I think it's time I draw you."

"I'm yours to do with what you will . . . after I make love to you," he said, grabbing her from behind and bringing her body full up against his so she could feel the urgency of his desire pressing into her backside. He nuzzled her neck as she struggled against him, and her writhing made him harder than the man of steel. "Feel that? It won't wait," he said, smelling the delicate fragrance of her curly hair when he buried his nose in it.

She wiggled with all her might until they tumbled onto the bed. "Let me . . ." The thought got lost somewhere between her brain and the kisses he was planting on her collarbone. She closed her eyes and drifted on the searing caresses from his capable hands. She ran an open palm across his broad shoulder and heard his quick intake of breath. The tension of ten years floated out of him when she pressed strong fingers into the unforgiving muscle. He moaned with weakness as her serene touches caused him to yield to her and experience a magnitude of awareness in so many places he had failed to pay attention to. His hands went limp, and his head lolled to one side.

"You always tilt your head to that side," she said. "It's where you carry your stress, and although it gives you that James Dean *Rebel Without a Cause* look, you hardly need it." Her chest hovered over his, and he could feel the linen of her shirt brush over him, and a cacophony of new sensations exploded in his head.

Jai massaged his tense muscles, leaning into him with

all of her weight. Each sigh, breath, and twitch of his body was a telltale sign that she was breaking through a physical barrier he had yet to acknowledge. His erection snuggled beneath her was a constant beat below ready, and Jai's body hummed with barely suppressed energy, waiting for that moment. She dug the pads of her fingers into each indentation in the dreamy landscape of his chest, which was the color of butterscotch, working her hands lower and moving her body down. His body was magnificent, with its taut muscle definition and the light dusting of downy golden hairs glowing against his skin. The mixture made him look like the hues of an Arizona sunset—all earthy, corporeal, and spiritual. Touching him was like exploring a vibrant new land, and she couldn't get enough of his arms thrown open wide and his lips parted just enough for her to hear his shaky breaths and groans.

As much as he wanted to take her, he also welcomed the deft movements of her hands. The simple state of melancholia she had introduced him to was erotic unto itself, but then he felt the merest brush over his manhood, and he was suddenly propelled into a new dimension. His hips bucked as she slowly took the length of him into her mouth. He feared she didn't know he wasn't completely at attention, but the more she wet his cock, swirled her tongue, and suckled the full and throbbing member, the more he came to realize she knew exactly what he had to offer and exactly how to get it.

He tried to sit up on his elbows, the sounds of her slurping him to fulfillment driving him insane, but his arms trembled and gave out once he saw the way she was spread eagle between his legs, her rear thrust into the air, the swell of her chestnut-colored bottom glowing in the light, her lush lips engulfing him to the curls of his groin, and her tongue lapping at the pulsating veins in his shaft. Her charcoal-colored hair brushed his thighs, her ebony eyes locked on his, and her long, dusky eyelashes blinked in slow motion. If her mouth wasn't stretched open wide, he would have believed she was smiling up at him.

The feeling of tightness in his stomach was building as she thrust him in and out of her mouth, her hand squeezing in tandem along the slick rod, his balls drawing up with a sharpness that forced an intake of breath. She laved the swelling flesh until the veins stood out like Braille, and with unwavering dedication, she continued to do tricks and spirals with her tongue, greedily sucking in a way that made his chest hurt and his buttocks clench.

A flush crept up his body, and beads of sweat broke out on his face, so that he glistened in the dim light. She felt his body convulse and push up off of the bed, his calves two hard marble stones and his manhood a long, huge, thick log. The churning that held him hostage suddenly burst, and like a firestorm, it ate everything in its path. A potent stream of hot fluid rushed from his phallus, and ripples of ecstasy rolled over him until he completely surrendered to them, his thunderous cry becoming a ragged whimper when the magnitude of his orgasm slowly subsided.

When a semblance of his energy returned, he heaved her up next to him. As much as he enjoyed seeing her curvaceous form do indecent things to an ordinary shirt, he stripped it from her body to better partake of her ample womanly assets. He ran a finger leisurely from her nose to her sensuous lips, past her upturned chin, and down her long neck, ending between her breasts. Admiring the auburn tinge her skin seemed to have in the low lights, he touched one weighty globe and dipped his head to capture one distended whiskey-colored nipple in his mouth. Her body rejoiced in the exquisite sensation. She felt the playful nips and the pressure from his tongue. His hand continued its slow journey until it found its way to her valley of love-scented curls. He found the little nub hard and wanting. He took it between his thumb and forefinger until her hips gyrated under the deluge of his affection. He moved his fingers down and found a fountain of her juices awaiting him. He plunged two fingers into her, and her tight canal clamped down on him.

Jai couldn't tell where he started and she ended; he was systematically tearing her soul from her and becoming her only need. Her legs opened wider for his pleasure and her own, her nails leaving their mark in his shoulders, the frenzied rapture just a touch away. His warm mouth burned a hot path to her other nipple, where his tongue fed with hungry urgency. His hard body covered hers as she humped his hand with mindless abandon, trying to find release. Her body was coursing ahead at an unbelievable pace, and he removed his hand, flipped her over onto all fours, and embedded himself in her in one flawlessly executed motion. Her breath caught. He was buried so deep within her wet folds that a thought couldn't pass between them without the other hearing it, but she was addicted to the feel of his thick cock impaled in her.

He moved with slow, deliberate motions at first, but her body bucked and heaved, ready to receive more, craving that jolt of euphoria that only he could give her. Her body was flush with the headboard and wall, and he matched her quickening pace until he rammed with such force that the pillows fell to the floor and the headboard pounded the wall. But all he could hear was the sound of Jai plummeting headfirst into a massive orgasm when he moved his hand down her body and rubbed a rough finger over the hardened nub in the cleft of her slick folds. He pulled her head back gruffly by the hair and rested it on his shoulder as he kissed her, swallowing the sounds of both of their climaxes. Her nails scratched the paint on the walls. His tenuous grasp on reality was severed; the only tangible was her.

The last quivers surged from her body. He waited for his own tremors to wane before he finally untangled himself from her and laid her down as if she were a priceless piece of work. She nestled her head in the crook of his shoulder and unconsciously curled her body into his. It was how they often slept. And as was often the case, he couldn't help but be astounded by her beauty. Even in sleep her face was alight with excitement, her body sensual, her presence formidable.

Even after their lovemaking, which satisfied the deepest parts of his soul, he was eager for more of her.

Chapter 31

Caleb gingerly opened one eye, not sure if he'd slept for a minute or a month, but there she was, basking in the glow of the candles she had lit around the room. A plate of food half eaten sat on the table near the kitchenette. Another, he was sure, was in the oven, waiting for him. A tall glass of water sat on the nightstand. It hadn't even started to sweat, so as usual she knew when he was about to wake.

"Are you psychic, or what?" he asked while appreciating all of her natural attributes as she stole into bed next to him. Her full breasts brushed his arm, the tips like raisins. Her body still smelled of their night together.

"No. You're still having nasty dreams," Jai said, concern evident in her voice.

"Are you naked in these dreams?" he asked, hoping to lighten the mood.

"Not that kind of nasty."

He played with one of her curls after polishing off the glass of water. "I can't talk about it."

"I didn't ask you to," she said, with a yawn.

"Maybe one day. One day soon," he said.

"You don't have to," Jai assured him, patting his chest and drifting off to sleep.

When she woke up, day and night were battling in the sky, casting a grey light over the room. She still clung to the memories of the night before as she reached across the bed to find nothing more than the cool, crisp sheets. A slow ache started somewhere in her, but she'd had practice pushing it away, denying it, ignoring it. To give it voice would just make it harder to ignore. Her cell phone tinkled a happy little song, and she smiled. He must have searched it out and plugged it into the charger for her, as he so often did.

"Good morning," she chirped.

"It's raining, and it's afternoon," came his terse reply. "Some of us have already put in a full day."

She was hit with the cold starkness of Caleb's unfriendly voice and the angry heat he possessed all at once. She was once again reminded of the painful changes that had taken place between them. "My business has been shut down. All my clients are gone. I have absolutely no reason to rise and shine at the crack of freakin' dawn, and my body is going through some serious shit right now. . . ."

"I called to talk," he said, with an exactness that contradicted the request. "Calling from Hawaii can be expensive, and walkie-talkies aren't an option."

"Okaaaay. So talk," she said, sitting up in bed.

"I have a friend Gary Tobin." He paused, but she remained silent. "We attended the same boarding school."

"Uh-huh," she remarked, clearly hearing the rain fall around him. She could see the silver drops like crystals against his honeyed skin and diamonds clinging to his untamed curls as he paced back and forth on the sidewalk, talking to her. His aristocratic voice, with the sexual undertones, had a magnetic pull, and she had to tread carefully lest he devour her whole. "Go on," she urged in her most aloof voice.

"He saved me once. It was my stepfather's problem, but let's just say my stepfather would have sold me like a slave if it got him off the hook. Tobin made sure it didn't go down like that. People think he walks a fine line, but he's always been straight with me."

"And what, pray tell, does this touching story about a boy and his friend have to do with me?" He didn't miss one glacial breath that she took.

"He's a good guy to know. So let me handle the federal government."

Although he tried to sound indifferent, there was something personal he was trying to tell her. But Jai decided what was hidden by the dark could be seen in the light, so if he wanted her to know, he'd have to just tell her.

"The FBI is looking for someone," she said. "And that someone has caused one of my partners and one of my account reps, who are suspected to have fled the country, to take a whole heap of money, leaving me holding the bag. I don't know if Gary Tobin has anything to do with it, but your father seems to have a pretty low opinion of the guy. I've also read that he most recently undercut several deserving architects on a multimillion-dollar resort deal in Hawaii, even though he wasn't invited to submit a proposal. A deal you had a bid in for. And now he's fucked it up so bad, you've been called in to save him. So explain to me again why he is good to know and why I should allow you to handle my problems."

Caleb spoke in lethal tones, "The whole world is not gumdrops and lollipops. You need to take off your rose-colored glasses and stop looking for rainbows, Pollyanna. And you and James need to stop acting like this is a game. This isn't a case of you smile and everyone smiles with you, and the nice music plays and the credits roll. This is life."

"Yeah, Caleb, my life. And if I smile, will things get worse?" There was silence on the phone. "I didn't think so."

"Great-grandpa Vincent served New England society as a master builder and mason. He could duplicate any style, recreate any stone face, and build some of the strongest and longest-lasting structures to date. He was so respected and sought after that he served only the elite and ultimately he joined the ranks of the elite.

"On a visit to New York, he met Carmelo Binetti, a big importer of raw materials for Vincent Masonry. Carmelo got him referrals in New Jersey, Pennsylvania, Maine, and Connecticut, where Great-grandpa eventually settled after meeting his future wife. VM is indelibly stamped on early New England history, and Binetti had a huge part of that. As organized crime took root in American society and wars over territory became bloody, Carmelo and Great-grand lost touch, and VM business slowed. Under my grandfather Whitey, it had a small rebirth, but my stepfather, Bradley Vincent, toppled everything but the reputation. So when Salvatore Binetti came to claim his silent share of VM and infuse it with money, Bradley was only too happy. Salvatore spent years away from his son and wife to ensure their safety. He sent money to them and continued investing in VM in order to provide a normal future for his son. But Brad squandered every last dime, maintaining the transparent and fading Vincent Masonry image even after wasting the financial fruits of marriage to my wealthy mother, Corrine."

"Caleb, this is a lot to take in," Jai said, clearly disturbed and upset by the fact that he had chosen this moment to confide in her. "We really should have had this conversation in person."

"I wasn't eager to have this conversation at all, and there's more. I found out about a week before meeting you that Bradley and my mother spent my college tuition, along with the rest of the Hamilton and Vincent fortunes, on themselves and that my biological father paid for my education. Although I wanted to believe Pop was always there for me, I didn't. I didn't really believe it, because if he had been he wouldn't have left me with Brad. He would have come to rescue me."

He was silent, and she was sure that his face was turned up to the sky and that the rain was washing away tears that he wouldn't allow to fall and the pain he'd been holding in all these years. He went on. "My mother stayed with a husband who couldn't stand who she really was and tried to make herself into the influential, wealthy Caucasian woman her parents and husband expected her to be. She lived her entire life never coming to terms with who she was."

"And you? How did you live?"

"I tried to live like their son, like a smart, well-to-do, suave, well-mannered Vincent. But it was never good enough. In the last moments of Bradley Vincent's bleak life, he chose to sacrifice his bastard child."

Jai gasped, unable to fully decipher the depravity of what Caleb was saying.

"Sal Binetti sacrificed everything for his son, and I had two fathers who I didn't trust."

"Knowing my dad would kill for me makes it hard to

believe a man like Brad exists. Your life is like something from a daytime soap."

"How 'bout a Mafia movie. When Sal finally confronted Brad, he called Tony in. Tony. Anthony Binetti is Gary Tobin. Now you're one of three people alive who know that. It shouldn't matter who his father was, but dead men are the only men who don't tell tales, and children carry their fathers' legacies and truths." Caleb didn't say it to scare her; he said it as a matter of fact. He wanted desperately for Jai to understand that Gary could be trusted and why he needed to help her so badly. "We thought for sure Sal wanted Tony to pull the trigger in order to show his loyalty and love. I told them to let me. I wanted to prove I was a man and a loyal friend."

"I already know Brad's dead, so please tell me this has a happy ending."

"Brad self-destructed. He was found at the airport, literally taking flight, when karma caught up to him and he had a heart attack. When Sal got sick, he wanted me to know what he had done for Tony. He trusted us to take care of our mothers and each other. So we both spent all of our time bringing VM back from the dead. With what money we made, we paid off the Hamilton-Vincent debts and Sal's hospital bills."

"Why didn't you ask your father for help or, at the very least, tell him what was going on?"

"I didn't know I could, and I didn't want to be rejected. So that's why I'm not waiting for you to ask for help. This is not a game. These guys are dangerous."

"Then let the police and the Feds handle it. You're not Superman, and I'm not as stupid as Lois Lane."

"Damn it, woman. Can't you stop being so pigheaded and let me help?"

"No. I told you before you came down, I didn't want your help," she said, annoyed at his presumptuousness. "I wanted you, and you became obsessed with saving me, just like my father did, to the extent of forgetting to love me. It's like setting me aside, and you'll get back to me when you've fixed everything. I don't need saving. I didn't need my father protecting me from life. I don't need you shoving it in my face, and I'm tired of watching it go by from the shadows, like I'm Ralph Ellison's Invisible Man. I'm not weak or afraid anymore, because I can live my life in the dark and in the light. I can even wear rose-colored glasses on a rainy day, and James Ross would probably drop gumdrops on my head just to make my fondest wish come true. And, Caleb, I've been handling things by myself all right so far, and I have a feeling today might be the day I see a rainbow."

"Jailyn . . ."

"Caleb, you have a plane to catch today, and a business deal to negotiate. I have my own stuff."

"Jailyn . . ."

"And unless I'm wrong about you, I'll see you at the wedding."

"Jai?"

"Good-bye, Caleb," she said, clicking the OFF button of her cell phone.

"I love you," he said, walking back into the terminal.

Chapter 32

Wind rustled through the trees, making a wonderfully soothing harmony with the melodic sounds of spring. Time was irrelevant as she enjoyed the brisk wind blowing her clothes, adding to her high spirits. The growling sound of the all-terrain four-wheeler hammered through the quiet as the vehicle went airborne over the crest of a hill before landing with a thud on the hard-packed dirt of the well-worn road she'd created just for herself.

Jai gunned the engine and roared down the last stretch of road, knowing her days of riding were coming to an end just as surely as the weather was breaking. Her husband would probably throw a fit if he knew the speeds she was pushing the mini-monster vehicle to while carrying his precious cargo.

She brought the bright bumblebee-colored ATV to a halt in the garage off to the side of the main offices, which had once been housed in a run-down, beat-up barn. Last year's barn raising had been more of a window-washing party, as the town had come out to assist with the completion of a glass-enclosed building. You could see every stairwell and elevator located on the outer shell of the four-story building. Inside was a multitude of businesses.

It was after six p.m. on a Friday, so she was unlikely to encounter anyone as she closed up the offices for the weekend. They were a strictly eight-to-four, five-day-a-week operation. Exceptions could be made, but with her new partner's stress-free philosophy, it was highly unlikely. And it suited her just fine to leave work while the sun still danced in the sky.

Jai walked down the gravel road to the big farmhouse, taking in the pretty summer colors beginning to blossom all around. She had left her Calvin Klein clients at the Hamilton Manor House Businessmen's Bed-and-Breakfast. Her campaign for CK cologne had been such a success that they had created an entire bath line dedicated to the scent, which you could almost smell through the phone. But this weekend they were there to launch the hair lotion they had created for her kinky locks and products geared toward African-American skin. They had hired her to handle the promotion for their new line of multiethnic products, aimed at a market that had largely gone untapped, because people usually associated themselves with one culture or another. CK-ME products addressed the cosmetic concerns of people of mixed heritage and, therefore, not any one particular concern but several. Jai and her family lived for the stuff, from the mild baby soap to the fruity-scented sunblocks. It had been her idea to have the guests of the Foxwoods Resort and Casino and all the surrounding B and Bs utilize the trial gift baskets from CK-ME and to invite the CK-ME execs to enjoy complimentary services at the newly revitalized B and B.

Kids of all ages and sizes came barreling out of the

house in a shower of screams and laughter. They were racing in all directions but were heading to one destination, the lake. "Be careful. Watch out for the small ones!" Jai shouted as bodies jumped down the porch steps and flew over the banister.

Tyrell came out, with his arm slung around a very pretty, brown-skinned girl with black braids, bad attitude emanating from her like skunk spray. Jai played along, giving hard, distrustful New York attitude right back.

"So you're in charge?" Jai asked, eyeing the girl suspiciously, looking her up and down, noting her size five jeans and cute little tank.

"Well, when you said I could come for the summer, I figured you wouldn't mind the extra help," said Tyrell. "Mickey has some pretty good applicants, but I figured you couldn't say no to my sister."

"Hello, Tyanna. Nice to finally meet you," Jai said, with a fake New York smile.

"Thank you, Ms. Wyatt," Tyanna said when Tyrell shook her.

"Did you bring any friends with you?" Jai asked.

Tyanna finally broke. Her eyes shined and there she was, looking like a young, excited teenager. "Tyrell told me not to," she whined, punching him in the arm.

"That's because you act stupid when you get around them," said Tyrell. "Tell them to apply just like everyone else. If they get Mickey's okay, then you'll see them. If not, oh well."

"Like you've never acted stupid," Tyanna said, rolling her eyes.

"I'll be in college in August, and I need to know you'll behave while you're living with Ms. Wyatt," said Tyrell.

"You're only gonna be, like, an hour away," muttered Tyanna.

"Yup. So I can drive up and kick your butt anytime it needs kicking," Tyrell said as he gazed at the meadow, getting a look at the rambling bunch heading toward the water.

Tyanna turned to Jai. She looked shy and scared, just as her brother had the first time he came in her office, looking for a paid internship so he could help out at home and stay in school. "Umm . . . I have a friend named Alana, and she's got like twelve brothers and sisters. Some are only halves, but she takes care of them all the time and she still keeps her grades up and she's never been out of New York. . . ."

"Get a permission slip from Mickey, and call her up so we can arrange a ticket. Now get a move on," Jai said, patting her shoulder. "Those twins move very fast."

Tyanna started running. "Hey, watch it. No hitting!" she shouted at the rowdy bunch.

Jai had barely gotten inside the door when James was on her with a big bear hug and a wet, sloppy kiss. "I was getting ready to come out there and rescue you," he said.

"I don't need rescuing," she said, laughing and wiggling out of his arms. "And stop kissing me. The whole world will hear us."

"Who cares?" he asked, making loud kissing noises toward the living room.

"I do. Now stop it. Is everyone in there?" Jai asked, fixing her clothes and looking down the hall with mild trepidation. This was a day almost two years in the making.

"Yeah, just about." James took her hand in his to lead her down the hall to the waiting group. Then he saw she wasn't moving. "Stop being nervous. These are your family and friends."

"It's been some time since I've seen some of them or even talked to them," Jai said in a small voice.

"Honey, look at me," he said, tilting her face to him. "You have been handling all of this better than anyone I know. You managed to bring some semblance of order to those first crazy weeks and to ride it out. They'll understand."

Jai leaned her head on his shoulder. It was a shoulder she had taken advantage of a lot in those dark days, and although no one, not even James, could have been certain she wasn't guilty of siphoning off the millions of dollars that had disappeared with the flight of Christian Meyer and Paul Reynolds, he had never spent a moment doubting her. He walked her into the room, and all eyes went to them.

"Everyone, the moment we have all been waiting for," James said like a ringmaster. He put a gentle kiss on Jai's forehead, gave a squeeze to her hand, and whispered, "Don't worry. You got this, babe," before taking a seat next to Eva.

Chapter 33

Jai scanned the room of familiar faces and felt the burning of tears behind her eyes. She felt like she'd let each of them down at one point or another. She met her mother's eyes across the room, filled with love and encouragement. Next to her mother was the massive frame of Seaghan Quinlan. Seeing the two most special people in her life together was a great motivator. It was time to see this thing through to the end.

"I want to thank everyone for clearing their schedules to be here. Mom, Quinn, Judith, Herbert, Toiji, Kevin, Eva, and James. First, because this is the opening weekend of the Quinlan Family Inn and, second, because I have some serious explaining to do."

Jai looked around at the faces watching her. "You've all seen the commercials and ads running for the inn and Hamilton Manor House, thanks to Visual Vibes, run by Toiji and Kevin Rhodes. 'If you want the comforts of home with none of the pitfalls, come to the Quinlan Family Inn.' The rooms are more comfortable and elaborate than home, there's always tons of closet space, and while you shower, your bed gets made. The kitchen is accessible twenty-four hours a day, a buffet is spread out from dawn till dusk, regular sit-down meals are prepared for residents, and there's never a dish to be washed. Shuttles run between here and Foxwoods, discounts are offered to our guests for all of their entertainment, and they can stop at a country store, go apple picking, make apple cider, take a hayride, enjoy horseback riding, have a dip in the lake, or come on back and bask in the tranquility of the inn.

"For the businessman and his family, we organize a weekly package. A portion of his day is spent at one of the private offices at Hamilton House, with a temporary secretary assigned to handle any number of regular office tasks and to coordinate with his home office. The rest of his itinerary is fun and relaxation with his family, anything from a hoedown, to making model planes, flying kites, or taking in a show with the wife and kids. We arrange it all so that no area of your life is neglected. Leave it to us, and it'll seem like home with none of the pitfalls."

"I thought it was too simplistic to catch on. Then I get here and find out you're booked solid for the next four months, and you haven't even opened yet," Kevin said, shaking his head. "Amazing."

Jai went on. "It comes from the idea of family and friends. Work often gets in the way, but what if we had a really efficient staff that scheduled in family time? Well, that's what the concept is. I get it from my mom. She literally puts family time in her agenda book so that it gets the same importance as a regular meeting. And from what I know, she's never cancelled or rescheduled me in my entire life." Jai looked at the woman who had loved her more than she could ever measure. Everyone looked at her mother. "I think everyone knows my mom and Quinn, who are huddled in the corner. Seaghan Quinlan owns Quinn's Pub and has a large stake here at the inn. He's also my mom's boyfriend, as well as a longtime family friend. And even though he doesn't think I know, he had a hand in selecting my husband."

"I can't imagine how. As of late, it doesn't seem anyone can convince you of anything," Toiji said.

"I'm just more cautious now. That's all. But Quinn is persuasive and sneaky."

"And sometimes he'll just outright threaten your life," James said.

"You smart mouthin' me, boy? I'll take you out to the barn for a whuppin' you'll none soon forget," Quinn said, going for his belt.

"See," James said, pointing animatedly until Eva pushed him back in his chair. Easy laughter rolled around the room before Jai continued.

"Now all of you have met Judith and her husband, Herbert Gannon," said Jai. "They met some years ago, when Creative decided to diversify its portfolio. But because they fell in love, we took our business elsewhere so we wouldn't be accused of anything illicit. Then Herb took a job overseas, and Judith joined him often and was able to go and see our investments at work and snag herself a husband."

Jai took a deep, cleansing breath before continuing. "Now knowing that tidbit of information, Eva and I took turns with the monthly financial audit. From one month to the next, you wouldn't notice a discrepancy, because you're so busy balancing debits and credits, you automatically allow for a margin of error. And we are talking a small margin. But when you have a memory like mine or are quick with numbers, like Eva and Jude, noticing discrepancies is inevitable. The money we were diverting to our stocks and personal portfolios was a small percentage of the overall net profit. 'Pay yourself right after you pay Uncle Sam,' my father would always say. But someone was dipping into the gross before the monies were fully accounted for." Jai found herself slowly winding down, the adrenaline having now been used up.

"Sit down, girl, before you fall down," Kevin said, taking her by the arm.

"Yeah. No more worrying us or keeping us in the dark," Toiji said, getting up out of his seat and allowing her to sit down in his comfortable chair.

Judith decided to pick up the thread of the story. "Herb and I were able to find several distinct points where the numbers fluctuated greatly, then disappeared, which would have remained an in-house problem if the IRS had gotten theirs."

"So you guys were skimming someone else?" Kevin asked.

"And everyone was helping to solve the crime except me and Kev here?" Toiji inquired.

"And me," James piped up.

"So what? At least none of you were being used," Eva huffed. "They used me without telling me boo. It was in the papers before I heard the first word."

"And for the last year, only you knew the whole story?" Toiji asked Jai.

"At first, I wasn't sure who to trust. The only one who couldn't possibly be in on it was Judith," Jai explained.

"You could've trusted Toiji. He lets his account team do his department books," Kevin said.

"You had someone else do your books?" Jai asked, with raised brows. "And Reynolds, at that."

"It's not like we knew the man was a criminal. You didn't give us a heads-up about the man," Kevin said. "You were on a one-woman crusade. . . ."

"Making decisions about our money without discussing it with us," Toiji ranted. "Treating us like we're too feebleminded to understand the inner workings of our business."

Jai thought it was endearing that Toiji and Kevin spoke like they were one person, finishing each other's thoughts, but it wasn't cute when they directed their frustration at her. Eva, however, came to her defense. "At least they were investing the money, paying the government, with each dime accounted for. And before you get all pissy, know that you all have a hefty chunk of change coming to you because of Jai's decisions. She's broke, and her dream, Creative Forces, is defunct, in case any of you want to know. But at least all of your reputations remain intact. . . ."

"Relax, Wind Runner. We're on the same side," Toiji said.

"Damn, Eva. You've known us for like what? Fifteen years?" Kevin said, taking offense. "We're not the kind of guys to place blame or take advantage of a situation. We would have done the same for Jailyn or anyone in this room. It would have been nice to be treated like equals. We're big boys. We can handle a little bullshit thrown our way."

"I just wanted to make sure we were separate but equal," said Jai. "I apologize, but I wanted to protect the ones I love. You and Toiji have a nice gig. If you had gotten stuck in the Creative muck, you wouldn't have been able to bounce back so quick."

"I kinda like my job with you," Eva said. "It's a bigger company than Creative. I like having power. Especially over him." Eva nodded in James's direction. He was one of the head photographers working in her department.

"So, wait a minute. Who has money coming to them?" James asked, honing in on the possibility of a payout. The room fell quiet. "What? I'm broke. I have a good job, but the paycheck is still small. My wife and I cannot survive on love alone." Eva shoved him and told him to stop being such a fool.

"I think my wife and I can help with that," Herb said, taking out a large, black metal briefcase that looked fortified enough to transport diamonds. "Here are the diversified investments that were made on your behalves over the course of the last seven years. We cashed in last quarter's investments from each portfolio so you'll have some travel money, play-around dough, start-up capital, or reinforcement funds."

Herb and his wife gave out thick accordion folders. Herb continued. "In each you'll find the name of the investment firms and contact persons. Some of you have similar accounts, and others are quite varied and unduplicated. In some cases, money was lost, but the earnings overall more than make up for it."

Judith took the floor next. "There are also separate banking statements for your employees. Each of your staff members from Creative has a nice nest egg for sticking by us through hard times. Even you, James." James pumped his hand in the air. "Now tell your wife you love her."

"I love you, wife," James said, pulling Eva kicking and fighting onto his lap and subduing her with the passion of his kiss.

"Eww, yuck." Caleb said, entering the room. "Get a room."

"My wife has enough moolah for us to take your very best, my good man," James said, giving him a pound.

"Can't," Caleb said, greeting all his guests in turn with hugs, kisses, and the like. "That room belongs to me and my wife." He looked down at Jai, who looked as if she was dozing off. "Right now I think someone needs to lie down and rest."

"I'm fine," Jai protested weakly from behind a yawn.

"Why you so sleepy? You need some chocolate," Kevin said.

"I saw some marshmallows and mint chocolate chip ice cream in the kitchen," James added.

"I think more like caramel syrup and nuts should do the trick," Toiji corrected.

"As long as you can put it in a blender, I'm good," Jai said, pulling her legs to her chest and then stretching them out.

"No more donuts, chocolate, cookies, chips, gummy bears, marshmallows, cotton candy, blue soda, or artificially flavored anything," Caleb announced to the room. "And even if you put it in a blender, it is still a banana split." He glared at Jai.

"I can take care of myself," Jai said.

"We took care of her for years before you showed up . . . ," Kevin said.

"We know what she needs before she does," Toiji added.

"I'm her buddy. I know what she likes," James quipped.

"I've known her since junior high school. I know what she doesn't like, " Eva challenged.

"I've got nothing," Judith remarked, shrugging her shoulders.

"What are you saying? At four a.m. who's the one boosting her morale and giving advice? You, Judith,"

Herbert pointed out. "You know her as well, if not better, than any of them."

"I've been spoiling her since she was in pampers," Quinn added proudly.

"Well, I trump that. I've known her since birth," her mother gleefully remarked. "And what I know is no one knows Jailyn Wyatt Vincent as well as her husband, so let the man take care of his wife the way he sees fit, without any grumblings from the lot of you."

"Thank you, Doe," Caleb said, tossing his mother-in-law a loving wink before bearing down on his beautiful, sexy wife. "And you, young lady, better listen to your mother, or else I'm going to tell Ann and Saoirse, and then you'll be sorry."

"Where are they, anyhow? They've been shadowing me like detectives for the last three months. What are they up to?" Jai asked.

"Taking the tires off of that ATV of yours," Caleb said, glaring at her. "By my request."

"You wouldn't," Jai said, horrified.

"I wouldn't, but Ann had no problem, and they'll make quick work of it, too," said Caleb. "Don't be surprised if those become tire swings in the next three days."

"Those are specially designed, fifteen-hundred-dollar tires. Ann would never do that," said Jai.

"You're worth way more than that to Ann right now," said Caleb.

"What? Are you crazy?" replied Jai.

"If I am, it's because you're my wife. Now do you walk up to bed on your own two feet, or do I carry you?"

"Carry me," Jai said, folding herself into a ball, determined to be dead weight and to make his job harder, because she knew he had no problem with physically removing her from the chair.

"I'll have you know, Gael is holding the blender hostage in the other room, so you best go with him nice and easy, or the blender gets it," Quinn said.

Caleb looked down at her with his sinfully wicked smile, his oceanic eyes flashing playfully, his muscled arms crossed over his broad expanse of chest, ready to lift her without a second thought.

"I'm going. I'm going," Jai said, getting up from the chair in a huff, her stomach protruding nicely at three days over three months of pregnancy.

Caleb admired all of her new curves and plumpness. He pulled her close to his side and kissed her. "As soon as I can liberate the blender, how about I make it up to you about the tires with a wheatgrass, blueberry, and peach yogurt smoothie?"

"Throw in some of Dolly's homemade whipped cream and strawberry syrup, and all is forgiven," said Jai.

"You two really should get a room," said a handsome man coming up the hall and blocking their path. He was dressed casually, which made his formidable bulk seem even bigger.

"Ah, so you made it, after all, Gary," Caleb said, giving the man a bear hug. Caleb was taller and firmer, and the man was wider and thick. It would be a contest if they ever fought.

"Better late than never," said Gary Tobin, his Brooklyn accent still one of his most prominent features. He gave Jai a kiss. "Always wonderful to see you."

"And you as well. Come in and meet my family and friends. Caleb's family is out back, in the family-room extension."

"Heard you got a big screen back there, with a satellite dish," Gary whispered to Jai as they went back in the living room. "For as long as I've known the man, all he's ever watched is CNN."

"I know almost three thousand channels, and all he watches is news feeds," Jai whispered back. "He also had Ann move the TV into the den in the basement. He said if guests need to watch sports, they don't have to disturb anyone else."

"Did Gael make it back? I've always had a crush on her," Gary said.

"You and half the men in Connecticut," replied Jai. "You'll be fighting for her attention, because Latham seems to have it all. But Maeve, Reaghann, Bridgid, Fidelma, and Ann are around."

"Saoirse and the other cousins?" asked Gary.

"Yup," said Jai.

"And Omar? I miss that little cuss always hanging around with me and Caleb," said Gary. "Used to get us into all kinds of trouble around town."

"He and Tammy will be back tonight from their honeymoon, so I won't expect them to be out much," said Jai.

"Quinn? What about Quinn? Tell me Caleb's father isn't here."

"Of course, he is. And chill. My mother has that man acting like a pussycat," Jai said.

"What is it with you Wyatt women? You have all these big Irishmen acting like sissies," said Gary.

Chapter 34

Jai entered the room arm in arm with Gary Tobin, and Caleb explained to everyone his role in the situation. "Uh," Jai whispered in the big man's ear.

"Don't worry, girl. Caleb won't find out from me that you went to meet DeAngelo, but you should tell him now so he won't spank your butt," said Gary.

"Stop making me scared," said Jai. "Dave and I are friends. There's nothing wrong with friends having drinks. Besides, I saw you following us the whole time. I knew I was smart trusting you."

Gary kissed her cheek and laid a hand on her stomach. "I think this is the best way to become a godfather." Jai's tinkling laughter caught the attention of the room.

Quinn made his way over to Gary, and Gary couldn't help but to start explaining under the big Irishman's glare. "Caleb is my friend, always has been, will be till they put one of us in the ground, and I will fight the devil to keep him around for as long as I can. I'm sorry, Mr. Quinlan, that you don't approve of our friendship."

"No need to apologize. I don't like you much. Don't

mean I never will. If my son says you're okay, then that'll be good enough for me."

Latham entered the room. "Listen, Ann and Saoirse are making their way back from the barn, so I suggest you all get back to the atrium. . . ."

"It's an enclosed porch," James said.

"Solarium," Jai's mother corrected.

"It doesn't matter," Quinn said, moving them all along. "Point is Dolly and Louise have been cooking for days, and we all better be ready to celebrate the birth of my grandbabies."

"Don't you think it's a little—" Judith started and then stopped, looking at a tired and slightly run-down Jai. "Oh my gosh! Did you say babies? I didn't know. Why didn't you say something?" she said, rushing over to the mommy to be. Since Judith couldn't have children and her one attempt to adopt recently had been foiled by the trouble with Creative Forces, Jai felt guilty.

"I didn't want to throw my good fortune in your face," said Jai.

"This pregnancy must have curdled your brain. Of course, I want to share in it with you. Herb and I have already started planning our next trip. We're taking all the kids to Disney. In Japan."

"All of them?" Jai asked

"Yeah, and I can't wait, 'cause as soon as we get back, I'm dropping all your little nieces and nephews back here for a month in the happiest place on earth, and then I'm gonna sleep for a month."

The two laughed their way to the sun-drenched porch, where Jai was swarmed with hugs and kisses, while Caleb was bombarded with handshakes and pats on the back. It took another fifteen minutes for

Caleb to whisk Jai away to the quiet of their private apartment.

"We're not going to have much alone time for at least the next year and a half," Caleb said, kissing her neck and stroking her back. "You should take advantage and take a nap."

"I could sleep through until morning if you'd stop kissing me," she said, tilting her head so that her lips met his in a provocative kiss that caused a frisson to stampede through his system.

His mouth became insistent against hers, his hands found the hardened areola, and his leg nudged her thighs apart. She felt a flush steal over her skin and set the natural force between them in motion. She unzipped his pants, releasing his fully engorged member. He moaned when she took him in her hand with long, firm, knowing strokes. He tugged at the buttons of the shirt she wore until they popped off and, with one hand, released the back clasp on her heavy-duty maternity bra. He salivated at her augmented endowments.

"You should be pregnant more often," he said, taking one ultra sensitive breast into his mouth.

Her nerves were amplified a million times over because of her state, and every flick of his tongue sent a rush skittering along her veins. He managed to free her pants and pulled her full up against him, his fingers massaging the tender and bounteous flesh of her rear. Her long nails dragged along his back, and he lifted his head at the intense sensation. He could smell the sharpness of her scent and lowered himself to bask in the liquid pool. He opened the slit wide and saw the pretty silver droplets waiting for his tongue, and with each lick, she moaned his name like a prayer.

Jai gripped at the sheets as he pleasured her with

his face. The way he loved her with his tongue caused her hips to pitch forward to meet each delicate little stroke. Her legs fell open as he lavished her clitoris with the attention she had been yearning for. Her heart beat erratically in her chest, her body reveling in the carnal abyss, her breathing turning shallow as he slid two fingers into her core.

"Come on, baby," said Caleb. "I can feel it. I know you're right there. Let me see you come." In that moment, her body yielded, hitting a crescendo and plummeting off the precipice, right into Caleb's arms. Down the sinewy length of him, she saw the bulbous head of his manhood jumping around.

She let her tongue roam his lips until his breathing became rapid gasps, his heavy erection standing straight out from between his legs. With as much care as he could manage, he entered her. His ramrod straight appendage sank into her tightening opening as if it were hungry for him. She twisted her hips beneath him, and with each stroke, his staff gave a shudder. He tried to hold himself back and control his seed, but seeing his wife lying before him like a goddess, her shapely curves more pronounced, her hair a shoulder-length onyx mass of curls, and her eyes bearing witness to his soul, he could not stop himself from gripping her hips and pressing into her. He kissed her deeply until the reeling pleasure he always experienced with her assailed him, sending him on a miraculous journey, with all his senses alive.

When he lifted his head, he saw angry red spots on her neck. "I'm so sorry, sweetie. I didn't know I bit you," he said, putting on his pants and getting a cold cloth.

"It's okay. Wait until you get a look at your back," she said, with a dimpled smile. "I guess there goes my nap."

She slipped on the oversized T-shirt and overalls that he handed to her.

"I'll go down and explain. You rest." There was a light knock on the door.

Before either one could answer, an Afroed, red-headed, caramel-colored little boy was carried into the room. He was clutching Tyanna for dear life. His huge blue green eyes were as big as saucers. "Sorry to disturb you, but Tyrell said he gets like this when too many new people come around," said Tyanna.

"Mama, Papa! Lay-lay?" Liam asked.

"Yes, Liam, Mama go lay-lay. You can lie down for a nap in your room," Caleb answered, reaching out for his son.

Liam clutched at Tyanna's shirt with all his might. "Papa lay-lay. I Tanna."

"Tanna, huh?" Jai asked.

Liam stuck out his chin haughtily and shouted, "Tanna mine!" before Tyanna or anyone could correct him.

"I'll be Tanna for you as long as you lie down in your room and take a nap for Tanna," said Tyanna. "How about I put you down, and you show me where you sleep?" As soon as his little brown feet hit the floor, Liam tugged with all his might on Tyanna's hand to make her move faster and to get her to follow him into his room through the connecting bath. "Someone has got to show me Liam's hill. He wanted to go to it, but I didn't know which one it was."

As soon as the door shut, Jai said, "I think our son is having his first crush."

"And here I'm thinking we got us a nanny."

"Guess it's a good thing you added more rooms up here," Jai said.

"I didn't plan on stopping with just three. Remember, my daddy is one of seven."

"So you call me when you get pregnant with your three, and we'll toss a coin to see who carries number seven," Jai said.

"You've only been pregnant twice, so you owe me one more."

"I'll still be pushing out two of your towheaded kids," she said, making Caleb laugh at the silly things she made him say around her. It felt so good to be able to laugh, dream, remember, and live with a woman whom he loved with his very being and who loved him exactly the way he was. She tolerated his downs, his confusion, and was blessed with him becoming a whole and giving man. He was glad to have been the one to hold her hand when she cried in her sleep when Liam was born. He looked so much like her father, it had made her weep, and every day Liam got a little darker, his eyes a little bluer, his hair turning a rust color, and she couldn't help but cherish him all the more.

Liam was already building planes and making kites, and he had barely learned to walk. All you had to do was show him something once, and it was etched in his little brain. Caleb could tell him anything, and Liam's mind held on to it like old cave writing. Caleb could not believe the traits that flourished in his son, and he wanted the world to see and his son to never be ashamed of all that was him.

"Who's gonna tell Tyanna that Liam's hill is where he was conceived one night, while my wife was out chasing rainbows in the rain?" Caleb said, leaning down to kiss his wife, who yelled, "Tanna!" right into his mouth.

"You are so not gonna tell her that right now!" he whispered into Jai's mouth.

"You're the Blarney expert," Jai said as Tyanna came through the door.

"Yes, Ms. Wyatt," Tyanna answered.

"I'm Mrs. Vincent," Jai said, with a smile, her husband glaring at her with squinted eyes.

"Oops, sorry, Mrs. Vincent."

"No prob. Can you make a decent milkshake?" Jai screamed.

"Peach yogurt, one banana, a drip of strawberry syrup, two spoons of fresh blueberry preserves, a tablespoon of wheatgrass, and a half teaspoon of Dolly's whipped cream to thicken it. Puree for fourteen seconds on high, right?" Tyanna said.

"I think I love this girl," Jai and Caleb whispered simultaneously.

"And keep your voice down. Liam's asleep," said Tyanna.

"I know I love this girl," Jai and Caleb whispered in wonder simultaneously.

"I'll make the shake downstairs, and I'll check on Liam when I bring it up," said Tyanna. "How long does he sleep? Never mind. I'll unpack while he's resting. Is it okay to take the little room at the end of the hall? It looks like the big one is gonna be Liam's room, but you should think about putting him in the smaller room, because he might be scared being alone for the first time and so far away. The smaller space might be comforting. But I figure I can pull my mattress in there and sleep there. Then, in the mornings, I will just put it in the other room. It makes sense to be close to him if the twins wake him. . . ." She gently closed the door leading out to the hall, still talking to herself.

"She's hired, and I'm doubling her pay," Caleb said, getting back in bed and kissing his wife. "I wonder if she has a twin."

"I think we can keep the hill thing to ourselves," Jai said, kissing her husband.

"Agreed. Now let's have that nap," he said, kissing his wife's neck.

"Seriously, Caleb, I'm going to go to sleep no matter what you do, oohhh, oohhh except for that. . . ."